D1502167

UNDISCOVERED COUNTRY

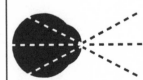

This Large Print Book carries the
Seal of Approval of N.A.V.H.

UNDISCOVERED COUNTRY

A NOVEL INSPIRED BY THE LIVES OF ELEANOR ROOSEVELT AND LORENA HICKOK

KELLY O'CONNOR MCNEES

THORNDIKE PRESS
A part of Gale, a Cengage Company

Farmington Hills, Mich • San Francisco • New York • Waterville, Maine
Meriden, Conn • Mason, Ohio • Chicago

Copyright © 2018 by Kelly O'Connor McNees.
Thorndike Press, a part of Gale, a Cengage Company.

ALL RIGHTS RESERVED
Thorndike Press® Large Print Historical Fiction.
The text of this Large Print edition is unabridged.
Other aspects of the book may vary from the original edition.
Set in 16 pt. Plantin.

LIBRARY OF CONGRESS CIP DATA ON FILE.
CATALOGUING IN PUBLICATION FOR THIS BOOK
IS AVAILABLE FROM THE LIBRARY OF CONGRESS

ISBN-13: 978-1-4328-5415-7 (hardcover)

Published in 2018 by arrangement with Pegasus Books Ltd.

Printed in Mexico
1 2 3 4 5 6 7 22 21 20 19 18

To Bob, for believing when I couldn't.

As often as not, we are homesick most for the places we have never known.

— Carson McCullers

When Lorena "Hick" Hickok died in 1968, she donated a sealed trove of her correspondence with Eleanor Roosevelt, who had died six years before, to the Franklin D. Roosevelt Library, on the condition that it not be opened until 1978. So it was not until then that archivists — and soon the rest of the world — learned what was in the more than three thousand letters the women exchanged over a span of thirty years. They shared the details of work and daily life, of worries over money, health, relationships. And they wrote about their love for each other.

In fact, Eleanor and Hick had exchanged well more than the letters preserved in the archive. Hick had made careful edits to this collection, destroying an untold number of letters. She was candid about why in a conversation with Eleanor's daughter, Anna: "Your mother wasn't always so very discreet when she wrote to me." The full picture of

Eleanor and Hick's relationship resides in those pages, lost to history.

But fiction can resurrect the story of Eleanor and Hick with its cardinal paradox: by making things up, we can finally get at the truth.

■ ■ ■ ■

PART ONE

■ ■ ■ ■

The fact is that our culture has sought to deny the truths and complexities about women's passion because it is one of the great keys to women's power.

— Blanche Wiesen Cook,
Eleanor Roosevelt: Volume I

CHAPTER ONE

October 1932

The luncheonette across the street from Potsdam's St. Mary's parish seemed as good a place as any to wait out the funeral, and we esteemed members of the press seized it like ants on a dropped lollipop. Inside, with the brass bell over the door still ringing, I had my cigarette lit before I even took off my coat. I passed it from the clenched fingers of my right hand to the clenched fingers of my left as I slipped out of the sleeves one by one. At the counter I took a stool next to John Bosco, a fellow reporter for the AP, who was still sore about the previous night's poker game. The boys were rowdy, and when the waitress came over, I had to shout my order to be heard above the din. *Pie and coffee, and leave a little room in the cup for the holy ghost.*

From the other end of the counter, Don Franks, from our rival wire service, United, couldn't resist the siren song of his own voice. "Don't go looking for Bosco to buy your lunch, Hick," he barked at us. "He's so broke he can't even pay attention."

"Ah, shut up, Franks," John said.

I could have reminded our cohort that Don was a confirmed boob who held his liquor so poorly he'd twice in the last week been wheeled back to his train compartment in a laundry cart. Instead, I looked at John.

"Do you hear something?" I asked. I pulled my flask from my pocket and topped off both our coffees.

John squinted at me and grinned. He wasn't quite ready to forgive me for cleaning him out with a pair of twos, but he was getting there.

Don kept on, though no one seemed to be listening. "His wallet's got a better echo than the Grand Canyon. It's emptier than Christ's tomb."

I took a sip of my coffee and felt its sting on my lips. "All in favor of Don Franks shoving his tired jokes up his ass?" I asked loudly.

Every last man at the counter raised his hand.

When the waitress brought my pie, she stuck a ticket under each of our saucers. I took John's ticket and put it on top of mine.

He nudged me with his elbow. "Thanks, Hick."

We weren't in Potsdam for our health, I can tell you that. In the church across the street — that redbrick monument to Irish grit — were Democratic presidential candidate Franklin Delano Roosevelt and his wife, among the other mourners. The gilded casket (paid for by Governor Roosevelt) contained the mother of Missy LeHand, Roosevelt's longtime personal secretary and, some said, his mistress. This funeral was off itinerary, an unexpected stop on a presidential campaign trail that was otherwise planned down to the minute. In the last few weeks, the press corps, including yours truly, had accompanied the whistle-stop tour through seventeen states. Speeches, handshaking, and enough renditions of "Happy Days Are Here Again" to make your ears bleed.

As we finished our food, we watched through the luncheonette's clouded windows as the church doors opened and people began to stream out into an inhospitable drizzle. Gus Gennerich, the stocky bodyguard who helped FDR get around, eased the governor's wheelchair awkwardly down the church steps, and a crowd formed around the candidate. FDR shoved himself to his feet so that he could shake hands. At the counter I scooped the last bite of too-sweet apple pie into my mouth and paid the bills.

I was slipping back into my coat when the bell on the door jangled once more and Mrs. Roosevelt walked in. The doorframe was decorated with orange paper jack-o'-lanterns that brushed her coat as she passed through. Though my fellow newsmen quieted right down, they didn't lunge toward her for a quote the way they would have if her husband had come in. There wasn't much of a scoop to be had with the missus, they knew. Any story about her was just going to be women's-page pabulum — her sensible shoes, the dreadful hairnets that sometimes sagged onto her forehead, her charitable causes.

This was, sadly, my domain, as the only woman from the AP assigned to the campaign. I had been trying to get Mrs. Roosevelt to talk candidly with me about the prospect of becoming first lady so that I could write the long feature my editor had assigned, but I couldn't get her to agree to an interview.

When she'd joined the second leg of the now-eastbound train tour more than a week ago, I'd made a nuisance of myself by appearing at her elbow after each of the governor's speeches from the back of the train — at a spare depot in Ash Fork, Arizona, where almost no one clapped; in Pueblo, Colorado, to forlorn steel workers; in Council Bluffs, Iowa, near the bank of the startlingly wide Missouri River. And yet she managed to duck me every time. She was never rude, but somehow, just as I would glance down for a second to flip open my steno pad, she would slip away in the crowd. One morning a few days before the funeral, while most of my cohort was sleeping off the previous night's escapades, I came into the dining car and found it empty save for Mrs. Roosevelt and her secretary Mrs. Thompson, whom everyone called Tommy. As they sat sipping their coffee and watching the sun rise over Tennessee, Tommy invited me to join them. I thought my ship might finally have come in.

Tommy — a career gal like me — was friendly, and we moaned and groaned for a few minutes about the train's tiny beds and our aching backs and how as old hens we weren't fit to do anything anymore. As the train flew toward Knoxville in order to get the candidate to his scheduled 9:00 a.m. speech, Mrs. Roosevelt kept her eyes on the trees. She seemed so lost in her own thoughts that I wondered if she even heard us. Before I had the chance to bend the conversation toward some questions, Mrs. Roosevelt stood abruptly and excused herself to deal with a "mountain of correspondence."

When she'd disappeared from the car, I sighed and put my head down on my forearm for a moment; then I rose and slumped against the seat. "I've been covering FDR for years, and I swear she still doesn't even know who I am."

Tommy threaded her fingers around the coffee cup's delicate handle, and, for a moment, I thought she was looking for a gentle way to agree. But instead she said, finally, "Mrs. Roosevelt was raised to believe that a woman's name should appear in print just twice in her lifetime: for her wedding and her obituary. Reporters make her nervous. Be patient."

A lesser scribe might have given up then and just used generic quotes from Mrs. Roosevelt's speeches to cobble something together, file the story, and move on. After all, I was on the most important beat in the country at the moment; I had bigger fish to fry. But I hadn't become a top reporter by taking the easy road, thank you very much.

I stubbornly refused to write a bland feature on a politician's wife. No one with half a brain gave a damn about her fond memories of finishing school or where she bought her gloves and hats. I had to find a way to sidestep that stodgy old yarn and show a different side of her. My hunch was that her still waters might run deep, if only I could keep her in the same room long enough to find out.

And now here she was walking my way. As I watched her move toward the luncheonette counter, I marveled at her height. Some people called her awkward, but I didn't see that. She seemed like a dancer, a prima ballerina from an entirely different, somewhat larger race of people, and she held her head still as she walked, as if the stack of books she no doubt had been compelled to balance there as a girl remained.

"Miss Hickok," Mrs. Roosevelt said, grasping my hand. She had pale blue eyes and spoke in a soft voice that seemed to apologize for interrupting. "I hear you want to interview me."

So Tommy had greased the wheels for me, God bless her. "I promise I don't bite," I said. I hoped my nonchalance covered my nerves. As I felt at my breast pocket for a pen, I cut my eyes at my cohort and willed them to stifle their *goddamns*. They all pretended not to be listening in, but the only sound in the room was the hiss of the griddle back behind the kitchen window.

"My husband has to stay here tonight," Mrs. Roosevelt began, glancing at the new cigarette in my hand. "But I have to teach in the morning in Manhattan."

I nodded, unsure whether there was a question in there. "All right."

She tipped her head slightly and seemed to study me, started to speak again but hesitated.

In a clumsy attempt to reassure her, I said, "You probably don't remember me, but I actually came to Hyde Park at Governor Roosevelt's invitation back in April. He and I sat by the fire to talk over the primaries. You were in the room too, but you were occupied with your . . . knitting . . ." I felt myself starting to babble, and the skin on my neck flushed.

"Of course I remember you," she said, and the steadiness of her voice compared to my own gave me a shiver. "As I recall, the two of you mainly talked repeal. Over cocktails."

I pressed my lips together to stifle a smile.

"Now, if you'd be willing to accompany me on the train tonight, you can have your interview. There will be plenty of time to talk — it's a long ride."

And just like that my fortune changed. I was finally going to get some decent copy out of her, and then I could get back to work covering the real story: the man who would soon be our president.

Mrs. Roosevelt smiled a tense, toothy smile. "The train leaves at nine. Don't be late."

I spent the rest of the afternoon at the office of Potsdam's *Courier and Freeman* typing up notes from the past few days and wiring the funeral story to my editor, Bill Chapin, in the city. When I finally left for the train station, the rain was coming down in sheets. I wedged my typewriter case between my elbow and ribs and tried to cover it with my coat; in the process, I soaked my skirt clear through to my girdle. *Farewell, dignity; I hardly knew ye.* I don't have to tell you I was dying for a drink about then, but my flask was empty and I had no time to refill. On the bench inside the station I disentangled myself from my wet coat and sat catching my breath. With my index finger, I plucked my necklace out from under my collar and rubbed the little wooden charm, its surface smooth as glass.

And just as I did every time I touched it, I remembered where I'd come from and where I was now. *Hey, old nobody: you're about to interview the future first lady of these united states.*

When I heard the clacking of her heels on the tile, I stubbed my cigarette out on the bottom of my shoe in a hurry. Slipping my necklace back under my collar, I stood.

"Well, Miss Hickok. Did you get any supper?" Mrs. Roosevelt carried a dripping umbrella and patted her blue leather satchel. The sleeves of her dowdy tweed suit were dark with rain, but the rest of her was dry, and her blue eyes were bright in the dim station. "I brought us sandwiches."

"That's great — I'm starving," I said, too quickly. I tended to turn fidgety around rich people because I was afraid there was no hiding the evidence of my humble beginnings, a yellowed slip hanging beneath the hem of a fine dress. But she seemed pleased by my candor.

"Me too," she said.

The train — the overnight to Grand Central — pulled up to the platform. Though the station was nearly empty, the dim cars were full of people coming from points farther north. With things so bad, the rail companies couldn't afford to run half-empty routes and had cut back on the number of cars for each line. There wasn't a seat to be found as we made our way through. Surely the governor's wife could have reserved one, but I was getting the sense that she tended not to take advantage of the special access her position afforded.

I watched the passengers' faces to see if any of them recognized her. She might have been the most photographed woman in America besides Jean Harlow, but in nearly every photo I'd seen, she was looking away from the camera — sometimes down at her lap, often over at her magnetic husband. One never quite got a view of her face head-on, I thought, as I watched her coiled gray-blond hair bob in front of me. A few women whispered, and a man jabbed his wife with his elbow and pointed our way, but no one spoke to her.

Finally we spotted an empty drawing room. Mrs. Roosevelt went in first and switched on the little brass light fixture. She sat on the narrow couch across from the single berth. I pulled the door closed to muffle a crying baby just outside.

"Oh, that's better," she said.

"Are you sure this will be all right?" At some point I knew she would want to go to sleep, and I would have to find somewhere else to go until we arrived in the city.

"Of course. Don't be shy." She gestured to the place beside her and then pulled the wax-paper-wrapped sandwiches from her satchel, along with two checkered napkins, and laid them between us. "They call you Hick, don't they?"

I nodded. "Yes, they do. I'm a proud Hick from the sticks, no matter how many years I've been in New York. And I never did like the name Lorena."

Mrs. Roosevelt took a crystal saltshaker out of the bag and dusted her sandwich with it before taking a bite. The bag sat beside her on the seat, its frame splayed open. I wondered what else she had in there — ice cream sundaes, cigars and brandy?

"The name suits you. No nonsense."

I watched her manicured hand slip the shaker back in the satchel. That small piece was probably worth more than all my housewares put together. I saw a flash of Mrs. Roosevelt's early years — finishing school and riding lessons, visiting her uncle Ted in the White House, cotillions written up in *Town Topics*. Only a former debutante would travel with crystal in her purse.

I tried to find a natural way to begin the interview. "So . . . Are you looking forward to living in Washington?"

24

Mrs. Roosevelt chewed her roast beef, dabbed her mouth with her napkin, and said, "Now, Hick, aren't we getting ahead of ourselves? Franklin hasn't won the election yet."

The polls had him leagues ahead at that point, and she and I both knew he was a lock. The train lurched forward, and I shot my arm out to brace myself on the berth.

"Well, *suppose* he wins," I said. "How do you think you will like your new address?" I thought I might at least get some intel on the changes she planned to make to the White House drapery. That was just the sort of terminally boring copy Bill said our female readership went nuts for. This country had a grand tradition of forcing brilliant women to fritter their lives away in domesticity, and, though I knew from my reporting on the family just how much more there was to Mrs. Roosevelt than people knew, I didn't think even she would be able to escape that fate.

Given her general gentle demeanor, her sharp tone in reply surprised me. "I think it will be a great interruption to my work. I'm writing more than ever. And I love teaching. But all that will end so that I can host teas and decorate."

I knew well the kind of woman Mrs. Roosevelt was — and the kind of work she was doing. She didn't just talk in parlors; she organized women. She didn't just give money away; she developed policy and put it under her husband's nose. And yet, I was astonished that she'd admitted as much.

My face must have revealed my thoughts about her response, as she quickly added a line more suitable for public consumption: "Though of course I am honored to have the chance to do it, for Franklin." She crinkled up the waxed paper and shifted her position on the couch, restless.

I felt my mouth turn up, amused. Her irritability made her much more interesting to me because I saw at once how the luxury and ceremony of the thing meant nothing to her. I got the feeling she had a whole lot to say but was trying to restrain herself, and that made her radiate a kind of energy that was hard to look away from. It was quiet in our drawing room, but the air felt charged, and I paused for a minute, thinking about what to say next. Outside the window, the lights of small upstate towns shone through the streaming rain, ghostly orbs appearing and disappearing, and they played on her skin.

She took advantage of my surprise and lobbed a question of her own. "You said you're from the 'sticks.' Where?" Out of the satchel of endless surprise, she took a skein of yarn and a half-finished baby sweater and began a complicated lace pattern from memory. I recalled my visit to the Roosevelt estate back in April, when she had sat in the corner knitting, and I'd assumed she was not listening to my conversation with her husband.

It seemed best to get my background out of the way, since there was no covering it up. "South Dakota, mostly, though I was born in Wisconsin and we moved around some. Dirt floors, the whole nine yards," I said, in case she hadn't gotten the message that we had been poor. Just thinking of those years gave me a shiver. "Of course, that was a long time ago."

"And you don't get back to visit?" she asked.

"Never," I said. "Nothing could make me go back there."

She examined my face and something un-spooled across her eyes, as if what she'd thought of me — if she thought anything at all — was changing. I wondered if it was pity, which would get under my skin, or worse — some kind of admiration for all that I had "overcome." Though my hackles were up, I had to remind myself I'd hardly revealed a thing. But somehow she had wrested this interview from me.

"That lipstick is a lovely shade of red," she said slowly. "It really brings out your eyes."

So the thing that had changed between us was something different still. I looked at her in surprise and felt the kind of jolt you get touching a metal doorknob on a dry winter day. My gaze slipped to her lips for a moment, dropped to the starched collar of her blouse. But I knew I had to be misreading the temperature of the room. It was only a cunning attempt to dodge a reporter's questions, nothing more.

"You really *don't* like being interviewed, do you?" I asked.

She didn't answer right away but finally smirked. "No. And Franklin told me to watch out for you especially. He knows your work. He thinks you're smarter than all the other reporters combined."

The future president was wary of me — now that was a compliment I could feel down to the arches of my feet. "Well, if I am that good at my job," I said wryly, "your resistance will be pointless in the end."

Mrs. Roosevelt laughed and tipped her head back to rest against the cushioned seat. The fabric pulled at the small hairs along the nape of her neck. She looked tired but a little more relaxed. "All right, all right, I give up, Hick. Ask away."

As the train chugged south, I got her to give up the biographical goods, most of which I already knew. But I needed the quotes. She told me about what it had meant to her to become a mother, how she learned through trial and error to take care of her six babies, including the first Franklin Jr., the one who had died.

"At seven months and fourteen days old," she said, and I could see she knew down to the hour too, down to the minute.

Through those years, she had been content to embrace a quiet family life, but eventually she got restless and began to stick her toe in the water of politics — both her husband's campaigns and her own work on women's rights, labor unions, better health care, housing, public parks.

When she began to talk fondly of her boarding school in England, I squared that with what I knew of her childhood and understood why she had wanted to escape New York. Her father, Elliott — Teddy's brother — had been quite the boozer, and his benders were the stuff of society legend: pie-eyed joyrides in hansom cabs around Central Park, whores and mistresses, a bastard son with a servant. Back in his day, Eleanor's father had kept reporters scribbling, and it couldn't have been easy for her to hold her head high when those stories ran in the papers.

She had loved boarding school so much, she said, that she'd founded one of her own, Todhunter, on the Upper East Side. "Just think of it, Hick. The unused potential in half the human race!" She jabbed the air with her knitting needle, and I grinned. "Think of what women know, just by nature of being women, and what they could *do* with that knowledge. What if the cures for diseases reside within those brains? The path to peace and justice and true democracy?"

I glanced up from my steno pad, my pencil racing, and nodded to encourage her. I could use it all. But it still sounded a little canned. I had yet to break through.

"It's not about *me*," she went on. "It's about making a way for those young women to contribute. *Nothing* could be more urgent." Then she yawned, and we both laughed. So much for urgency. She balled up the knitting. "I can hardly keep my eyes open. Do you mind if I stretch out?"

"Of course," I said, looking at my watch. "I lost track of time — I apologize. Please get some rest." I stood and tucked my notebook in my bag. My hand was on the door, and I was just about to bid her good night when she touched my shoulder.

"Oh, I didn't mean you needed to go," she said. "There isn't another open seat on this train. Please stay. You won't get a minute of sleep otherwise."

Again I felt that strange crackle in the small room; again I reminded myself that I would have to be out of my goddamned mind to think she was trying to send me a signal. But then it had been a little like that with my old flame Ellie at first, telling myself it was all in my head. Of course, Ellie had not been American royalty. The consequences of guessing wrong, in this place, with this person, were not for the lily-livered. Right then, I wanted a drink so bad I could have wailed.

I stood paralyzed with indecision. "Well . . . if you're sure . . ."

"Of course," she said, and handed me a pillow.

She took the couch and I took the berth, which she claimed she was too tall for.

"Well," I said, "good night, Mrs. Roosevelt."

"Yes, good night."

The train swayed; I heard the baby begin

31

to wail again, and then, in the distance, a man laughing. I glanced at her without turning my head, petrified of saying or doing the wrong thing. I knew there wasn't a chance in hell I'd be able to fall asleep.

She took off her jacket and spread it over her like a blanket. Embarrassed that I hadn't thought to do it immediately, I tried to hand her the blanket that came with my berth, but she waved it away. "So how did you become a reporter?" she asked.

I watched the clothes hangers that hung on straps from the ceiling sway back and forth above me. I thought about that for a minute. "The hard way," I finally replied. "I had a hundred jobs after I ran away from home. Servant in a rooming house. Cook on a farm. In that one, they gave me a little portable kitchen I had to wheel out into the fields every day at noon to make potatoes for the hands. And then my last job before I found reporting was in a saloon in town — Mrs. O'Malley's."

"Ran away? How old were you?"

"About fourteen. There were some tough years in there, but also some extraordinary kindnesses. Mrs. O'Malley made me suits with trimmings," I said, remembering that fact for the first time in decades as I said the words, "so I had something to wear to school. And she made sure I *went.* If it hadn't been for her, I never would have made it out of Bowdle, South Dakota, or become a reporter. Never would be riding on this train."

"Hm," she said, a knowing laugh. "Now, I should let you get some rest."

"Yes. Well. Good night again."

The train chugged on. Thoughts of my childhood always left me unsettled. Awareness of the many accidents on which my fortune had depended could give me a haunted feeling — haunted and hunted both. I knew I had gotten out of South Dakota by the skin of my teeth, though I tried not to think about it too much. But now my mind was whirring. *Go to sleep, Hick,* I told myself.

Mrs. Roosevelt turned on her side and made a pillow of her elbow. "I just want to say, God bless the Mrs. O'Malleys of the world. I for one am glad she was there so that you can be here now."

It was as if she'd read my mournful thoughts. I shivered and tried to cover with a joke. "Now you have more dirt on me than I have on you," I griped. This seemed to delight her. I could see her smile in the dark.

"Good night, Hick."

Here I was, with all the access I could wish

for, and I was taking my eye off the ball. I decided to try one more time to get a good quote for my story. "You really don't want to be first lady?" I asked. "There's got to be more to the job than watercress sandwiches and tea parties."

"I do not," she said, rolling onto her back once more with a sigh. "It doesn't interest me in the slightest."

"But what if —" I blurted. Then I stopped myself. The first-lady-to-be had not asked for my advice.

"What if what?" Mrs. Roosevelt said. Her voice revealed curiosity and wariness in equal measure.

The motion of the swaying car and the darkness of the night had me too relaxed for my own good. I didn't want to let her friendliness lead me to the false conclusion that she saw me as her equal.

"What?" she said, more softly this time, and turned on her side again.

"What if you set out to change the job itself?" I said. "What if you ignore the trappings — let someone else worry about the parties and the china. The office of first lady is one of the most visible posts in the country. You could use it as your platform, for whatever you want to do." As I spoke, the stodgy job seemed suddenly full of possibility if she were the one who would hold it.

She was quiet for so long I wondered if I had overstepped.

"And have them fight me every minute? I dread it," she said. "Just between you and me, I would be glad if he lost."

And there it was, the scoop of the decade. Eleanor Roosevelt would have liked her husband to lose the election. Who knows — she might even have been planning to vote for Hoover. Any reporter worth her salt would have asked her that, point-blank, but did I? Did I set my mind to hustle from Grand Central to the AP office and file that story at 4:00 a.m., my fingers tearing like hell across the typewriter keys?

I did not. I did not think of what I would do in two hours, or ten minutes. Instead, I watched the curve of her cheek where it rested on her elbow, the closed lids of her eyes, delicate as eggshells. She was pulling me in. I was fascinated by her, longed to help her — and longed, I realized with fear, to reach across the train car and touch her.

CHAPTER TWO

November 8, 1932

On the night of the election, a little more than a week later, the Roosevelts invited a troop of family and friends as well as all the reporters assigned to the campaign trail over to their town house on Sixty-Fifth Street for a buffet supper. FDR was heavily favored, of course; the only suspense was over the margin of victory. Just how severe a drubbing would Hoover take? We reporters had been traveling the country for months, ostensibly to cover the campaign, but, as a free gift with purchase, we got an eyeful of just what was going on in America in 1932, and, my, was it bleak. Bedraggled men and women were building towns out of garbage — flattened tin cans and squares of cardboard and stained canvas sacks lashed together with cord — and they were naming those towns after the current president of the United States. We thought Hoover deserved whatever he was going to get.

It was already getting dark when I took Prinz, my German shepherd, out one last time. Then I walked him back into the apartment and closed him in the bathroom. My poor boy had a tendency to destroy every object in sight when I was not around, and this way he could lounge in the bathtub, as befitted a royal, until I came home. I changed into a fresh blouse and then smoothed my hair and slipped my notebook into my coat pocket. On the way to the door, I switched off the record player and the anvils of Wagner's *Das Rheingold* clanged their last. I caught a cab uptown.

The Roosevelts' town house was lit up like it was Christmas Eve, a lamp in every window and a red, white, and blue paper garland hanging over the doorway. A campaign poster on the door featured FDR's picture with the caption HERE IS THE MAN WE HAVE BEEN WAITING FOR. Just like that — so solemn you'd have thought he was a prophet. I could hear someone inside giving a toast as I tapped the iron knocker hanging from the lion's mouth on the door.

A servant in a black uniform answered and whisked my coat away while I switched my notebook and pencil to the pocket of my skirt and went into the parlor. About fifty people were crowded into the room, draped over couches or standing in clusters of two or three, the taller men with their elbows resting on the mantel. Anna, Mrs. Roosevelt's daughter, was there with her sulking stockbroker husband, Curtis Dall. It was an open secret that she was involved with John Boettiger, a reporter from Chicago, and intended to seek a divorce, and I couldn't help but feel sorry for her two-timed husband, dull as he seemed. Anna's younger brothers, Franklin Jr. and John, were home from Groton School for the week. James Roosevelt — the favored, eldest son — was at his father's elbow, and problem-child Elliott was just as reliably at the bar.

In the back of the dining room was a table heaped with chafing dishes, where servants doled out plates of ham, sliced beef, potatoes, and vegetables. A bartender mixed drinks in the corner. Prohibition may still have been the law of the land, but few people let that stand in the way of their God-given right to imbibe. I was headed the bartender's way when I saw her.

She was swathed in a regal chiffon dress, a far cry from the tweeds she'd worn that night on the train, and the color was high in her cheeks from the room's heat. I tried to catch her eye, but she either didn't see me or pretended not to. I felt my chest constrict with the thought that I was wrong about whatever I imagined had passed between us on the train, and I glimpsed the humiliation I could have brought down on myself had I acted on it. I felt as though I had stepped off the curb and back up just in time to avoid being mowed down by a taxi.

I didn't recognize the man ahead of me in line for the bar. His jacket was too well-made for a member of the fourth estate. He had to be a Roosevelt, or Roosevelt-adjacent. "All the news is good, eh?" I saw Tommy across the room and gave her a wave.

He nodded at me and munched a cracker. "They are saying turnout is very high. In South Carolina, the polls couldn't find one man on the street who said he voted for Hoover."

Women can vote too now, you know, I felt like saying, but didn't.

The good news indeed was that Manhattan shared South Carolina's opinion, at least as far as I could tell from speaking to people leaving my own polling place that morning. Unlike his ghoulish predecessor, FDR could charm the stink off an onion. Of course, his supporters weren't exactly sure what he planned to *do* when he got elected — he was too good a politician to make any concrete promises — but we had faith he would do *something.* Three years of inaction had plunged the country into the worst depression it had seen in anyone's lifetime. The choice couldn't be simpler: something had to be better than nothing.

Louis Howe approached Mrs. Roosevelt on the other side of the room. A bent little man in a wretched brown suit, he was the governor's campaign manager, adviser, and fixer. He looked like an undertaker, with his gaunt face and bulging eyes, and he smoked about a hundred cigarettes a day, sometimes two at a time, but he was a gifted political strategist, the engine of the Roosevelt machine. He got his start as a reporter himself and was a genius at coaxing favorable stories out of the New York papers. Even though the governor seemed to have clinched the race, there would be no rest tonight for poor Louis. He and Mrs. Roosevelt were putting their heads together over by the window — quite a feat as she had to stoop by about a foot to do it. I turned around to check the status of the bar line and nearly plowed into John Bosco.

"Easy!" he said. He was a hayseed like me, from Ohio, and kept his hair cut too short for his giant ears. "I was just bringing you this."

I took the cocktail, something fizzy with a curl of lemon peel floating on top. "Thanks," I said, and took a sip, waited for the kick that didn't come. I peered into the glass. "Did you put the bourbon in with an eyedropper?"

"Blame the bartender," John said, and took a swig from his own glass. "You coming to the Biltmore after this to wait on the returns?"

"You bet." I looked back at the window, but Mrs. Roosevelt had disappeared. I wondered if I would even talk to her at all that night. It now seemed entirely insane that I'd gotten my brain so scrambled over those unguarded moments on the train.

FDR was seated at the dining room table, receiving well-wishers and talking with reporters. It went without saying among the press that we wouldn't dwell on his physical condition unless it was to mention his various strengths — arms like a prizefighter's and beautiful posture, as well as that winning smile. A photographer who dared to snap a picture of him rolling into the room on the wheeled dining chair would have been asked to surrender his film and leave the party. Louis Howe in particular had devoted his life to ensuring that this man he admired was never seen as a cripple or an invalid. Most of America thought Governor Roosevelt's polio had been merely a mild case from which he had almost completely recovered. When you heard him on the radio, you felt like you would follow him into battle. You never thought about how he'd have to be wheeled to the front.

I felt the whisper of fingertips at my elbow, and Mrs. Roosevelt was there. My heart sprang up like a grasshopper.

"Hick, how lovely to see you."

"Likewise," I said, trying to sound calm. I couldn't help searching her face; she wouldn't quite look at me. With so many guests to attend to, she could have passed me by. Did it mean anything that she'd come to say hello? Probably not. I had told myself a little story about her, but it was all in my imagination.

"Franklin will want to say hello," she said, gesturing to the table.

I looked at John. "Want to meet him?" His eyebrows jumped. Though John had been on the trail for about a month, he griped to me every day that FDR never once called on him at the daily press conferences.

When we approached, Mrs. Roosevelt put her hand on her husband's shoulder. "Darling, you remember Lorena Hickok from the Associated Press?" John and I sat in the chairs to his right, and Mrs. Roosevelt sat to the left. It felt rude to stand while he was seated.

The governor fixed me with his laughing eyes, and his ivory cigarette holder smoldered in the ashtray in front of him. "Of course! Hello, Hick!" He shook my hand heartily. "You've had a busy summer — your pieces on convention politics are some of the best I've ever seen. Well done."

Hoo. I knew I'd be trotting that praise out later on when I needed a pick-me-up. "Thank you, sir. This is my colleague John Bosco." The men shook hands, and I could feel John trying to keep his cool, though his pinkening ears gave him away. In the presence of greatness, physiology can go haywire.

"You'll be seeing a lot of Miss Hickok," Mrs. Roosevelt leaned down and told her husband over the din, "now that she has been assigned to write about me."

I looked at her in surprise. I hadn't said anything like that on the train. After I finished the feature on her, I wasn't sure there would be much else to write. My focus was supposed to be on the candidate himself, what he would say tonight in his victory speech. She met my eyes for a fluttering moment.

"If I might," Governor Roosevelt said to me, "let me give you a piece of advice: you must never get into an argument with my wife." Mrs. Roosevelt rolled her eyes as FDR's grin broke out like a sunrise. "I mean it. You can't win. You think you've got her pinned down over here," he said, pressing his finger on the tabletop, "and she pops up over there" — he moved his finger to the other side of the table and smacked his palm flat — "and deals you the death blow. Take it from one who knows, Miss Hickok."

"Yes, sir," I said.

Mrs. Roosevelt gave a little laugh and then stood up and we got the picture that the exchange was over.

"Good luck tonight, sir," John said, the earnestness making him seem much younger than his thirty years.

Roosevelt folded his hands across his chest, as if he were relaxing in a club chair at the Knickerbocker, just waiting for his brandy. "Don't need luck. I've got the votes."

Mrs. Roosevelt grasped the back of his chair to wheel him toward the kitchen door. I waited for her to turn back to look at me again; she didn't.

"I guess that means we're moving over to the hotel," John said, still a little stunned by his contact with the candidate.

I threw back the rest of my poor excuse for a drink, and then John and I hurried down the front steps with the other news hawks. If we were quick, we could beat the limo to the hotel and get a feel for the room before Roosevelt arrived. Hundreds of campaign volunteers had already amassed there to celebrate what they'd spent months working to achieve, and they'd be clamoring to get a glimpse of the man it was all for.

John limped beside me on account of an old football injury to his right knee. He offered me a shrimp; he had grabbed a fistful of them as we'd left the town house. It dangled from his hand like a sad pink comma.

"John, are you really that hard up? Next thing I know I'll find you eating out of the trash. Doesn't Bill pay you anything these days?"

"Easy come, easy go," he said, trying to be casual, but I had a feeling his debts were even worse than I knew. I lit a cigarette without breaking my stride and tried to change the subject.

"Did you get anything on FDR's speech?" I asked.

He laughed and wiped his buttery hands on his jacket. "And you think I'd tell you if I did?"

"But, John," I said, feigning shock, "aren't we colleagues?"

"I've seen you scoop far better men than me," he said.

"Than *I*."

"Ha! Point to Hick. See — everything's a competition with you. I don't trust you any further than I could throw you."

That was a fat joke, but I didn't mind. As my stepmother had liked to tell me, I'd be the perfect wife for a blind man, except I talked too much. Anyway, John and I were about even now, after all the money I'd taken from him at the poker table.

"What do you think of Mrs. Roosevelt?" I asked next, trying to slip the question in as casually as I could. First she had revealed herself to me on the train; then she had pinched closed like a morning glory at night. And, just now, she'd made some kind of play I couldn't quite interpret. Was I the only one who'd noticed it?

As we walked, he flipped through his notes and frowned. "What do you mean what do I think of her?"

"I mean . . . what kind of first lady do you think she'll be?"

John shrugged, looking at me like I had a screw loose. "I guess this is your department, Hick, but how many kinds are there? She can pour a teapot, can't she? Tie on a bonnet for the Easter Egg Roll on the White House lawn?"

I liked John a lot, but this made me so mad I couldn't even speak for a moment. I thought back to what Mrs. Roosevelt had said on the train about the great interruption of becoming first lady, and I understood more than ever her dread about life in the White House. It had never occurred to John to think about a woman as anything other than a droopy piece of wallpaper behind her husband. Here was a woman who understood the nuance of law, the complexity of economic policy, the checkered history of the government's service to the poor. She had founded a school, published magazines, organized women to get out to vote, spoke impeccable French. And now she would be selecting table linens. I felt despair by proxy.

"To tell you the truth," John said as we ran up the steps to the Biltmore's lobby and I threw my cigarette in the brass urn, "she looks a little dazed to me. Sometimes it seems like there isn't any grain in the silo, if

47

you know what I mean."

We didn't beat the limo there. When John and I walked into the suite on the second floor, Roosevelt and his aides were already seated at a long table dotted with telephones and radios. On either side of them were rows of telephone operators wearing pearls and red lipstick, plying their trade with manicured hands. You could hear their "good evenings" echo one on top of the other like the parts of a madrigal. In the center of the table, Roosevelt sat grinning like a king, the lamplight reflecting off his tanned forehead, as he took calls from his regional directors. New England was a lost cause. All that old money tended to follow the candidate who promised not to tax too much of it. But the calls from Ohio and everything to the west and south were full of good news.

Every time one of the men spoke to a delegate, he tallied the electoral votes on a little card. It seemed silly that there was any suspense in the room at all. We knew how things were going to turn out. Still, I couldn't seem to take a full breath. My chest was tight, my heart pounding. Finally the people had made a move to take their country back from the top-hatted thieves who had reduced them to ruin. Roosevelt had pledged it: a new deal. And it was thrilling. But I felt something else dogging me — I was worried about *her,* Mrs. Roosevelt. I was worried about what his winning was going to do to her. Whatever else had happened in that Pullman car, she'd been quite clear about her trepidation of the fate that awaited her. And for some reason she had trusted me with that fact.

Just then, she materialized at the other end of the table. She waved to me quickly and then turned to shake somebody's hand with both of hers, the left one on top for good measure. She made her way from one bevy of reporters to the next, threading among the clusters of party bigwigs and donors who'd come to collect the flattery they'd paid for; she smiled and kissed cheeks and laughed at bad jokes and put everyone at ease. To look at her, you would think she was relaxed and happy, but it was like a picture painted on a window shade. If you rolled it up to let the light in, you would find an entirely different scene. Back in September, I had written a story about her husband's campaign stop in Chicago, when the family went to see the Cubs play the Yankees in the World Series. While everyone around her heckled the umpire or leaped to their feet to urge a runner into base, she sat with her head tipped back and *slept*. No kidding. The woman slept through Babe Ruth's two home runs. It just broke my heart right open to see how out of sync she was with everyone around her. But, again, I seemed to be the only one who noticed.

When a messenger ran down the stairs to the ballroom to announce that FDR had won Virginia, the volunteers cheered. You could hear the roar coming up through the floor. I scribbled some things down for the story I would file later. One of the telephone operators told me it was the most exciting night of her life, and that was saying something, considering how tight her sweater was.

In the chaotic room, I started to compose a lead in my head for the feature article. After hearing the way John had dismissed Mrs. Roosevelt on the walk over, my sense of duty about the piece surged; maybe I could try to help people understand her. She had plenty of detractors, on the left and the right, who thought she was either a socialist or simply a failure at being an heiress. I would include as much as I thought readers could stomach about her vast accomplishments, but I'd need to sweeten it too, with anecdotes that showed she was a real person. She had a little Scottie dog named Meggy, which she loved and took everywhere with her. And she really did buy ten-dollar dresses off the rack, the way the gossip rags said. Maybe, if I handled the information just right, I could make my readers see how wonderful she was.

I nearly sounded like a publicity hack, I realized, but ushered the thought away.

A commotion at the table with all the telephones claimed my attention. Louis Howe and another man were helping Roosevelt to his feet. You could see the outline of the braces he wore beneath his baggy trousers, two long pieces of steel that ran on either side of each leg and hinged at the knee. The apparatus was secured around his waist and beneath the sole of each foot with leather straps. Once he hoisted himself upright, he could stand with the help of a cane. The whole process took about fifteen long seconds, and the room was full of the nervous anxiety of people trying to steal glances and yet seem like they weren't looking. Louis saw over his shoulder one of our men from the AP with a camera ready to go, but he held up his hand. He lowered it only once Roosevelt was up and steady. The president-to-be flashed a broad smile. His good looks were wasted on politics — he could have been a film star. He used his handkerchief to wipe a thin layer of sweat from his brow and then he shoved it back into his pocket.

"Congratulations, Mr. President," Louis said. He shook FDR's left hand; the right one was on the cane. The photographer's flashbulb flared and a rumble of voices surged through the room like a wave crashing to the shore. *He's done it! They've called it! Don't let the door hit you on the ass on the way out, Hoover!*

A crowd of people lined up to shake his hand. The telephone operators were flinging their arms around one another, and a trio of musicians started to play the campaign song. As disappointed as I was for the future first lady, I was happy for the rest of the country. And yet still I knew: these people thought they had found a savior, but they were wrong. He was just a man. They believed in their hearts that FDR could snap his fingers and put everyone back to work, put all the residents of Hoovervilles in brand-new homes tomorrow. It wasn't going to happen, not without a long, painful slog — one that felt a little like the process a man with useless legs had to endure in order to balance on sharp pieces of steel so that he could pretend to stand.

The hope that was in this room was going to turn inside out into disappointment, guaranteed. But I suppose this kind of foresight was just the sort of thing that kept me from being able to have a good time. Who was I to rain on their parade?

American flags appeared out of thin air, and dozens of bottles of illegal whiskey started making the rounds. Waiters came in with trays full of empty glasses and distributed them. Louis Howe gave himself a few minutes to soak it in and down a couple of large glasses of booze before he became the preoccupied tactician once more, assessing what needed to be done next. FDR would wait for Hoover to concede, and then he would make his acceptance speech and go downstairs to the ballroom to thank the volunteers who, at the moment, sounded a little like rioters locked in a pen. Louis felt at his pocket for his cigarettes and extracted one from the packet. With a smoke bobbing on his lips, he began corralling the reporters to one corner of the room, where they could take a statement from the president-elect.

I let myself be ushered with the others but not before glancing back at the new first lady. She stood just a few feet away at the window, staring out at Madison Avenue.

Her palm was pressed to her diaphragm as if she couldn't quite take a breath. The look on her face was like a hunted animal's fear, but it passed away in an instant and she turned to the reporters.

Somebody shouted, "Are you glad, Mrs. Roosevelt?"

She didn't hesitate for a second. "Of course I am," she said, and I alone in the room knew it was a lie. "You're always pleased to have someone you're very devoted to have what he wants."

Those were her exact words, and all the reporters wrote them down.

CHAPTER THREE

November 9–11, 1932

I was fairly pickled by the time I stumbled down Madison to the AP's offices, but that didn't stop me from unlocking the tin box labeled first aid that sat on Bill's desk. That was where we kept the newsroom reserves. (The previous year, one of the higher-ups had called Bill to ask about this line item in the budget, curious about how in the hell our bureau spent so much on bandages and iodine.) With my drink beside me, I typed up my straight news piece on the outcome of the election and filed it. Then I worked on my feature on the new first lady. I also took time to call over to the *Post* and place a classified ad announcing a charity drive for down-on-their-luck farmers upstate. All donations of feed corn and oats should be directed to John Bosco, Office of the Associated Press, New York, NY. John had said he thought Mrs. Roosevelt didn't have any grain in her silo. Well, we'd see about that.

I returned home at dawn to find that poor old Prinz had just about given me up for dead. I opened the bathroom door and he raced out, knocked me clean over with joy at our reunion. After a quick walk, I brought him back inside and filled his bowl with cold water. He crouched in the kitchen, lapping it up, while I sat on the day bed with my feet on a pillow, smoking like a barn on fire.

What in the hell is wrong with me? I wondered, but I was beginning to have an inkling. I probably don't have to explain by this point that I was not the typical single gal on the hunt for a husband. I never made any bones about who I was, not to my colleagues, not to my bosses. And nobody seemed to care one way or the other, as long as I kept being good at my job. Which was just the way I liked it.

I had no plans to change; at nearly forty, I knew who I was and liked it just fine. Freud probably would have said that the whole thing had something to do with my father and what he had done to me, but that seems like a lot of horseshit. People are who they are. My whole life, I liked the things boys like — football, cowboys, trousers, cursing, and smoking. And every damned time I fell in love — and believe me, every time *was* damned, right from the start — it was with a woman.

Around one o'clock that afternoon, I took the Third Avenue train back to the office. The newsroom was a microcosm of America that day: jubilant and a little worse for wear.

" 'Morning, John," I said. He was in his chair a few desks over, skimming the crime bulletin.

"Did you get any sleep, Hick?"

"She who sleeps gets scooped, my friend." I handed him the typed pages of my feature. "Would you look this over for me?"

"Sure thing."

While I waited for him to read it, I listened to the most beautiful sound in the world: the clatter of dozens of typewriters. *Chick-chick-chick-chicka-chick-chick-zing.* Like the sound of the dancing feet of Fred Astaire.

I looked back at John to see if he had any reaction at all to the last part of the article. I'd included a version of Mrs. Roosevelt's quote on not wanting to be first lady but altered it so that it sounded more like a deferential wife shying away from the spotlight than a restless woman eager for independence. He shrugged and handed the pages back.

"Looks good to me, Hick."

"No big bombshells there," I said.

"Same old, same old. Want to get a little hair of the dog in a bit?"

"Is the pope Catholic?"

I took my pages back to my desk. I was being true to the letter of the law, reporting what Mrs. Roosevelt had told me, while violating its spirit by bending the truth to cast her in the best light. I had never done anything like that before in my work, and I was surprised by how easy it was. A victimless crime, I supposed. I felt buoyed knowing that I had found a way to protect her and still do my job.

The following day, I was just returning from taking Prinz for a walk when I heard the shared telephone ringing in the hallway. Assuming it was for Mrs. Jansen, the woman across the hall who was in constant contact with the members of her quilting circle, I went to the kitchen to fill Prinz's bowl. Thanks to Mrs. Jansen's piercing voice, I knew all about whose hair was dyed and whose slip was showing at the church supper and whose son had been seen lingering outside the window of a young woman known to walk around in her underwear. But now the phone continued to wail and she did not emerge. Could the call possibly be for me? I made plenty of outgoing calls from that phone, hunting down sources or calling in to my editor, Bill, but I didn't receive many. The only family I had left were my sisters. Myrtle and I hadn't spoken in more than ten years; I honestly didn't even know whether she was still alive. And as for Ruby, she lived here in New York with *Julian,* a man whose name I could not utter without the italics, but they didn't have a telephone of their own, and we rarely spoke.

I picked up a pad and a pencil, prepared to be supremely annoyed if I had to take a message for Mrs. Jansen.

I snatched up the receiver. "Yes?"

"Miss Hickok?"

"Speaking."

"This is Eleanor Roosevelt."

The pencil slipped from my hand and I watched it roll across the hallway tile. When I tried to speak, my tongue only shifted like wet cement.

"Hello?" she said. "Can you hear me?"

I finally jolted myself back to attention. "Mrs. Roosevelt. Good evening." Had she called the office to get my number? Why hadn't anyone warned me? I groped with my stockinged foot to pull the pencil back my way. I guessed she had to be calling about her schedule, upcoming lunches, speeches, ceremonies — something that I might want to cover.

"Hick, I'm calling to see if you are free for dinner tomorrow."

I squinted, trying to call up the editorial calendar tacked up over my desk in the newsroom. I couldn't remember what I had booked for the following day, but I could probably get out of it. Was she always this bad at delegating work? I wondered. The scheduling seemed like a matter for her secretary.

"Thank you for letting me know, Mrs. Roosevelt. Where will you and the president-elect be dining? We can keep it candid and light — just a piece about how you are celebrating his victory."

She laughed. "Oh, no. It's just me. I am teaching in the morning, you see, and I hate coming all the way from Albany without at least seeing a friend."

It took my addled brain a moment to understand that by "friend" she meant *me*. "Well . . . sure," I said. "I'd be honored."

"Oh, don't talk that way — please, you must promise."

"All right, then," I said. "Well, where shall we go?" My mind spiraled. Dinner with Eleanor Roosevelt, just the two of us. I could only imagine what she would think of my typical haunts, chosen for their cheap

60

food in large portions and bootleg booze only slightly less caustic than paint thinner. She'd probably never eaten a meal that didn't involve white tablecloths, tuxedoed waiters with silver trays. I tried to think on my feet. "Do you like Armenian? There's a great little place in my neighborhood."

"Oh," she said. "That sounds . . . interesting."

A misstep. What was I thinking? People of her class disdained garlic as if it were a contagious disease. "Or not," I said. "We can go wherever you like."

She hesitated. "In the past few months, it has gotten . . . more difficult for me to go about my routine without reporters following me around — the green ones, I mean. Not you. They ride in the same car with me on the train and then follow ten steps behind on the sidewalk. Last week, a young woman waited outside Todhunter for me all day. I watched her from the window of my classroom, sitting on the curb with her handbag in her lap. They don't let me alone!"

I laughed. "Well, forgive me, but I think you have to look at things from their point of view. They have a job to do, after all. They have editors breathing down their necks." I sat back down beside the telephone table and rested my steno pad on my knees.

Mrs. Roosevelt sighed. "I don't see why anything I say or do would interest anyone." Then she brightened. "What about this — do you know how to cook?"

"I do," I sputtered. Was I understanding what she was asking? Did she want to come to my apartment?

"Would that be a terrible intrusion, if I were to invite myself over for dinner?"

"Not at all!" I tried to sound casual. "It will be a lark." I tried to picture this heiress sitting at my flea market dining table, eating off one of my chipped plates. The balloon that had been expanding in my chest deflated into a listless rind. We would be alone together, as we had been on the train. The image of her cheek resting on her elbow flashed through my mind and I felt a spark of confused hope.

"Ten Mitchell Place," I managed to squawk when she asked for my address.

I set the telephone down and walked slowly back into my apartment. Just two days ago, I had been standing in the parlor of her town house, where they employed a person whose entire job it was to dust things. Her *butlers* probably had butlers. I took a deep breath and reassured myself that it was small-minded to assume she would judge my apartment beneath her standards. Maybe it would be an adventure for her, like camping.

Back when Ellie and I were together, we lived for seven years in the Leamington Hotel in Minneapolis, so neither of us had ever really gone to housekeeping. Since our split, I had lived on my own, and, as I looked at my living room, I could see now that I had let things go quite to hell. I picked up an empty coffee cup and a glass sticky with the remnants of yesterday's bourbon and carried them into the kitchen. Over the narrow sink was a window with a small shelf mounted on it, and, miracle of miracles, my African violets seemed to thrive there despite the soot and grime the alley coughed up. New Yorkers complained about how dirty the city was, but I knew better. Bowdle, South Dakota — now that was a filthy place. Out there the dust had nothing to cling to and so it gathered in roving clouds that would burst through a kitchen window at a moment's notice. My mother had once laid the most beautiful — if humble — supper on the table when one of those clouds coughed in and coated every last piece of food with red dirt. She hadn't even cried; she had been beyond crying by then. Oh, how I hated thinking about those years. The blessing of New York was its anonymity, its pastlessness. When the AP hired me — a dirt-poor nobody with the lineage of an alley rat and a college degree it took me four tries to get — I had learned that you could erase your whole story and start again. The city had wiped me clean, and reporting had saved me. It was the bone running down my back.

All I could be was what I was, so I got to work. I did the dishes and peeled off the daybed cover; I attacked all four corners and the ceiling cobwebs with a broom, scooping the dust and dog hair into the dustpan. Prinz padded over and looked from me to all his old hair in a heap. He seemed a little hurt when he saw me tip the dustpan into the pail, but I just said to him, "Look, bub, the past is dead and gone."

I polished the scuffed surface of the dining table and ironed a linen tablecloth I had found at a rummage sale the previous spring. Then I hauled the daybed cover and my dusty drapes to the launderette.

"Aren't I virtuous?" I asked Prinz when I took him out for his evening stroll. He was stoic, but I knew he was impressed. If I got hit by a bus now, I thought, everyone would marvel at what a fastidious housekeeper I'd been.

In the morning, I woke gasping out of a dream of curdled hollandaise and too-rare lamb, as if I had a clue how to prepare either. Steaks, I thought, steaks in the oven. Then I combed the apartment — cookie jar, summer pocketbooks, junk drawer — in search of funds. At the office, I filed the last part of my profile, wondering if Mrs. Roosevelt had read the installment that had run in the morning edition.

By six o'clock, I had the steaks slathered in ketchup and baking in the oven. I put on the first act of *La Traviata,* and, while I set the table, I amused myself imagining what Wagner would say about Verdi's masterpiece. Too beautiful; too satisfying. Better to make the audience long for resolution but never give it to them. Better to torture them with dissonant chords that kept relief just out of reach. I aspired, in opera as in life, to the Italian way, but Wagner had his thumb on my heart, I knew. I was doomed to unrequited longing.

I opened a bottle of Chianti but drank down a bourbon first, lit a cigarette, and stood in the middle of the kitchen to smoke it. I clutched the wooden pendant on my necklace with my left hand as if it were a rosary with a single bead and the prayer was *Don't screw this up.*

The door buzzed.

I opened it and there she stood, with a dark-suited man behind her.

I tried to breathe. "Hello there."

"Hello, Hick!" she said, and glanced down. "And who's this?" She knelt and put out her hand. I introduced Prinz and, gentleman that he was, he offered his paw. She rubbed his ears and then gestured to the man standing in the hallway. "This is Marcus, who is here to protect me from you or anyone hiding in your apartment who means me harm. Franklin insists, but he will lose this argument eventually."

Poor Marcus, I thought. I shook his hand.

He didn't smile — perhaps he wasn't allowed — but his kind brown eyes were full of patience. "Would you like to take a look around?" I asked.

"Just quickly," he said, "and then I will be out of your way."

Marcus stepped inside and poked his head into the kitchen. He peeked in the small pantry and cased the living room, glancing under the overhanging tablecloth and in the alcove where I slept. The whole thing took about ten seconds.

"All clear," he said.

"Thank heavens," Mrs. Roosevelt said, and took off her gloves.

66

"Enjoy your supper, ladies." He went out the door and closed it behind him.

"Let's start over," she said. "Thank you for having me, Hick."

"Oh, it's my pleasure, Mrs. Roosevelt. May I take your coat?"

"We need to talk about that."

"About your coat?" I asked as she slipped it off and handed it to me. It was navy cashmere with silver buttons, and I hung it in the front closet. The first lady's coat, just hanging in my closet.

"No, about my name. Won't you please call me Eleanor?"

I cleared my throat and tried to say it, but I couldn't get my gums around it. "I don't think so," I said.

She made a dismissive cluck with her tongue. "Did you know that Marcus is going to sit downstairs in the car and wait until we are finished with our supper? And then I am going to have to argue with him about letting me take the train back to Albany instead of riding with him?"

"Well, he has his orders." She seemed not to understand the gravity of what had happened to her, that her husband had just been elected to the highest office in the land.

"And I probably *should* let him drive me, because when I get to Grand Central, that woman reporter is going to be waiting for me on the platform. She followed me all the way here and, when I walked out to Forty-Second Street, would you believe she had the gall to ask me where I was going? She wanted an address!"

I laughed, but I actually felt myself getting my back up over it a little. "Marcus there, that lady reporter — you know, they aren't setting out to annoy you. They have jobs. They have bills to pay. If they don't do the work they've been assigned, they'll be fired. Lord knows there will be a line of people waiting out the door to take their jobs. We don't all live like Roosevelts."

Suddenly it was very quiet in my apartment. I had blurted many idiotic things in my time, but that was one of the more harrowing. My throat started closing up, and I fumbled to apologize but failed. Her face cycled through a few emotions — surprise, irritation, and then amusement. It gave me a little zing to speak to her frankly and get away with it.

"Hick, I am being an absolute bore. Let's talk about something else." She glanced around the living room. "Your apartment is wonderful. How long have you been here?"

"About four years."

"And it's all yours?"

"All three leaky faucets and a radiator loud enough to rattle your teeth. Lucky me." But I did love it, my little kitchen, my violets, listening to my opera records as loudly as I pleased. When I was with Ellie, we had lived in the Leamington Hotel as if we were on vacation, everything temporary and subject to change. And change it did when she announced she would marry to please her family, leaving me in the lurch. I had lugged my broken heart to Manhattan then and found this grand Tudor building in Turtle Bay, an oddity among the laundries and slaughterhouses that churned out soot. I loved its herringbone brickwork, its enormous fireplace in the lobby. It was the closest I'd ever come to making a real home, a refuge from the world's strife. The only hitch was that I'd had to do it alone.

"Lucky indeed," she said. "What's for supper?"

"Steaks." I stepped into the kitchen and peeked into the oven. "Would you like some wine?"

"Half a glass. I don't really drink, but when in Rome . . ."

"Oh, dear," I said. "Don't follow my example, or you'll really be in trouble."

"You don't drink *that* much, do you?" she said with a soft laugh.

If she only knew, I thought.

Then she sat down and I handed her the wine to pour while I fixed our plates and carried them to the table. She seemed very relaxed and, all of a sudden, I felt silly for having worried so much about what she would think of my humble abode. Of course, to someone who can have anything she wants, any piece of jewelry or furniture, any fine hotel suite, lobster for breakfast, no indulgence holds much interest. Solitude and autonomy were the only luxuries she could not obtain, and I had them in spades. I couldn't believe it, but she envied me.

"I love it here," she said. "May I move in?"

I unfolded my napkin and draped it in my lap. "Yes, if you will chip in for groceries."

Prinz trotted over to us and lay down beneath the table, placing one paw on the top of my stockinged foot as he liked to do. After a while, I noticed that her glass was empty. "Would you like some more wine, Mrs. Roosevelt?"

Her mouth drooped. "Eleanor! Just say it!"

"I want to," I said as I poured for her. "I really do. But I just can't."

"You have a very nice nickname. I've never even heard anyone call you Lorena.

Why can't I have one?"

I laughed. "You are about to become the first lady of the United States of America," I said. "I am fairly sure you can have anything you want." I thought about it a moment, trying to come up with a solution. "And no one ever called you anything else when you were a girl?"

She shook her head. "My father did call me Little Nell, after the character from Dickens. But that name reminds me of him, and, well —"

I nodded so that she didn't feel she had to explain. My eyes went to the triple strand of pearls at her throat. Had they belonged to her mother before her, her grandmother before that? I wondered how heavy they were with the weight of the past. "I know all about those kinds of memories," I said. "The ones that dog you."

"You do?"

"My father's only nickname for me was You Little Bitch." I felt my face color and laughed a hard, awkward laugh, trying to shrug off my candor. "I'm sorry," I said. "I can't believe I just told you that."

She held my gaze and pushed her wineglass aside so that she could put her elbow on the table and rest her chin on her palm. Her long forearm extended beyond her cuff like the pale branch of a birch tree. "There is nothing more cowardly than a man who would be cruel to a child."

I laughed that same laugh, uneasy that I had brought the conversation anywhere near this topic. "Well." I blinked. My eyes had started to fill. "It's all decades behind me now."

"And he has passed away?" she asked.

I nodded. "Several years ago."

"Well, then. You are free."

Beneath the table, Prinz changed position, and when he settled, he moved his paw from my foot to hers. I felt dizzy. I never talked about these things with anyone, so I didn't have much experience with a person standing up for my side of things. Even my mother hadn't intervened to save me. Then she died and my father remarried, and my stepmother was no better. When I was a child, I had had a kitten named Tweezer, on account of her legs being so skinny. She had a beautiful face and fur like feathers. And one night when I was seven, my father dashed her brains out on the side of the barn for no reason at all. I saw her lying in the weeds, all bloodied, as I walked to school the next day and had to wait until I got home to bury her. And no one in my house ever said a thing. Mrs. Roosevelt

72

would have been sixteen that year, already taller than everyone in my one-room schoolhouse. What if I had known her then? Would she have stood up to him?

Now her hand rested on the table, the long graceful fingers free of scars and the knobs left by broken bones, her nails painted a pale pink. I wanted very badly to touch her hand, but that was out of the question. Instead, I slid my wineglass closer to hers until the rims touched with a soft clink.

"I hope I haven't upset you," she said.

"*I* brought it up. And anyway, don't we all have wounds like these and try like the devil to pretend them away?"

"Yes, indeed."

I looked at her expectantly.

She laughed. "Oh, I see. You've shared your tale of difficult times, and you'd like me to respond in kind."

I grinned. "It seems only fair. It doesn't have to be on the record."

"I can see why everyone says you're such a good reporter. Now you have me wondering whether those things you said about your father are even true."

"If only they weren't."

She didn't say anything for so long that I wondered whether she was going to stand up and leave. Then, finally, she started talking. "I guess it was about ten years ago — in '18, so that would make it a few more than ten — when Franklin's mother and I received a telegram at Hyde Park that we should come to the city and summon an ambulance to meet Franklin's ship, which was just returning from Europe. He had pneumonia in both lungs, they told me, plus a case of influenza that concerned them even more."

"I can see why," I said. "An awful lot of people were dying from it around then." I wondered where the story was going. Would she tell me that this brush with death helped strengthen her marriage for the unknown challenges that lurked in years to come, like his polio, his political scandals, the grueling campaigns? The idea of so tidy a narrative disappointed me. I wanted to bypass the public image, yearned to get at her secret truths the way a hand wants to find its way inside a blouse.

She continued. "So his mother and I rushed to the port and got him home under a doctor's care. While I let him rest, I began to unpack his bags, sorting out what papers required attention, which dispatches should be filed — that sort of thing. And that's when I found the letters."

I raised my eyebrows.

"There were so *many* of them. The bundle must have been three inches thick, and it was tied together with red string. He had only been gone for two months. So she must have sent at least one every day."

"Did you know her?" I was trying not to tip my hand — I wasn't completely shocked by this story, as plenty of rumors swirled about FDR's dalliances. And as assistant secretary of the navy and then governor, he would have had access to plenty of adoring women, in addition to well-appointed offices in which to meet with them.

"Oh, yes," she said. "It was Lucy Mercer, my secretary."

"*Your* secretary!"

"Apparently his own secretary was too busy with actual work to make herself available."

I groaned. "You must have been devastated."

She tipped her head from side to side, weighing whether that word described what she had felt. "I certainly was shocked — foolishly. The hardest part was realizing that not only had Franklin betrayed me, but so had my friends. She had gone with him to dinners that I could not attend, sat next to him as if she were his wife, and they said nothing. My real fear was that they all liked her better than me."

I didn't know a thing about Lucy Mercer, but she must have been quite young and was likely docile as a cow. She probably petted and pleased him, but what a meager offering compared with the qualities of the woman sitting before me.

"So I offered him a divorce."

"Really." Now that did shock me. It was an unthinkable word in her circle. For a moment, I thought of what a scoop that would be for a reporter who wanted to hurt the Roosevelts. The truth was a dangerous thing in the wrong hands, and yet she was trusting me with it.

"His affections clearly lay elsewhere. Why shouldn't he be able to pursue them out in the open?"

I took a sip of wine. "I can think of a few reasons."

"Yes, well, so could he. Even then, he and Louis had a plan to put him up for president someday, and a divorce would make that impossible. Add to that the fact that his mother — who controlled the purse strings — expressly forbade it, and, well . . ."

"So you forgave him." Out in the hall I could hear Mrs. Jansen talking on the telephone, and in the unit above, children thundering down the hallway. None of it seemed to faze her.

"I forgave him. Conditionally. We would remain married, but I no longer asked for his fidelity. I was tired of his insulting my intelligence by lying. We really always have been great friends, and I didn't want to lose that. I would be the political wife. I would continue with my writing and organizing, so long as it didn't conflict with his policy work. I would take care of the children."

"I fail to see how this arrangement offered any benefit to you," I said.

"As I said, I told him that he would have his freedom." Her soft eyes locked on mine then, belying the plan that was behind them, what she had already made up her mind to do. "But I would also have mine."

She was watching me carefully. I thought of Marcus, supposedly down in the car. What if he had decided to stay in the hallway; what if he walked in now? Something thrilling or dangerous or both was happening here — something that had to be concealed. I could not look away from her eyes, and so I allowed myself to fall into them, like tipping forward to dive into the smooth surface of a swimming pool.

"I'd like you to write to me," I said, trying not to come undone. "Dispatches of your new life as it is unfolding. Off the record, of course. Things you might not say in an interview, things you'll have to trust me with." The idea had come to me when John had shrugged at the draft of my feature. I hadn't planned on writing more about her, but suddenly it was all I wanted to do.

She looked surprised. I was dodging the question she had all but come out and asked: did I want her as she wanted me?

"Letters? To what end?"

"Someone will write your biography someday. Why not me?"

We had finished the bottle of wine by then and she seemed a little tipsy, emboldened. Beneath the table, her shoe hung off the back of her foot and I felt the smooth block of its heel grace my ankle. "And what shall I have in return for bringing you into my confidence?"

"I'll never write anything that could hurt you," I said. I tried to catch my breath. "You can read my drafts." The words shocked me as they bolted from my mouth — what a promise! The cardinal rule of reporting, objectivity, abandoned in a heartbeat. "I'll help people see who you really are." She nodded patiently, as if waiting for more. I twisted my lips sideways. "And I'll give you a nickname. Nora."

She threw her head back and laughed, and

I saw her beauty then, the beauty of a gleaming mare that knows she can leap a fence without effort, that knows down the whole length of her body what she is.

"I would like it very much," she said, "if you would call me Nora. And only you."

And then she pressed both palms on the table, rose up, and kissed me on the mouth. I remained inert for a moment, stunned and yet not stunned at all because I had known that this would happen from the moment we had lain side by side in the Pullman car as it raced to Manhattan. My mouth awakened to her soft lips on mine, the hunger rising up, and we slid out of our chairs and stood. The space between us disappeared into fingertips, the coiled promise of our bodies. And if you think I am going to tell you what happened after that — remember, I had promised to protect her, and later I would lose the most important thing in my life trying to do just that — well, I guess you haven't been paying attention.

November 14, 1932

Dear Hick,

Well, here it is, my first dispatch. Ask and ye shall receive — I hope you won't be bored to tears.

Now that the election is settled, one would think that the hubbub might have died down, but it has not, not in the slightest. Franklin has been in Albany tying up loose ends, and I am here in Manhattan packing the boys up to get back to school and writing letters with sincere gratitude to all the people who helped on the campaign, so many my hand may never uncurl. Likewise, we skate across the front hall on all the mail. Every man, woman, and child promised a favor has written to remind Franklin of it, and the savvier among them are calling on the telephone to arrange dinners, lunches, and fishing trips. But this is the way of the world, and we are happy to help supporters.

I am keen to get him my suggestions for his cabinet before the cavalry of new advisers come thundering across the drawbridge. I hope it will not be too scandalous to say that he does listen to me, and if not me then surely Louis, and, thank heavens, Louis listens to me. We must have Frances Perkins for labor, without question. She is the most qualified, and can you imagine how much more efficient she would be than any man? No drink, no dalliances, no bombast. Just solid policy, step by step, until we can look working people in the eye again. Good governance should be boring but steadfast as the moon.

And of course we face going to housekeeping in that drafty white barn in the middle of the swamp. Many decisions await, and a role that has doomed far better women than I. We all know about poor Mrs. Lincoln's temperament, but did you know that Ida McKinley transformed into an invalid when she walked through the White House's doors and was miraculously healed when her husband died and she got to go home?

I rose early to write this so that you could reply today. Let me have your letter by tonight — please, darling. I miss you and long to be near you.

Nora

November
14
15
16 Saw <u>Grand Hotel</u> with N
17 New suits to tailor
18
19 Met N, NYPL
20
21 N over for a nightcap
22 Took Prinz to vet — poor boy!
23
24 Turkey Day
25 Saw <u>Andrea Chénier</u> at Met (soprano disappointing!)
26 Bosco's b-day party at Dom's
27 Hung over!
28 Recovered for nightcap with N
29
30 Saw the Benton murals at the Whitney w/ N. Wish he'd do Mitchell Pl for me!

December
1 Rent paid — reserves lean
2
3 Saw Stanwyck in <u>The Purchase Price</u> and N came for a n.c.
4
5 Heard Jane Addams speak at NYPL. I

go to too many movies.

6
7

CHAPTER FOUR

December 18, 1932

The weeks went by, and my days were filled
with work and Nora, Nora and work. When-
ever I was engaged with one, I was thinking
about the other. One Saturday, we sat in
Nora's third-floor sitting room at the Roosevelt town house, a fire crackling and
Nora's terrier Meggy snoring on the rug. I
was admiring a piece John had written on a
high-profile murder in the Hamptons and
my eye wandered to Nora, where she sat
scribbling at her escritoire with her reading
glasses on the end of her nose. She wrote
hundreds of pages of correspondence each
week, keeping up with dozens of issues.
There were committees, boards, agencies,
clubs. I had never known that so much of
helping people was in the paperwork. The
sleeves of her dress were threadbare from
the hours she spent at the desk.

"You're going to need a patch," I said,

pointing to her right arm where I could see a little skin exposed. "You are quite literally out at the elbows."

"These?" she said, crossing her arms to touch her elbows. "I like the holes. They're my badges of honor."

I laughed, and Nora moved from her chair to the couch beside me. She handed me the letter she had been writing. Over the last few weeks, in our "working" evenings together, she sometimes asked me to proof her work, but this one, I saw, was for me. She folded her hands to wait while I read it.

Hick,

You asked me to write some notes on the League of Women Voters and our outreach. You know it has been a long slog — at times our greatest hindrance is these women themselves. No longer is anyone blocking their path to the ballot box, but they are not convinced they are smart enough, qualified enough, to have a say. "I let my husband speak for the family" is what I hear again and again, as if that has done them much good so far. Still, I believe we made great strides in turnout this time, though of course there is always more to do.

Ho hum . . . I am writing this as we sit

across from one another and you are reading the evening edition of the paper. You look quite serious, dear, and I long to reach over with my thumb and press the crease out of your forehead. Darling, I am undone by the sweet corner of your lovely mouth. When will I have all of you again?

N

I looked up at her. "Nora. Don't you think we had better be careful? Putting things like this in writing?"

She sat back, looking a little wounded. "I just wanted you to know that I was thinking of you."

I squeezed her hand and then stepped over to the fire. The paper flared when I dropped it into the flames, and I felt both reassured and miserable at destroying her lovely words. "That's for your own good," I said.

Back on the couch, she touched the edge of my ear with her finger and I looked to the door behind her, half open to the third-floor hallway. Servants, campaign volunteers, and friends came and went throughout the day. Louis had an office downstairs. Nora's daughter, Anna, often came for dinner. We were never truly alone, yet each time she was in town, she invited me over. It was easier to explain my presence at the town house than to make up a reason to meet with me at my apartment, especially since she was supposed to report everything on her schedule to Marcus. We did find time to steal away, but those moments were few and far between.

"When we're at my place, it's different," I whispered. And it was. It was nearly possible on those nights to imagine that she was just a regular person, a gal from New Jersey, say, about whom nobody gave a hoot. And I was me and Prinz was Prinz and 10 Mitchell Place was our cozy little home. For days after her visits, I would find scribbled notes hidden around my apartment. "Je t'aime," read the one under the milk bottle. Another, tucked inside the medicine cabinet: "Je t'adore."

"But here, Nora, we can't be reckless. Maybe . . . it's because you haven't been through this before? Well, I have. You should listen to me."

Nora rolled her eyes. She was in a funny mood, more relaxed than I could imagine feeling. "Darling, you worry too much. What can anyone do to us?"

I pulled back from her hand. "Is that a serious question?"

"Franklin and I have our freedom — I told you."

"Surely *this* is not what he imagined when he granted it."

She smiled, thinking it over. "I am not sure he is even capable of imagining what goes on between two women. If I were carrying on with a man, it would be something else, something threatening. But this, we can explain it all away. You and I are new friends, the best of friends, and friends are affectionate. We can hide in plain sight."

"It's one thing to look the other way," I said. "It's another to have something brazen shoved in your face." Everything was happening so fast. But that was how she was when she made up her mind about something. God help you if you tried to slow her down. And we both knew that once the president-elect was sworn in in March, she would be off to Washington and the White House. We had to make the most of every second.

I might be afraid of being found out, but Nora wasn't. She set her jaw. "I won't let anyone try to control me."

"And what about me?" My voice grew shrill. "You are at once the smartest woman I've ever known and as naive as a child. What do you think would happen to *me* if we were found out?"

"We won't be."

"I could be fired, Nora. They could keep us apart."

She gave me a skeptical look. "Who? Who is 'they'?"

"You don't think Louis will do whatever he has to do in order to protect your husband? To protect his office? He would dispense with me in a heartbeat."

A change came over her face as she thought about this, and I saw that I was getting through to her, if only a little. For my part, it was all too clear. Without my job, I would be nothing again, nobody. I might as well hop on the train back to Bowdle. If this were a poker game, I had all my chips on the table.

Meanwhile, the threat of discovery seemed only to embolden Nora. So much had been denied to her over the years — there was a brief chaste romance with another girl back in boarding school, but she had been a faithful wife in a marriage enlivened by intellectual connection but not passion — and it was as if, to butcher Whitman, she had unscrewed the door from its jamb.

I felt her fingertips slip north of my knee. A warmth spread in my belly, and I longed to give in to it, but I heard the sound of footsteps on the stairs, voices in the hall exclaiming over the driving rain outside.

I leaped to my feet. "Let's go out."

We decided to go to a matinee at the Met. I could tell she was angry as we walked because she was careless with the umbrella she held over both of us, and water dripped down my left cheek. Marcus didn't know we had left, and I wondered whether we should stop in somewhere and call the town house to report in.

"We could take a taxi," I said, wiping my cheek with my sleeve.

"No."

Her shoes clacked against the pavement, and I had to rush to keep up with her. When we reached the corner of Sixty-Fifth and Fifth, we waited for the light to change. She would want to walk south along the park, I knew, even in the rain. I tried to understand her anger — had she felt I was rejecting her?

"Nora, everything you feel for me, I feel for you," I said, touching her sleeve. "Probably more."

Her jaw was tight. "I do not like to think someone could take it away."

"They won't — if we take care."

After a few more miserable blocks, she consented to a taxi and we rode in silence.

As the car crawled past the southeast corner of the park, I saw a group of women hanging long underwear to be rinsed by the rain. Behind them, near the pond, was a little shantytown that had grown up over the last year, with tin huts and fires in barrels. I saw that Nora too noticed the women, standing in the rain with their heads uncovered as they spread the stained, gray garments over the fence.

The driver seemed not to recognize Nora, but the day had made me paranoid, and I imagined him calling up a newspaper to tell someone he had seen us together. And yet what details could he report that would threaten us? When I was with her, I felt exposed, as though my face betrayed everything I felt, but perhaps Nora was right. Perhaps what was between us really was invisible.

Under the awning at the entrance to the opera house, Nora brushed her damp hair off her forehead. I could tell she was trying to compose her public face before we stepped inside. There we would be among her set, wealthy Manhattanites, the cream of society, the powerful.

"Hick," she sighed, closing the umbrella, "you have to understand. From the day I turned sixteen, my name has controlled my fate." The women in furs rushed past us, foxes lunging for their dens. "My name has ordered my days. I am forty-eight years old now, and I've only just begun to see how I could make a life of my own. I'm not angry at you. I'm angry at them." She pointed at the foxes. "At all that I have lost in taking such care to follow the rules."

I didn't know what to say. I had not faced the problem of enormous wealth and the ways it curtailed a woman's freedom; in fact it was tempting to laugh at that problem, as a person who had not seen a bathtub with plumbing until she was fourteen years old. But the truth was, in running away from home, I really had gained my freedom once and for all, and I hadn't needed to look back. I was haunted by other things in other ways, of course, but at least my life was my own.

I was grateful to see the lights inside flicker, calling us to our seats. The opera was *Aida* — fitting for us as a story of star-crossed lovers — and the music worked its usual magic on me. The tenor in the role of Radamès sang of the slave he loved: *"Celeste Aida,"* heavenly Aida. I marveled that a body could make such a sound; that a sound could become an entity, a physical thing. To experience an aria was to have your heart plucked from your chest, washed, shined, and reinstalled. By the end of the second act, I was so thoroughly transported that I had forgotten Nora was sitting beside me.

But she had not been transported. When the house lights came on, she sprang from her seat and climbed the stairs to the stage.

"Good afternoon," she called into the cavernous space, and there was a pause before the whispering began: *Is that Eleanor Roosevelt?* I stayed frozen in my seat, baffled.

She clasped her hands in front of her and called out in her signature warble, "I am here tonight as a representative of the Emergency Unemployment Relief Committee. As we enjoy this spectacular performance, we must remember that many citizens of our state are, at this moment, wanting for the most basic necessities of life. While we sit here in comfort and luxury, the unemployed go back to homes without food, without heat. I'm sure you will agree that when we see people in need, we absolutely *must* do something about it."

It took everyone, including me, a moment to understand what she was after, but soon the bejeweled pocketbooks began to click open. A laugh rose in my chest, and I pressed my hand over my mouth to contain it. She wouldn't let them sit comfortably beneath the crystal chandelier, these people who held all the power over the weak and out of luck — the people who had held such power over *her*. While I had been swept away in the love story, she had been plotting to shake down the audience.

As ushers rushed to collect the donations in time for the second act to begin, Nora walked back up the aisle to our seats in that gait that apologized for itself, her shoulders hunched to mask her height. The anger had gone out of her.

"You were right, Hick," she said as she sat back down. "We cannot act as if society does not exist. I was thinking only of myself, of us. But if we could run away tomorrow and live as we pleased, what would happen to the work we've spent our lives on?"

"Who cares?" I said, and mugged to make her laugh. But if she had asked me to run away right then, I would have left with nothing but the clothes on my back, apologies to Prinz.

She tilted her head like a school marm. "There is more at stake than just our own happiness."

"I've got to hand it to you," I said. "There are very few people who have both access to high society *and* the gall to hit them up for cash."

"Well, why shouldn't I, when the need is so great? What good am I to this country if I do not make use of every possibility to help people?" I was starting to understand that this was classic Nora: she denied herself a thing she wanted until desire bubbled up, uncontrollable. And then she tamped it down with shame at her selfishness and made herself atone.

As the lights dimmed in advance of act three, I was left somewhat unsettled by Nora's stunt. I couldn't help but notice that the possibility of my own ruination — the very real chance that I might be fired and lose everything that mattered to me — had failed to move her to action. I supposed the specter of my loss was insignificant in the face of the widespread suffering of the poor women forced to do their laundry in Central Park. But aren't we all the heroes of our own little operas? Didn't I have the right to live inside my particular tale?

I shifted my attention forcefully back to the stage, where the new act opened on the eve of Radamès's wedding to a woman he is forced to marry in order to form a political alliance; he and Aida make a secret vow to run away together. I longed to take Nora's hand in the dark but could not, and so, instead, imagined invisible wires linking us and tried to telegraph my affection.

"Do you remember that night on the train from Potsdam?" she whispered close to my ear, "when you said I should reimagine what the first lady could be?"

The White House was the last thing on my mind, and I couldn't help but think that at the moment we were being galvanized by two very different forces. But I remembered everything from the night on the train as if I had transcribed it line by line into my notebook. I nodded. "You said they would fight you at every turn."

"Well," Nora said, her breath warm on my skin, "I am ready for a fight."

My dear heart,

I want to tell you of matters that concern me greatly at present, both to give a sense of what this country faces and to hold myself accountable. If I write here that I will take action, then I must keep my vow. Or you will not be able to put it in the book someday!

I am working up an initiative for the Junior League and other women's clubs; maybe we will call it "Spare a Room." Those who run in our set tend to have space to spare in their country houses and even in the city — more rooms than people — and I'd like to propose that they fix up an extra room as an efficiency and take in someone who is down on his luck. A kind of temporary shelter initiative but dispersed across households instead of institutionalized. Certainly it is warmer and more cheerful to be in a real home, with good food and company. The members will howl, I know, and maybe it sounds ridiculous — what do you think?

Housing is on my mind constantly. Seeing those women in the park was an admonishment that we must not rest until we have people sleeping safely indoors. Good gracious, in this richest country on earth, you would not think this should be a radical statement. I think of how hard it must be for people in the city, how rural life offers a more peaceful and economical option.

Why aren't we building homes, building towns? With jobs and schools and big gardens that will yield food inexpensively? Back to the land we must go, to teach out-of-work people how to grow their own food and depend upon themselves instead of factory jobs, and raise up whole towns full of children who have what they need to become productive citizens. It is such a trial to be patient with committees and policy briefs when daring action is required.

Tonight is Scrambled Eggs and Brains, when we invite all manner of policy makers over to the town house for supper to discuss the issues of the day, and I mean to bring this up, these subsistence towns, though the first step is getting reports from the field. But I must take care not to bring it up until all are served because at the last session I went on a tear about trade unions and burned the eggs.

Now, let me apologize for my stunt at the opera. We <u>will</u> take care and guard what is ours and I promise to behave much better if you will promise to be patient with my restless nature. Will you take me this week to the Armenian restaurant you mentioned once on the phone? I have looked up the names of the dishes and am practicing how to say them — dzhash, dolmas, lavash — so that I may order my own supper.

All my love, darling, in all the ways I am learning to give it and long to give it, and only to you,

Nora

Chapter Five

On Monday I walked into the newsroom to find John Bosco standing in front of his desk with one hand on his hip and the other over his eyes, laughing. Eight hundred-pound sacks of feed corn were stacked on his desk and the surrounding floor. A corner of one of the sacks had torn, and the yellow grain pooled on the carpet below.

He looked up when he saw me come in. "Oh, are you ever in for it."

"Whatever do you mean, sir?" I said, fluttering my lashes like an innocent doe.

Just then, our editor, Bill, strode through the room with his eyes glued to his steno pad. He was a firecracker of a guy, compact and combustible. "Bosco. Hick," he said, wishing us good morning without looking up. He crossed the room to the coffeepot, poured, and stalked back in our direction. John sat down on the piled sacks.

100

Bill sipped his coffee and flipped a page. "Bosco, you're on the seaport fire. The marshal is saying arson. Hick, I want ten inches on —" He looked up when he heard us snickering. Bill blinked for a moment at John's desk. "Bosco, what the hell?"

"Don't ask me," John said. "Ask this hayseed what she's up to. Eleanor Roosevelt is turning her into some kind of do-gooder."

I gave John a sideways glance, wondering what he meant by that and whether it should worry me. "It was just a prank," I rushed to say.

Bill looked thoughtful. He had a habit of adjusting his tie and then pulling on his collar with his index finger — a tick of a man constantly on the lookout for disaster. "Hick, let's talk in my office," he said. Then he pointed at John. "Bosco, I hope you have a plan for getting that out of here that does not involve a flock of chickens."

I hustled over to my desk to call the classified department to get them to remove the ad.

"This is great stuff, Hick," Bill said as he waved the previous day's issue of the *Times*. He smoothed his black hair. "This thing about blisters from her sensible shoes? I mean, you've got to be kidding me."

I sat down across from him at his desk. "If Mrs. Roosevelt's shoes aren't breaking news, I don't know what is."

Over the previous few weeks, I had written about Nora's penchant for those ten-dollar dresses and cheap hats and the way she walked everywhere to save on cab fare. Hand to God, she packed her own lunch most days, and I had seen her mend a torn glove rather than buy a new one. Perhaps I'd been laying it on a little thick. It was only that I wanted people to see she was just a regular person like them, that she didn't live as an heiress. But I was not breaking any big stories. Day after day in our time together, I watched scoops sail by — the things she told me! — but I did nothing with the intel, having promised her it was all off the record, that she could see my pieces before I filed them. I felt like someone I hardly recognized.

"Well, they're eating it up." Bill sat back in his chair and folded his hands across his belly. "We've gotten a dozen letters about this piece. You make her seem so warm, comfortable around you. Does she ever confide more than her spending habits?"

I froze for a second, on high alert to discern his implication. "We talk," I said. "She tells me things for background."

Bill nodded and seemed to accept my lie. "Well, I don't have to tell you that we can't underestimate her reach. She's going to have her fingerprints on every political appointment. She's probably got lists of candidates on her desk right now."

In fact, she *did.* I had seen her working on them, though for my own sanity I had begged her not to divulge any more names — she'd already mentioned Frances Perkins in her first dispatch — until all was said and done. I didn't want to know how carefully her husband was considering her suggestions. See no evil, print no evil. Some other reporter would find out eventually and speculate in print. And that would be one more scoop dead and gone. But at least I wouldn't have betrayed her.

Bill was still looking at me. I shrugged, as if to say, *When would a peon like me have the chance to see her desk?*

"Well, I think it's brilliant, the way you're ingratiating yourself," he said. "If she trusts you, you'll have unfettered access to anything the president-elect tells her."

"You know this job is my life, Bill," I said, answering a different question than the one he had asked me. "I'll bring you anything I can get."

He eyed me with care, and I saw there

was duplicity in his praise. He tapped yesterday's paper again. The headline was THE DAME HAS DIGNITY; the piece contained zero actual news. At this point, I had nearly run out of uncontroversial things to say about her.

"I hope you're right about that, Hick. Because I'm sure you know I'm going to need more meat on the bone going forward. Readers are all over this stuff about her because he hasn't taken office yet. They know he can't *do* anything yet. But once he can, they are going to turn on you if you can't deliver the goods. After all, it is your job."

I gave him a weak smile. Suddenly my blouse felt tight across my shoulders, the room too warm. Threats called up my old recklessness from my girlhood days on the farm, when I'd sometimes provoke my father to anger just to get the lashing over with, just to keep him from being able to take me by surprise. I bit down on my urge to tell Bill to go to hell. Keeping him happy, I reminded myself, was the main thing that kept me in New York and kept Bowdle a distant memory.

But Bill wasn't going to let it drop. "In the meantime, why don't you get me something on the daughter's affair." It was a statement more than a question. Nora had told me she was helping Anna expedite the divorce, though the president had urged her to wait and see if her marriage would improve. *Life is too short to be miserable,* Nora had said, though of course I wouldn't print that for all the bourbon in Kentucky.

"What's the news peg?" I asked Bill, trying to turn his own demands back on him. "It's just dirty laundry, rumors."

Bill counted the potential angles on his pudgy fingers. "Embarrassment for the president-elect? Stress on the family? Her children running wild while she is distracted with her causes? While Anna's off having her affair, I hear Elliott has left *his* wife to run off to be a cowboy in Texas."

I gaped at him, though he wasn't wrong. Elliott Roosevelt *had* lost his mind and bought a cattle ranch, abandoned his wife and child. The Roosevelt children could not be said to have the clean reputations most people expected of members of the first family, and yet I did not see what this had to do with Nora. "Anna is a twenty-six-year-old woman, not a child. What in the world do you think her mother could do about her love life? And what do you propose she should do about Elliott — ride out to his ranch on a horse and drag him home? It wouldn't be fair to write about those things, Bill. It would be very hurtful to Mrs. Roosevelt."

"Well, then," Bill said, "it's a good thing you work for me instead of her."

John went out for a while and came back just as I was getting ready to leave the office for the day. He sat down at his desk with his unbuttoned coat still on; it splayed out on either side of the chair, revealing the torn blue lining. His demeanor was totally changed, his face ashen.

"Everything all right?" I asked.

He nodded once. "Just found out I lost some money."

"Some?"

"A lot. A hell of a lot." He scratched the whiskers on his neck. "*Damn.* I just finally got out of the last hole."

I took a bottle out of my desk and poured us each a drink. "Have you been to see Marina?" Another nod. He took the glass I offered. "What does she say?"

He threw his thumb over his shoulder like an umpire. "I'm out. She says this is the last straw."

John's girlfriend had said it before, but it seemed this time was different. And even though I was fond of John, I found myself thinking, *Good for her.* Marina was smart — smart enough to know John's problems would make her life miserable if she married him. I'd met her at a few AP functions over the years and always thought John was punching above his weight. She was a dark Italian beauty, devout but with a rebellious streak, the kind whose murmured confession was known to make the priest drop his Bible. But wild colts made the best horses and she was trustworthy, steadfast. John, on the other hand . . .

"You're thinking she's right," he said, and gave me a miserable smile.

I shook my head. What I was actually thinking was that I was a lot more like John than I was like Marina. At the moment, I was fairly on the wagon as I defined it — abstention before 10:00 a.m. — but my drinking came and went like the weather, and I knew it was only a matter of time. It takes one problem child to know another — what might change, what probably never would. John and I each had our vices, and the problem with quitting was that our vices were, for us, both causes and effects — the disease *and* the cure. We clung to them, despite the wreckage they caused.

"How are you fixed for cash?" I asked.

He held up a finger. "Don't." Then he

laughed. "As if you have anything to give me."

"I could come up with a little, if you're really in a jam."

"Don't," he said again. "Because I'll say yes and then I'll feel like shit."

I shrugged. "But it's Christmas."

He considered this and his misery seemed to deepen. "Marina's cooking for her family, and I am now officially uninvited. Hal Richards in sports is having some stragglers over — I guess that's what I'll do. I'm not exactly on stellar terms with my father at the moment either."

I drained my glass. Since I had taken up with Nora, a funny thing had happened to me: I could finally look at myself in the mirror. For the first time in I couldn't think how long, I didn't mind what I saw. There was the dark brown hair streaked with gray, the glower I'd retained from childhood on, but the red lips too — remembering how Nora had praised them gave me a jolt — and the laughing eyes. Behind them, my brain like a windup toy, and in my chest a gypsy heart that had roamed from the plains to the prairie to the island of Manhattan. I was hardly a sight for sore eyes, but love was giving me aspirations. I wanted to do better. I wanted John to see that he could too.

"John," I said and took a breath. "The gambling . . . I think . . . I think you need some help." Someone had to say it.

He pursed his lips and, standing up, shrugged out of his coat and flung it on the chair. Next to his typewriter was a cup full of pencils the secretaries sharpened each morning. He selected one with great care and slid it over his ear. "I'll get right on that, my dear," he said, turning to me with a smirk and pointing to my empty glass. "Soon as you quit drinking."

"Hoo," I said, stung. "You can be a mean son of a bitch when you're cornered."

He tilted his head and fixed me with a curious look. "You know, you went to an awful lot of trouble with this feed-corn gag," he said.

"What are you talking about?"

"The feed corn. The ad."

I smirked. "It was worth it for the laugh."

"But you did all that just because of what I said about Mrs. Roosevelt?" He searched my eyes like he was still waiting for the punch line. "Why do you care so much what I think of her?"

"I don't." I laughed, trying to appear casual though my mind was spongy with fear. Did everyone around me know? Did Bill? Did John? I pulled up my cuff and held my bare wrist up to my eyes. The whereabouts of my watch were anyone's guess — another casualty of my inebriated ways. "Well, would you look at the time. I need a drink."

"And I need to call my bookie," he said, misery in his voice once more. "I'll meet you there."

December 21 — late late late

My darling Hick,

It has been a devil of a day and I cannot sleep.

I am still thinking about those homeless families in the park and how we have failed them and what it means to lose one's home. I imagine that when most people hear the name Roosevelt they think of a life of privilege, and of course they would be right, though I hope that my family has balanced its advantages with service to this nation. It might surprise some to learn, however, that I myself have never had a home of my own. As a girl, I was whisked away to my grandmother's house when my parents died. Then off to boarding school, then marriage, after which I lived in my mother-in-law's house (and under her thumb, which you are welcome to print once she has passed away). When Franklin entered public service we lived in a rented house in Washington, and later the governor's mansion in Albany. And now it is off to the White House. Some would call that the best address in the land, but I might take issue with that claim.

111

What is a home, really, but a warm, dry place with a comfortable chair, and a table filled with the ones you love? That — the freedom and privacy of that place — is something I have not known. I hope it won't sound to you as though I am complaining. All over this land as I write there are people suffering in ways I cannot imagine: hunger, sickness, and despair. It can bring me to my knees if I let it. But what I do think I have a little knowledge of is the forlorn heart of one who has no place of refuge that is all her own, however humble it might appear. I hope when I am gone someone might say of me that I tried to make of that displaced feeling some good action that changed things for the better, that put more solid roofs over the heads of my fellow citizens. I see now how my work is just beginning, and I am getting all kinds of notions about the programs and things I'd like to do. That I intend to do. And watch out or I will recruit you for the effort.

Though for now I am content, my darling, to make my home in the crook of your elbow, in the soft shelter of your chin. How I miss you every minute we're apart.

Nora

chin. How I miss you every minute we're apart.

Nora

CHAPTER SIX

Christmas Eve 1932

Most years, the holidays meant little to me. Ruby and Julian and I might get together for supper at a diner near their apartment. My quilting-circle neighbor, Mrs. Jansen, would cross-stich me a pillow and leave it wrapped in tissue paper in front of my door. In turn, I'd give her a box of stationery from Terrapin — a sort of nudge that she might consider another mode of communication to reduce the endless hours she spent yammering on the hallway telephone.

But this year was going to be different. Nora and I had made plans — real plans — to celebrate Christmas Eve together at my place, just the two of us. The president-elect was stuck in Albany finishing up his gubernatorial duties, and his mother had joined him there. The children wouldn't be back in Manhattan until Christmas Day. Surely over at the town house the servants were breaking their backs to hang garlands of holly on that endless banister, but Nora said she planned to send them home to their families at five.

We picked out a tree together, and I decorated it in anticipation of her arrival. On the way home from work, I detoured to Macy's to splurge on a box of ornaments, pink and green and blue bubbled glass blown into the shape of bells. They looked a little showy alongside the popcorn garland and paper snowflakes I'd made — I hadn't cut paper snowflakes since my one-room schoolhouse days — but I didn't care. In the oven, a meatloaf was baking. On the stove was a pot of mashed parsnips drowning in butter, and a chocolate cake waited in its bakery box. The door buzzed and I threw back what was left in my glass, rinsed it and put it in the drain board so that she wouldn't know I had already been drinking.

"Merry Christmas!" Nora said when I opened the door. She wore a dark coat with a mink collar and on the lapel was a sparkling pin shaped like a poinsettia. Marcus stood behind her. Prinz greeted them with a woof, and Nora rubbed his ears.

"Merry Christmas, madam," I said, careful not to be too familiar. "And to you, Marcus."

He nodded without smiling, never breaking form. "Thank you, Miss Hickok." Nora moved out of the doorway to let him pass, and he took a couple steps into the apartment and gave a cursory glance around. While he was occupied, her eyes found mine and we shared one of our birdbrained grins of infatuation. She put her hand in her pocket and pulled out a small wrapped gift, about the size of a book. My heart plunged and I felt my nerves start to jangle like a bunch of old keys. Shouldn't I have known that the gift I planned to give her was too much, too extravagant? And now it would seem so all the more in comparison with a mere book.

I chewed the inside of my bottom lip. I could pretend I hadn't gotten her anything — that was one solution. I could take the book and be overjoyed, and then act embarrassed at my oversight. Or I could tell her that I had bought us tickets to something, that they would be waiting at will call. I racked my brain trying to remember the rest of the operas on the season's schedule.

"Now, listen to me, Marcus," Nora was saying as she slipped the gift back into her pocket. "It's Christmas Eve, and my husband and I are not going to hear of your working. Do you understand?"

116

"Well, I —"

"I can't stand the thought of you out there in the cold car, and your wife sitting home alone."

"Mrs. Roosevelt," he said, "it's my job."

"But I am *fine* — can't you see?"

Though his face remained blank I spied a new tension in his jaw. "Mrs. Roosevelt, with all respect: I understand your frustration, but I answer to your husband and Mr. Howe. We can take no threat lightly. I will stay out of your way, downstairs. Please enjoy your dinner. And Merry Christmas, Miss Hickok."

He went away down the hall and I closed the door. "What was that all about?" Prinz tapped across the room, back to his bed.

Nora shook her head. "It's nothing. They are alarmists." I raised my eyebrows, waiting for more, and she sighed. "We receive an awful lot of mail these days and there are . . . factions that hate the government no matter who is running it."

"All right," I said, uneasy. It was her way to underplay things, but Marcus seemed to be on high alert.

"Sometimes they make the president's family the target of a threat."

My mind filled with violent images — a man bursting in with a gun, someone wait-

117

ing for her outside the elevator door. The reporter in me went to work. "Is it credible?"

"No," she said, unperturbed. "Maniacs write things just to waste our time."

I didn't say anything for a minute; then I went into the kitchen and poured myself another bourbon. Nora glanced at the tumbler when I came back to the living room. She had a certain expression that I was sure her husband had been on the wrong end of a time or two. Her extreme self-discipline made it impossible for her to understand how some people really could come to rely on a crutch. She would have made a marvelous Puritan, I thought.

"You're making me anxious," I said. I was afraid for her and afraid for myself. If something happened to her, I would be devastated and I would never be able to tell anyone why.

"Don't think about it anymore," she said. "I wish he wouldn't have mentioned it."

Over dinner, she calmed my nerves with idle talk. After that we ate our cake at the coffee table, listening to carols on the radio. I found my missing watch in the ice cube tray and we both had a good laugh. Again I wondered what to do about our exchange of gifts, but in the end I decided to go ahead with what I had planned. Even if she hadn't brought me anything at all, I still would have handed over the little silk pouch cinched at the top with grosgrain ribbon. I'd been walking around with it in my pocket all day.

"This is for you," I said as I dropped it in her hand.

"Oh," she said with glee. "Is it time for gifts?" She set the pouch on the coffee table unopened and went to the closet where I had hung her coat. She came back with her package and set it next to my crumb-speckled plate. "You go first. It has been such a trial keeping this a secret!"

I glanced uneasily at her gift and drained my drink. "Nora, I just want to tell you that nothing you could give me now could mean more than what you have already given me." My voice sounded hoarse and I realized with horror that I might cry. "These last weeks . . ." I felt as though we'd crammed a lifelong relationship into them, marching past the typical fits and starts of new love. And for good reason. We both knew the clock was ticking until the inauguration.

She shook her head, her eyes kind. "You don't have to say anything, Hick. I know. I feel it too."

The moment I picked up the wrapped gift,

I realized that it couldn't be a book. The contents of the package were flexible, soft. I gave her a questioning look and she clapped her hands. "Go on," she said.

I pulled away the paper to find five folded squares of fabric in various patterns — sheer silk and linen and one bouclé — tied together with ribbon.

"Swatches!" Nora said. "If you hate any of them, you can tell me. We've got plenty of time to keep looking and make our plan."

"You're having a pillow made for me?" I asked, struggling to keep the disappointment out of my voice. This was worse than a book. Between Mrs. Jansen and Nora, I was going to have pillows coming out my ears — and, in about five minutes, enough embarrassment to last me the rest of my days.

She laughed. "Well sure, if you want one. But I was thinking of a sofa, curtains . . ." She raised her eyebrows, waiting to see if I understood.

"You're going to redecorate my apartment?"

Again she laughed. "Well, this is rather fun." She tapped her chin with her index finger. "I wonder if I should just keep you in the dark a while longer."

"Nora!"

Finally she put me out of my misery. "We have a lot of property at Hyde Park, as you know," she said. "There's the big house, where Franklin grew up and where his mother lives when she is there." I nodded. "And, a few miles away, Val-Kill, my cottage with the furniture workshop. But when all of this is over" — and by *all of this* I gathered she meant the presidency, her public life — "I am going to build a new house, a little cottage. And you and I will live there together."

I stared at her, stunned. "I don't understand."

"A home of our own, Hick. A *real* home. A life that is just ours."

The emotion I'd been trying to restrain a moment before rushed up and my eyes spilled over.

"Nora," I said. I couldn't string together any other words.

"You see what I want to tell you, don't you, Hick?" She put her hand on my arm. "*You* are the one I want to be with. You are the one I love."

This really wasn't just a lark, an infatuation. That was why it seemed I'd already forgotten what my life had been like before. This was love. And hearing her say it was like an incantation. I let my mind drift over what could be — a quiet life in the country, cups of coffee in the mornings. I saw our dogs running together in the woods, nipping and wrestling in a patch of sunny meadow. I saw a porch swing, and, in the winter, a wood stove fragrant with cedar. Nora had talked in her last dispatch about the forlorn heart of the homeless, and I wondered if she knew she was talking about me too. My years as a girl were a horror to me, and home then was a prison; in the decades since I'd left South Dakota I had doubted I would ever lay my head somewhere that would finally let me breathe easy.

And doubt had made me skeptical. The scene I imagined was nearly painful, because the images were so sweet and so unlikely. I wondered whether she really believed we could have that life. And, even if we could, how many long years would we have to wait for it? I wanted it now, today.

But to her the plans were as good as under way. "We'll have all the furniture custom-made at the workshop and choose everything together. It really will belong to both of us."

She took care not to mention, of course, that the cottage would be on Roosevelt land, with her lawful husband just a short drive away. Still, it was a beautiful thing to imagine, and I took solace in the fact that my gift to her no longer seemed extravagant. "You make me so happy. Nora," I said, and nudged the silk pouch closer to her. She untied the ribbon and turned it over. The ring fell into her hand and its sapphire caught the light from the kitchen.

She looked at me with wide eyes. "Hick, it's too much."

"It's not enough. Nothing could be." I held out my palm and she placed her right hand on top of mine. When I looked at her, she nodded — she wanted me to slip it on her finger.

"With this ring," I joked, trying to cheer myself out of a sudden darkness that had engulfed me. How torn I was — to love her as I did, to know in my bones that she loved me in return. But she wasn't really free to give me that love. Every expression we made of our feelings had a bassline of sorrow, love at once uttered and negated. For now we lived in the same city, but soon she would move three hours and a universe away. It was terrible, and the only way I could bear it was to lie to myself in the way that boozers can — to make this night an island, untouched by yesterday or tomorrow, and believe there would be no consequences for the promises we made now.

"I thee wed," she finished, her eyes still on mine, her face free of guile, and that was it: we were joined by a vow to love fully and secretly, and I felt as protected as I ever could be. We had created a world of our own in which we could be our true selves, invincible.

In the privacy of my apartment, we felt free and unafraid. Time slipped as we listened to one record after another and drank a bottle of wine, and it was into this scene of relaxed abandon that, hours later, Marcus burst, the door banging against the wall in his wake.

Nora and I leaped apart. I stood frozen, my hand clutching the open placket of my blouse. She quickly fixed her dress. Marcus stared not at us but at the blanket that, just a moment ago, had covered us. Now, it draped from the couch to the floor. I could see his thoughts race from shock to confusion. And then his face filled with disgust.

Panic bloomed in my chest as Marcus turned to face the open door to give us a moment to collect ourselves.

"I thought you said you would be waiting in the car," Nora spat. As if righteousness could save us. She shoved pins into her hair, and I saw at once that we had lost our cover. There was no explaining that what Marcus had seen was friends merely sharing affection. We were no longer hiding in plain sight. And it was the disgust on his face that woke me to how much trouble we were in — how could I have let us be so careless? How could I have forgotten that the world would twist the love we shared into something ugly, perverted?

Marcus cleared his throat. "I was in the car, ma'am, but you said your evening would be finished by midnight and it is twelve forty-five. I knocked, but . . . there was no answer. With the recent threats, I became concerned."

I realized he was shouting to be heard over the music, and I crossed the room to turn off the record player, swallowing the urge to vomit. In the bathroom, Prinz was barking his head off and I didn't dare let him out for fear he would attack the Secret Service man. Lord, what had we brought down on our heads? What would Marcus do? Nora would have to ride home to the town house in the car with him. I cringed imagining how awkward it would be for them both.

I looked at her, hoping to see some reassurance — Marcus still had his back to us — but her features were slack. She too was nearly frantic and seemed to hear the question I was all but shouting: *What should we do?*

She shook her head as if to say she would handle it — if it could be handled, that is.

My fingers worried the pendant at my neck as I shuffled through the possibilities. Marcus might go to Louis with it, if he was afraid Nora would try to have him fired. Louis might go to Bill. Of course, Louis could never let the tale reflect poorly on Nora. He would tell an altered story, say that I had fallen into an obsession with Mrs. Roosevelt and forgotten my place, that I should be removed. I would be ruined.

Marcus went into the hall while she slipped on her coat. I saw the flash of the blue sapphire when her hand emerged from her cuff and thought that there was nothing crueler than to finally have the thing you had longed for. Because the world always takes it away — always. For those few hours, we had lived as if we were free, and now we would pay the price. We did not embrace as they left, only shared a final glance before she followed Marcus out. I stood with my back against the wall, listening to her footsteps and the click of the elevator door as it sealed her inside.

CHAPTER SEVEN

New Year's

It snowed on Christmas Day, and I holed up in my apartment, combing notes and recent papers to generate ideas for stories on things other than the Roosevelts. I had once covered crime and the courts, and I could do it again if I had to. I wanted to be ready to change gears and prove my worth if Bill confronted me — or *when* he did. I couldn't stop imagining how it might unfold and called in sick with the flu so I didn't have to face him.

As the days passed, I slowly consumed all the food in my refrigerator, too afraid I'd miss Nora's phone call if I went down the block to the market. But the phone did not ring, and as the last day of the year approached, I received no mail other than bills. Left to its own devices, my mind worked up a few awful possibilities: That Nora would throw me off as if there were nothing between us. Or that she was taking the blame for it all, trying to protect me. I couldn't decide which was worse. The precious time we had left together in New York before she moved to Washington and the White House was leaking away.

Finally, it was the need for more bourbon that ejected me, like a pilot from a plane that was going down in flames.

"Ice or no ice?"

That was the only choice with which one was faced at Dom's, a speakeasy accessed by a steel door covered in peeling brown paint that was hidden by a garbage bin in an alley off Forty-Seventh Street. John and I often found ourselves sitting across from each other at a wobbly table in the dank warehouse that still smelled of the pickles that had once been canned there. We liked it because it was close to our office and made no pretense of glamour, romance, or even heat in the winter. Dom kept a fifty-year-old wood stove next to the bar, which vented through a leaking collection of makeshift pipes that ran up to the street. Everybody kept their coats on until they had drunk enough to warm up.

"No ice," I said.

After Christmas, John had somehow

talked Marina into taking him back and was trying like hell to stay on the straight and narrow. As far as I knew, he had stayed away from Atlantic City, and of course it would be months until the horse racing started again. But there were plenty of ways he could get himself into trouble right here in Midtown, private poker games and the like, so I had been keeping my eye on him. In a way, Dom's was the safest place for him. Drinking kept him mellow.

I was half in the bag already when we carried our drinks from the bar to a table, and John noticed some of mine slosh up onto my wrist.

"You all right, Hick?"

"Couldn't be better."

He narrowed his eyes at me. "You sure? Your neck is red. Your neck always gets red when you're in a lather."

"Maybe I'm just drunk." I smirked. We sat down.

"Well," John said, "you probably are. But your cheeks get red when you're drunk. Your *neck* gets red when you're bent out of shape about something."

"Who knew you paid so much attention to my complexion?"

John held up his hands in surrender and leaned back in his chair until it balanced on its two back legs. "How's the Roosevelt beat?"

"A little sparse with the holidays. Things should pick up with the inauguration."

"No warm-fuzzy exposé on their Christmas traditions?"

I smiled, but it was a hard smile full of my secret pain, and John lowered his chair. "Come on, Hick. What's going on?"

My eyes skittered across the tabletop, over to the chopped wood piled on the floor. "I'm just in a jam. That's all. It will work out."

"But it's something to do with her?"

I looked down into my drink — anything to avoid his eyes. I was dying to have somebody to talk to, but one of the hazards of being me was never being able to say a thing head-on.

John should have known to back off then, but instead he pressed me. I couldn't tell if he was just clueless or actually trying to be cruel. "Can I ask you something?" he said. "But you have to promise not to get mad." He took a cigarette out of his case and offered one to me.

Oh boy, I thought as he lit it. I nodded.

"Does the first dame read your pieces?"

I looked at him in surprise, felt myself relax. "I suspect she does now and then,

130

but not the ones that only run in the Mid-west papers."

He shook his head and exhaled a cloud. "No, I mean does she read your drafts before you file them?"

I sat up. "Of course not. Where the hell do you get off, John?" He'd hit a nerve there. Nora never had to ask to see my articles ahead of time because I now showed them to her as a matter of course and kept my promise to steer clear of stories that made her uncomfortable. I knew I was hopelessly compromised, a disgrace to the profession I held dear. The last thing I needed was to hear it from John. "I can't believe you would ask me that."

John held up a conciliatory palm. "All right, all right. I can only handle one angry woman at a time, and Marina has that market cornered. I'm sorry."

I glared at him. "I believe you were just about to say the next round is on you."

He went over to the bar and came back with two fresh drinks. I pouted a little while longer, through my first few sips. Finally John ventured another question.

"Tell me the truth, Hick. What is it between you two?"

Now we're getting to the heart of the matter, I thought. "We're friends," I said.

He nodded. "Good friends?"

"I guess you could say that."

"Better friends than you and me, Hick? You sure know how to make a guy feel left out."

Something about his face — mock hangdog but with those puckish eyes, enormous ears — made me laugh. I was getting plenty drunk, and it felt so very good.

"Hick, you know what I think about you." He leaned on his elbows and laced his fingers together. "You're the best reporter, man or woman, I've ever known. You're true-blue. You've taught me a lot."

"Oh brother," I said. "Is this where you bring up my advanced age? Call me your 'mentor'? This night keeps getting worse and worse."

"What I'm trying to say is that I'm worried about you. I —"

"You don't need to worry about me."

He bobbed his head, absorbing my words. "I hope you're right."

My instinct for self-preservation was at war with a desire to get things out on the table. "Is there something you want to ask me?" I said, almost taunting him.

"No." He held up his hands again. "It's none of my business."

"Oh, come on. We're both adults. And I've

never hidden who I am."

"Well." He took a drag on his cigarette. "Maybe you should."

"What does *that* mean?"

"Look, Hick. It doesn't make any difference to me whom you like to see. I'm not going to lie — it *is* hard for me to understand. I'm from Ohio!"

"And I'm from South Dakota! What of it?"

He laughed. "I mean I'm not a worldly guy — I don't pretend to understand it. But that's your business, just like Marina is my sad affair. What I'm talking about is your professional reputation. You've got to be careful. You've got to protect yourself. It seems like Bill has his eye on you. Have you thought about what kind of career you're going to have left when this is all over?"

I sucked down my drink. The dark barroom swam; the curved backs of the workingmen who drank there shifted like whales in the swell. I looked at John and I so badly wanted to tell him everything right then: that I was in love; that my heart was breaking; that I knew I was ruining my work but didn't know how to stop.

"Hick, I'd hate like hell to see you get hurt."

I swallowed it all down with the last of my

133

drink. "You know me. I always land on my feet." I ordered another.

For a while we sat in silence. In my stupor, I reminisced about the day the previous year when John and I, along with every other reporter in the solar system, had stalked the countryside around the Lindbergh estate when that baby went missing. We had tromped through muddy fields and old barns, looking for what we were afraid to find: a shallow grave or, if a miracle was in order, some sign of life. Near the Princeton highway, we had found an abandoned house hidden from the road, and I got a haunted feeling when I saw muddy tracks that looked fresh. Armed with a hockey stick from John's trunk, we had walked through the rooms in the dark, afraid out of our minds. But we found nothing. Two months later, when we'd long been back in the city, a truck driver found the baby's remains across the street from that very house. We had followed the tracks in the wrong direction. The AP man in Trenton caught the story and got a Pulitzer for his trouble.

Was that what I was doing now? Following the tracks in the wrong direction?

John slid his glass in a circle on the tabletop. "I'll tell you something I've learned, Hick, for what it's worth. Maybe it'll make you feel better, in a strange way. In the end, we all pay the price to get what we get. Not even to get what we *want,*" he said wearily. "Just what we get."

The weeks passed and I filed my columns on Nora, describing her activities without a single quote from her and hoping no one would notice. I took care to get in before Bill in the mornings and then make myself scarce during the parts of the day when he tended to roam the newsroom. John promised to tell him I was out pounding the pavement. I felt like I was waiting for the blade of the guillotine to come down on my neck. And the only thing worse than fearing Bill's wrath was not knowing what was happening over at Sixty-Fifth Street. It was driving me batty, but I didn't dare write or call. I had to wait to hear from Nora first.

One early February afternoon, I topped off my flask from the bottle in my desk drawer and hustled over to the Paramount in Times Square to see a matinee of *Grand Hotel.* If opera was my first love, then film was her wayward younger sister — more sloppily dressed but with jokes that were dirtier and funnier. A few dozen people were scattered across the rows of burgundy velvet seats. I took one near the back, off the center aisle, just as the curtains opened and the projector clattered to life like a wheel on a rutted road. I tried to let the story carry me away from my problems. Nora and I had seen the film together back in November and loved it — all the intertwining stories, all the big stars. Something about it reminded me of reporting. As the man in the lobby says in the beginning, "People come; people go. Nothing ever happens." That was it, exactly, all these years of my career. I had written thousands of stories, but I could never stick around long enough to find out how they ended.

As the film unfolded, I delighted in the way John Barrymore and Joan Crawford circled each other. She was beautiful in the way a statue was beautiful — even her eyebrows seemed like lines etched in stone — but it was delicious to watch her brazen flirtation, how she could say just the right thing to keep Barrymore's character coming back to her at the balcony, to ask her whether she had a gentleman, to ask whether she, a stenographer, might consider "taking dictation" from him one day. The line was so ribald you had to laugh, and yet I felt the thrum of recognition in it because I could see he longed for her like a thirsty man in the desert. And that was like me and

Nora. Two starlets whose screen tests might break the camera, who shrugged at leading men and instead made eyes at each other across the set. Soon I might know just what sort of price we'd pay for going off script.

A couple weeks later, I came home to a letter.

Feb 12

Dear Hick,
Please meet me Wednesday at 2 on the corner of 65th and First.

Nora

I stared at the single sentence, dashed off in a hurry without so much as a *darling.* Was I supposed to read between the lines? Was I being invited solely as a reporter, once more, to cover a story? I wondered whether Louis Howe would be there too, or the president himself.

I wore my heavy wool coat and took my steno pad with me. The wind off the river was cold and the sun reflected off the gray water. To the south, power plants and slaughterhouses churned soot into the sky, but I faced north, toward upward mobility. The corner on which she wanted to meet

137

was just a residential block, with dormant gardens in front of row houses and an iron bench on the ice-crusted strip of grass near the street. I stood waiting in confusion in the cold for a few minutes until I finally saw her coming around the corner, just Nora alone.

"Hick," she said, and squeezed my hand with her leather glove.

The tenderness I felt for her washed over me. I had nearly forgotten it, nearly drunk it away over the six weeks of worry since Christmas.

"Nora, I have been so empty without you," I said. She wasn't angry with me; she wasn't going to deny what we had. Relief overwhelmed me.

She nodded. "I even miss your dreadful handwriting," she said. I laughed and felt more at ease. "But I wanted to settle things."

My chest was tight. "And have you?"

"I asked Louis to reassign Marcus to the boys at school. He is obviously vigilant."

I closed my eyes. "Is he ever."

"I *do* worry about them. It's not as if I want Marcus to be punished. He didn't intend to . . . do what he did. The boys will be in good hands with him."

"And what did Louis say?"

" 'Fine, Mrs. R.' He barely reacted. I don't

think he knows anything."

I shivered. "Oh, it's so awful."

"We have had a terrible shock. I won't say we are free from worry, but perhaps the worst is over?"

I tried to let that sink in. Nora was ever the optimist, and I wanted to breathe easy too, but something sinister had been unleashed that night and it flared again in my mind when I recalled the disgust on Marcus's face. It was hard to shake.

"Is there a reason we are standing on this corner?"

Nora looked at her watch and pointed to a Juliette balcony at the nearest row house. After a moment, someone opened the French doors and the drapes inside curled in the breeze. I heard the trill of a piano and then the familiar voice of a tenor, singing the role from *Aida*.

I looked at Nora.

"He rehearses at the same time each day," she whispered. "Sometimes I come to hear it."

"Tu sei regina," he sang. *"Tu di mia vita sei lo splendor."* It meant something like "Queen that reigns over me, you are the splendor of my life."

We stood side by side and faced the window, and the backs of our hands hung

139

an inch apart. The biggest threat to both of us in all of New York City was not a sniper or a runaway bus but just the thing that hovered in that inch of space — the longing to close it. The longing to forget that we never could.

A few hours later, I walked into the newsroom and headed straight to the first aid kit. My heart was as frayed as an old hanky, and I was ready for a drink. Over the last few weeks, I had managed to stay pickled morning, noon, and night, and today was going to be no exception. But before I got to the bottle, Bill rocketed out of his office.

"Where is Mrs. Roosevelt?" he shouted. About a dozen heads turned my way. He was all coiled up, his eyes wild.

"I don't know," I said, startled. "Home at the town house, I think. Why?"

"Get the hell up there quick. Some crackpot in Miami just tried to shoot her husband."

CHAPTER EIGHT

February 15, 1933

I buttoned my coat as I ran across the lobby and out onto Madison. It had started to snow, and several taxis sailed by without slowing down. Finally, one pulled over and I barked the address.

The crackpot "tried" to shoot FDR, Bill had said. What did that mean? Had he succeeded? My mind scrambled to understand it. In a crowd, the president-elect was a sitting duck in his open car, since he couldn't run from the scene or quietly slip away through a crowd. He traveled with Secret Service men and bodyguards, but they couldn't cover every angle. Whatever had happened, I was at that moment one of the only people in the country who knew about it.

I thought of the millions of dollars and thousands of hours that had gone into raising this man up to the highest office in the land; I thought of all the hopes that rested on his shoulders. The taxi jerked through an intersection, and I braced myself against the seat with my hand. The entire American democratic experiment was in peril if that assassin were a good shot. Tomorrow's articles could incite panic. Was FDR lying dead in some hospital bed? And was Nora in danger?

Traffic crawled and the chorus of horns was like a church organ at a funeral. When the driver pulled up in front of the town house, I threw my money into the front seat and jumped out, racing up the wide stone steps. A servant moved the curtain aside and peered out before I had the chance to ring the bell. She opened the door and ushered me inside.

"Good evening, Miss Hickok," she said. Her eyes were puffy from crying.

"Have they told you not to let anyone in?"

She nodded.

"Good girl."

"No one but you or Tommy, but she is upstate at a party meeting. We haven't heard anything about Mr. Roosevelt." She closed the door and took my coat.

"It's going to be all right," I said, though I wasn't in the least convinced of it.

The parlor was empty, so I went upstairs

and into a room I had never entered: the president-elect's bedroom. Nora sat on the foot of his bed clutching a handkerchief, though her eyes were dry. Her back was very straight and she looked pale. Behind her on the wall were dozens of framed pictures of family and friends, houses, horses, dogs, boats — the retinue of a wealthy, powerful man.

"Hick, thank God," she said. "What have they heard at the AP?"

I shook my head. "Nothing more than you know already, sounds like. Someone tried to shoot him."

"We don't know if he was hit. Louis has been trying to get through."

On the other side of the large room, Louis stood by a small oak table, jiggling the receiver with a cigarette between his fingers. "Operator?" he shouted a few times. "I need Miami. Hello?" He kicked the wall. "Damnit."

"Louis, *please*," Nora said. I could see she was making a mighty effort to keep her composure.

He shook his head with the handset pressed to his ear. "I knew I should have gone on that trip with him." He slammed down the telephone and then lifted it to try again. "Operator!"

"But it was a pleasure trip." Nora looked at me, bewildered. "He was supposed to be on Vincent Astor's yacht for his birthday. I don't understand why he was even giving a speech." Her eyes shot to Louis. "Has anyone called the boys? Or Anna? We can't let them hear it on the radio."

I thought of Anna's beau, the reporter from Chicago. "If she's with Mr. Boettiger, she may know already. But first things first, Mrs. Roosevelt," I said, addressing her with care in Louis's presence. "Let's confirm that he's all right." I stepped carefully toward the telephone. "May I try?"

He nodded, but, as soon as he set the telephone down, it rang. He snatched it up.

"Hello?" Louis closed his eyes and the tension went out of his narrow shoulders. "Son of a bitch." He looked at Nora. "It's him. He's fine. He didn't even get hit."

Nora emitted a wail of relief that made the hair on the back of my neck stand up. She leaped over the bed and grabbed the handset from Louis. I could hear her husband shouting — the connection was bad — but laughing too, and I let out the breath I'd been holding for what felt like an hour. Suddenly, I was exhausted. On behalf of the United States of America, I was relieved he was all right. But watching her talk to him forced me to remember his primacy in her life, and it made me sorry for myself. I wondered whether his mistress Missy Le-Hand was down in Miami with him, listening while he talked with his wife. I was no better than Missy was; both of us were playing bit parts in this tale.

Nora didn't say much, just murmured "thank heavens" and "that's terrible." A moment later, she said "All right, goodbye" and hung up.

"Well? What the hell happened?" I asked.

She sat back down. "He decided on a whim to go to a rally tonight in Miami — they had docked there this morning — and, outside the hall, he gave a speech from his car. He was talking about fishing and he had just reached over the side of the car to shake Tony Cermak's hand when shots rang out. He said Tony fell instantly, and Gus threw his body over Franklin. The driver tried to pull off through the crowd, but Franklin made them wait to load Tony into the car so they could get him to the hospital."

Louis lit another cigarette. "So this nut tried to kill the president but hit the mayor of Chicago instead?"

"That's what Franklin said. That poor man. There must have been a lot of blood.

145

My husband cannot stand the sight of blood," she said, almost to herself. "Another bullet hit the back of the car and a handful of bystanders. But Franklin says the only thing that's wrong with him is sore ribs, because Gus is no lightweight."

Louis sat down in a chair in the corner with his short legs sprawled out and unbuttoned his collar. "Well, I'll be goddamned." He pulled a flask out of his jacket.

"I'll take some of that," I said with a little too much enthusiasm.

Louis handed it to me. It was gin, which I hated, but I choked it down. "Will Cermak be all right?"

Nora shook her head. "The doctors are working on him now. So we'll wait for word." She stood and straightened the front of her jacket. "What time is it?"

"Time to take a breath," I said. I glanced at the brass clock on the mantel. "Nine thirty."

"I have to call the children before they hear something and start to worry. My speech is in the morning and the overnight train to Cornell leaves at eleven. Hick, if you're going to cover it, we'd better get a move on. I assume you'll need to stop in at home before we head to the train?"

"You still want to go?"

"Why wouldn't I? Franklin is fine. There's nothing I can do for the mayor at the moment, and I won't tie up the line calling his wife now. Why should I disappoint people who are counting on me to show up?"

I laughed. "I think they'd understand."

"I'm going," she said, and I knew there was no dissuading her. It was both impressive and a little frightening to see how deftly she could harness her emotions and pivot to the next item on the agenda.

I took one last pull on the gin and handed the flask back to Louis. "All right," I said to her. "Why don't you make your calls, and I'll take down some notes. I don't need to stop at home — I have a toothbrush in my desk drawer at the office. And I need to stop there anyway to check in, or Bill will have my head."

Nora nodded. "Louis will call downstairs for the car," she said, all business, and went down the hall to the telephone in her bedroom.

I leaned against the wall and pulled my notepad and pencil from my pocket. Eager to preserve the details, I began writing down everything that had just happened. Without looking up, I asked, "All of this is up for grabs, right, Louis?"

As soon as the words were out, I regretted

them, but it was too late to retreat. I hoped he hadn't heard me, but it was clear from his arched eyebrows that he had. No reporter worth her weight in steno pads would ask for approval before filing a story of this magnitude: the near assassination of the leader of the free world. I might not encounter a bigger story in my lifetime, and here I was giving him the chance to massage the facts. I could read the complex panoply of thoughts on his face. As a former reporter himself, it had to make him queasy to see my commitment to journalism go down in flames. And yet perhaps my failing could be useful to him.

"Hick," he began, but then stopped and appeared to change course. "How are things going for you over at the AP?"

"Fine," I said quickly. "Great."

"And Bill is happy with your coverage of Mrs. Roosevelt?"

I wondered if he knew the answer to that and decided to keep my mouth shut.

He took one last drag and stubbed his cigarette out in the overflowing ashtray next to the telephone. "Would you ever think about crossing over to our side, working for me in public relations for the Roosevelts? You could have a real hand in shaping her image." He opened his cigarette case and

148

offered it to me. I pulled out a Lucky Strike.

I balked at this suggestion — my training had taught me to consider working in the city dump before I resorted to public relations — even though building Nora's image was precisely what I'd been doing with my less-than-objective articles about her. I rolled the cigarette between my thumb and forefinger. "I don't think so, Louis. I'm a reporter to the bone. Can't say I'd be very good at toeing the line."

Louis nodded, weighing my answer. He wore his thin hair slicked to his scalp with oil, and the trying day had pried a few strands loose. They'd migrated to his forehead, making him look a little off-kilter. "You two spend an awful lot of time together," he said. "I wonder — are you sure you'll still be able to do the job when the time comes? Call her out when she makes a mistake? Dig around for dirt?"

I knew the answer was no, but I couldn't say it.

He looked at the end of his cigarette as he lit it, not at me, as he spoke out of the side of his mouth. "There's a reason why editors tell you to keep a healthy distance from a source, don't you think?"

That remark contained the shadow of a threat, and I snapped to attention.

149

Finally he met my eyes. "Like I said, you've been spending a lot of time with the incoming first lady."

In that moment, I understood that he knew. Either Marcus had reported what he had seen, or Louis had discerned it himself. He was certainly no dummy and had nearly worked himself to death to secure a Roosevelt presidency. He was not in the business of leaving anything up to chance.

Louis could have told me right then to stay away from her and put the whole thing to bed, but instead he said nothing, only rolled his thumb on the striker of the crystal lighter so that I could finally light the cigarette I'd nearly pressed flat in my fingers.

At the other end of the hallway, Nora's door swung open and she stalked toward us. "Are you all set here, Hick? We can't miss that train."

"She's ready," Louis said with a disingenuous smile that came off like a wince. "And she's got a pretty big scoop on her hands, so you'd better get her over to the AP." He wasn't going to tell me what to write. The phone call, Nora's reaction to it, and the details of what had transpired in Miami — all of it was fair game. And he wasn't going to tell me to stay away from Nora, not today, anyway. Though I almost wished he would.

We emerged from the front door to find it flanked with more Secret Service men than I'd ever seen at once. As they scanned Sixty-Fifth Street, I tried to imagine how they would react if some evildoer came barreling out of the shadows and tried to tackle Nora. Did they have guns at the ready? Across the street was an apartment building ten stories tall, and each window was a tableau of some private existence — a man with a late-night ham sandwich, drawn curtains in another concealing lovers, a lonely dog waiting for its owner to come home. Behind any of those windows could be a man with a rifle, waiting for Nora to step outside. I put my hand on her lower back and ushered her toward the waiting car. For once she didn't complain about not being able to walk to the train station.

"Would you rather go on to Cornell alone, Nora?" I whispered. I wondered if I should tell her that I thought Louis was onto us, but it seemed cruel to add to her troubles.

She gave me a severe look. "Don't you dare leave me right now, Hick." She swallowed, and when she spoke again her voice was faint. "Please."

It took me only ten minutes to type up my piece at the office. Someone else would write the lead story on the assassination attempt, with help from a reporter in the Miami bureau. My contribution was the reaction on the home front.

At Grand Central, more Secret Service agents sprouted like black cornstalks, and they kept the throng away from her path between the entrance and the track. Our footsteps echoed through the hall. We boarded a special car that had been cleared by agents; once we entered, it was sealed off from other passengers.

In the darkness of the tunnel, as we waited for the train to move, she held my hand and finally her erect shoulders slumped forward; she let her head hang down and cried. I swept my palm in slow circles over her back.

"It has been a terrible night," I said.

She shook her head and wept for another minute before she could take a breath and speak. "If only you knew some of the thoughts that went through my head."

"You are under a tremendous amount of stress." It felt like something near treason, what we were skirting around, and I didn't want her to give it voice. The train began to rumble and crawl through the tunnel below the streets.

"When I heard what happened, I only wanted you, Hick. You know what I mean, don't you?" She looked up at me. "What I was thinking?"

I glanced around to confirm that we were still alone. "I do," I said. That if he had died we could be together for good and without compromise — a notion as dangerous as an electrified rail. "But I don't think we should talk about it anymore."

"You're right. It will do us no good. It already seems impossible again — the world without Franklin."

She took a handkerchief out of her pocket and wiped her face; then she turned on the lamp beside her head and took out her papers and reading glasses. The car was flooded with light and it ushered all the invisible things — the unsayable, the impossible — back into hiding.

The image of a man holding a rifle in the shadows appeared in my mind again. Brief contemplation of the world without *Nora* landed like a hard smack on my cheekbone, and I drew in a breath. I knew she didn't belong to me, but before that night, I had not understood how fully she was owned by the world at large, how she had ceded her autonomy to the greater good, despite the dark elements it contained.

153

I longed to take her in my arms to quell the anxious cells that vibrated in my chest. But a steward was coming into the car to ask whether we needed anything, and I felt the familiar dismay that our relationship had to be conducted in whispers and glances, that even in a matter of life and death I did not have the right to bring my grief into the open. What did it mean to be joined if we could never let anyone else know? Her blue satchel sat on her lap, and I remembered our sandwiches on that first train ride together, the checkered napkins and the way I'd laughed at her carrying the fine salt-shaker. I wondered if at least a few crumbs of bread remained at the bottom of her bag.

March 1

My darling,
  Thank you for helping me with all the
shopping. You know I dread it and hate
to spend so very much on what seems to
me so frivolous, but the calendar is full
of events in the next few weeks and I
suppose I would be ridiculed if I wore
my old tweeds to them all. I especially
like the dress you chose at the Milgrim
shop, the camel cashmere with the flared
hem. And the hats from Lilly Dache
really are lovely. You are welcome to bor-
row them anytime!
  Please say you will come with me on
the train to Washington. I will give you
the exclusive interview in the W.H. Bill
is asking for — but only for you. I rely
on you, Hick, now more than ever. I feel
so wretched when I think how we will
be separated by the long miles. But we
can talk on the telephone when I can
slip away, and I promise to write all the
time. You will just have to burn the letters if I am indiscreet.
  All my love to you, darling. It is your
face I think of as I fall asleep, your hands
in mine.

Love,
Nora

CHAPTER NINE

March 3, 1933

The lobby of the Mayflower Hotel in Washington was empty when the Roosevelt family filed through a secure back entrance, followed by handlers and helpers carrying luggage, and Secret Service agents guarding each window and door.

In the months since the jubilation of election night, the celebration had turned somber. Unemployment and homelessness were growing worse each week. Farmers were burning down their barns to collect insurance money and slaughtering their livestock to save the cost of feeding them. The tent village in Central Park had grown to a city. And an anarchist had nearly succeeded at assassinating the president-elect.

"People are getting antsy as hell," Bill said when I called in to the office from a phone in the Mayflower's lavish lobby. "What kind of security will they have at the Capitol tomorrow?"

"A whole lot," I said. "Snipers, armored cars, the whole gamut." They were worried about more maniacs like the man in Miami, but they knew the greater threat was from the crowds of regular people who would gather around the East Portico. They were not unlike religious pilgrims who knelt before the pope — they were helpless and broken down, but they *believed*. FDR held a tremendous amount of power for them, but I had the sense that the wind could change direction at any moment. If he said the wrong thing, or if he didn't go far enough in his promises of help, the supplicants might transform into a violent mob.

"And when will they let reporters into the hotel?"

I hesitated. In my pocket was the key to my own room, which Nora had reserved for me under her name. It was a floor below the suites where she and the president-elect would make final preparations for the next day's ceremony. Bill, of course, had no idea where I was calling from. All the other reporters were cooling their heels across the street. "We are waiting to hear," I lied. "Maybe this evening, but it could be hard to get very close."

"Well, now's the time to call in all your

157

favors, Hick. I'd sure like to know what they're talking about in their suite right now. We're hearing Hoover's thinking of closing the banks. Hard to believe, after all these years of doing nothing."

That day, every newspaper in the country had run photos of the runs on the banks: close-ups of panicked faces, and wide shots of the lines stretching around the block, the fights breaking out.

"I'll try to get you something," I said.

Bill laughed. "You'd better do more than try, Hick. If you like your job."

Later that evening, Nora called my room and asked me to come up, and one of the agents brought me to her floor in the secure elevator. I had expected a quiet sanctum, but the hallway bustled with aides and advisers. A porter carrying a tray of sandwiches entered a door about halfway down, and I spotted Nora's eldest son, James, wheeling a bar cart in behind him.

"Miss Hickok." I turned to the open door beside me to find Louis leaning on the frame.

"Mr. Howe." I shook his hand. "Looks like you're running a tight ship up here."

He nodded. "I wondered if we might see you tonight. We let your colleagues into the hotel, but they're still moping about being stuck downstairs. Pays to have access, I guess."

I gave him an uneasy smile. I had not seen him since the night at the town house, and Nora and I had been keeping a low profile. "N—" I stopped. "Mrs. Roosevelt invited me, and you know her: she doesn't take no for an answer."

"Yes, I do know her," Louis said. "And I work for her, so I am in the business of making sure she has what she wants. But also what she *needs*."

I was taking in that remark as the porter came out of the suite and passed between us on his way to the elevator. Before the door swung closed, I heard a snippet of energetic discussion, Roosevelt's voice and then Nora's. Without thinking, my reporter's muscle memory engaged and I strained to decipher their words.

Louis watched me for a moment. "Miss Hickok, we need to get something straight. You are here tonight as Mrs. Roosevelt's guest — not as a reporter. Do we understand each other?"

Bill had made his threat on the phone, and now Louis was chiming in with demands of his own. I saw that no matter what I did next, I would regret it.

Louis pointed at me. "Whatever you might hear is off the record. We let the reporters into the lobby, but that's as close as any of them are going to get. No one is coming up here. I won't have any leaks."

He must have seen on my face that I was still torn. "If you can't abide by that, you should go now," he said. "Mrs. Roosevelt will understand — you have a job to do. And you can do it from the lobby."

I wish I could say that I stood my ground, but at that moment my career didn't amount to a hill of beans compared with the chance to be in that room with Nora. The next day she would be off to the White House for four years, at least. It was our last chance to be together, our last chance to say goodbye, even if we had to do it through silent glances and a passed note or two.

I held up my empty palms and tried to look relaxed. "I didn't even bring my notebook," I said. It was still in my suitcase, one floor down.

"All right," he nodded, looking a little surprised — and perhaps even a little disappointed — at how easily I'd acquiesced. "I'm glad we could settle that."

He went back into his room and I exhaled a long breath.

I knocked softly on the suite door, half hoping I wouldn't be heard over the noise within, but Nora answered.

"Hick," she said, her lips painted pale pink and her reading glasses pushed up on her hair. "I'm so glad you're here."

Over her shoulder, I saw FDR sitting with his back to us, and James standing beside him.

"I won't do it," the president-elect said, more irritated than I'd ever seen him.

"It's the right call, Father. He's well out of line to ask."

I gave Nora a curious look. "Let's go across the hall and leave them to it," she whispered.

We passed into an identical suite, this one empty except for her luggage and a rack of dresses. The dining table was cluttered with vases of flowers and bottles of champagne with cards taped to their necks.

"People have been lovely." She fluffed up a spray of roses so that the stems draped more evenly in the vase. "The bellman has been delivering gifts all morning."

I nodded at the door. "What were they talking about over there?"

She didn't hesitate to tell me; for Nora, the matter of my trust had been settled long ago. "Hoover. He wants Franklin to issue a joint order *tonight*, before he is sworn in. If they close the banks together, I suppose the thinking goes, then they can share the blame if it goes to pieces."

"Sounds like the president-elect is not too keen on that plan." My gears were turning, and I imagined James's quote — that Hoover was "well out of line to ask" — in my lead. I could attribute it to an unnamed source inside the Roosevelt circle. Bill would be giddy.

"They spoke this morning and Franklin told him to do nothing. That it is a matter for the states."

"Is that what he believes?" The Roosevelt campaign had leaned heavily on symbolism and sentiment, but when you got down to brass tacks, no one quite knew what sort of policy the man intended to enact. Folks had mostly taken it on faith that he had better ideas than his predecessor, but "a matter for the states" sounded a lot like business as usual.

"We will soon find out, won't we?" She snapped a carnation off its stem and then came close to me and threaded it through the buttonhole on my lapel. My eyes rose to hers and I longed to kiss her. But she was still thinking of politics. "I have a feeling he has something up his sleeve," she said.

"Is that so?" Whatever he decided, if I could get the story, on the eve of FDR's swearing in, no less, it would be a scoop for the ages. The urge to start typing it made my fingertips tingle. If he went along with Hoover, the people would be disappointed to see him in league with the devil. If he went his own way and did nothing, the people would be outraged that he was maintaining the status quo after all his promises. Either way, they might need to deploy the National Guard to control the crowds at the banks. Perhaps they already had their orders. If I went to the major general's office in Arlington with a tip from the incoming administration, I might be able to get someone to confirm the plans. I pushed up my sleeve to look at my watch. I had about an hour to make the evening editions.

Just then there was a knock on the door and Louis entered, followed by James, Anna, the bar cart — with its reserves of whiskey renewed — and, finally, the president-elect.

I backed up to the window to get out of the way and watched as Nora scurried over to help her husband get settled at the table. She cleared away the wine and flowers and the stacks of papers that made up her own work. Anna made a round of horse's necks — her father's favorite drink, of whiskey and ginger ale — for the table.

"May I fix you a drink, Miss Hickok?" she said, and the eyes of all the Roosevelts, who stood between me and the door, turned my way. Roosevelt gave Louis a look to confirm that he had dealt with the matter of my access on this most historic of nights. Was I here as friend or interloper? Could they trust me?

I felt as though I were being split in half with a hatchet. Part of me was dying to bolt for the door, for the phone in the lobby, for my typewriter downstairs. But then there was Nora, her gray-blond hair piled high on her head, the vulnerable slump of her shoulders that I loved so dearly. She relied on me *now more than ever,* she had said. If only I could proclaim what I felt for her. How many hours had I lost to daydreams of the front porch of our someday cottage? I saw Nora on the swing, maintaining a gentle sway with the tip of her toe against the porch rail. In moments like these, my love for her kept me calm, but it had an undertow, like the sea, and I felt at any moment it might pull me down.

Louis was the only one who wasn't staring at me; his eyes stayed on the papers he held, and he made a note with a red pencil and handed the pages to his boss. It was the inaugural address, I realized. And if I stayed in the room, I might hear it. Good Lord.

He lit his next cigarette, unconcerned. "I've never known Miss Hickok to turn down a drink," he said.

Everyone laughed, and I felt the blade sever me completely. It left a raw edge exposed, and the next breath I took hurt a little. *I am giving up everything for you,* I thought, telegraphing the words to Nora across the table. *Please tell me it will be worth it.*

When I pulled up a chair and sat down, the president-elect relaxed and looked at his wife. "Eleanor, I want you to read it." He passed the pages across the table to her and rolled the red pencil after them. She snatched it up with glee.

She began to skim it in silence, but he interrupted her. "No, let's have it aloud."

Nora cleared her throat and sat up straight. "This is a day of national consecration," she began in a bold voice, and Roosevelt smiled at Louis, his right-hand man. In that smile was the shared knowledge of countless handshakes and rallies, late nights on trains, mind-numbing fund-raisers, deals and counterdeals and strategy and execution. Finally his day had come.

As Nora read, she used the pencil to add missing punctuation a time or two. When she got to the line about fear — "Let me assert my firm belief that the only thing we have to fear is fear itself: nameless, unreasoning, unjustified terror, which paralyzes needed efforts to convert retreat into advance" — she stopped.

"So you read the Thoreau I gave you."

Her husband grinned. There was an electricity between them and it seemed to be fueled by the game of the speech. Point to Franklin for choosing the words that evoked the intended feeling; point to Eleanor for the influence that led to the words. Roosevelt quoted from the work, " 'Nothing is so much to be feared as fear' — that's the Thoreau. We decided to add the line yesterday."

"Well, then it is a good thing I lent you the book," she shot back. Louis hooted and the children smiled, but I felt a sting watching them volley with such pleasure. When Nora and I were alone, the world made sense, but I would never be able to understand what role I should play in this baffling circle. A minor one, no doubt.

Nora read on and, as the words rang out, I tried to listen, not as a reporter but as a

166

regular American citizen. How would the speech strike me, I wondered, if I wasn't thinking of the machinations behind it but was instead an average Jane listening to my new president? I saw at once that it was written like a clever sermon, in which FDR compared America's bankers to the money changers in the temple. They had no vision, those men compelled by greed, but now that they had been chased from the seat of power, we had to decide what to replace them with. Could we be good neighbors to each other, finally, and work together to wage a war — an actual war — on economic chaos?

I pictured crowds that would gather in the morning cold to hear the speech and could feel how their throats would grow tight, their eyes full. It *wasn't* too good to be true. With this man as our president, change might really come.

"It's a good speech," Nora said, laying the pages back on the table when she'd finished. "Full of hope. I just pray it goes far enough."

The phone rang and Louis sprang for it. After listening a moment, he said, "Let me call you back" and hung up. He turned to his boss. "Hoover is asking to speak to you tonight, sir." He looked at the clock on the mantel. "It's eleven thirty already."

FDR pursed his lips and nodded. "I'll call him. And I'll say what I said before: do nothing. Let the governors decide."

"And then?" Nora asked. She leaned forward on her elbows. Anna and James looked at their father. Louis held his cigarette as the ash crept toward his fingers. The moment held more expectation than I could stand; whatever he said next, I couldn't do a thing with it.

"At 12:01, put it out to the press — *I* will close the banks."

I needed a walk. When Louis heard me murmur to Nora that I was going out for cigarettes, he shot me a look, but I held up three fingers. "Scout's honor," I said.

And I wasn't lying. I had no plans to call Bill on the sly. My bed was made; my goose was cooked. I just needed to get out of that room.

I took the private elevator down and exited through the back door, where two Secret Service agents stood at attention. I thought of Marcus and wondered whether he was somewhere in the hotel and how he would react if we bumped into each other in the dining room. Poor old Marcus had probably seen a thing or two in his time, but nothing quite like what he had seen on

Christmas Eve.

I went around the corner to an all-night shop and bought my cigarettes, plus a couple of packs of Louis's brand as a gesture of goodwill. I smoked one of mine under a streetlamp. Something about the light's yellow glow called up the quality of sunlight on the prairie of my girlhood. There was a patch of meadow on the land we rented that my father didn't farm. The bluestem and wild rye grew tall there, and cabbage white butterflies danced above the grass in the sun; it was the perfect place for me to hide from my father. One summer, I lay in the long grass and read *Rough Riders* so many times that I had dreams of the kickback of the Gatling gun, of digging graves for the men who died of strange fevers in the Cuban jungle. Roosevelt — the first one — had awakened me to adventure, to the intricate stories the world had to tell. He made me want to tell them and to be among others who told them too. In reporting, I had found not just my work but a fellowship, my strange tribe. That work ordered my life.

Back at the rear entrance, the guards' shift had changed and the new ones didn't believe that I had a right to come through. There was no phone outside, and I had no

ID on me to prove my case.

"Journalists to the lobby, ma'am," one of them said.

"Come on. I was just here ten minutes ago."

"Journalists to the lobby," he said again, looking, as he'd been trained to do, not *at* me but at something about three inches to the left of my head.

I sighed and walked around to the grand front entrance of the Mayflower, where I stepped into a kind of chaos rarely seen in the stately room of marble and silk and majestic low-hanging chandeliers. The lobby was packed, and people were also crammed up against the ornate rail of the mezzanine balcony. On the far side of the room, controlling access to the elevators, more agents stood in their standard-issue black suits. Back by the entrance was a cluster of men who were the agents' exact opposite: my proud cohort. Wise-cracking, half-drunk, or both; dressed in threadbare suits five years out of fashion, clutching pens with ink-stained fingers. In the middle of the crowd I spotted John.

I kept my head down and tried to pass through the lobby along the wall, but just when I thought I'd succeeded, I heard John's voice calling me: "Hick!" It was like buckshot in my back, but I didn't turn around.

"Gentlemen," I said to the agents blocking the hall. "I am expected upstairs."

"Nice try," one said.

"Hick!" I heard John yell again. It was agony not to turn around, but agony too to imagine the look on his face if I acknowledged him and continued on to the elevator instead of joining him where I belonged. I remembered what John had said to me that night at Dom's — *we all pay the price to get what we get.*

"Please," I said to the agents, desperation in my voice. "Just call up to Mrs. Roosevelt. My name is Lorena Hickok. She'll tell you — I'm supposed to be up there."

The second agent walked over to the phone at the desk. By now, some of the other reporters had spotted me and began to protest. "What a crock!" I heard, and then a terrible wave of booing rose up behind me. My heart was hammering.

The agent finally met my eyes and I clung to this spark of humanity. "And who are you with?" he asked. "*Times?* AP? *Globe?*" His partner returned and gave him a nod. The men moved aside to let me pass into the hallway and I felt simultaneous explosions of victory and defeat.

"I'm not *with* anybody," I answered him. "I'm here for Mrs. Roosevelt."

Late Saturday, March 4

Darling,

I must apologize that your historic interview of a first lady in the White House today became such a comedy of errors. So many interruptions and prying eyes and ears. Did you get a single quote you can use? And poor Hick, how resourceful of you to suggest escaping to the powder room, only to have me dash your plans. You must know by now that when we are alone I cannot think of politics or historic interviews but only my beloved — your eyes, the soft lobes of your ears. Oh, my darling, how will we bear being apart? I miss you so much already that it is like a physical pain.

There I go again. Maybe I can help rescue your piece with a few notes on the day. And what a day it has been! Years long, it seems. It began rather drearily with a raw wind that seemed to claw our hats from our heads. After church, we followed the custom of separating into two cars. I rode with Mrs. and Franklin rode with Hoover, who is furious about last night. He wouldn't speak, Franklin says, wouldn't even smile for the photographers. We had the agents on motorcycles zipping all around us like horseflies, and all the people in the grandstands to watch the procession. The scale of the thing!

What did you think of the speech? I must say I was very afraid to take my eyes off him and look out at the crowd. So many thousands of people, and I could feel the great weight of all of them hanging on his words. It's as if they are willing to do anything, if only someone will tell them what to do.

But then the feeling changed when he got to the end, didn't it, and everyone cheered? We were all so enormously relieved, as if he had changed the ship's course just in time to avoid the iceberg.

And then our interview and then luncheon, and receptions and parties and meetings. Franklin swore in his cabinet. It has never been done so quickly before. In fact, there was so much to do today, solemn work, that he declined to go out again in the evening. I dressed in my silly gown and fur and was off to the ball, Eleanor alone. Or that is what they all will write. They don't know, do they, whose ring I wear, whose signature is on my heart?

Good night, my dear one. My love

enfold thee all the night through.

Nora

CHAPTER TEN

March 6, 1933

I brought Prinz with me to the AP offices on Monday. Mrs. Jansen had looked after him while I was gone to Washington, and I feared that with all that exposure to her vapid conversations he might lose his intellectual edge. I also knew that, after my colleagues' reaction to my access to the Roosevelts' private suite in DC, I might be glad for a little protection. Prinz settled on the old army blanket I kept under my desk for him. When he rested his chin on his paws, he snorted at me. The snort said, "Screw your courage to the sticking place, Hick."

Bill was at his desk when I came into his office and handed him the mug of coffee I'd fixed for him. The window behind him faced Madison and the two buildings across the street, between which shone a rare patch of Manhattan sky. The city seemed like an optical illusion to me. From what vantage was it possible, really, to see it? From any given place, one could only see a handful of windows across the way, or one-fifth of a spire, or a couple of cables on a bridge. Perhaps we'd all been tricked into faith in this city's existence.

On Bill's blotter were the Sunday editions of the *Times, Post, Tribune,* and more. He took off his reading glasses and slid them into the pocket of his vest.

"Hick, I wonder," he said, swallowing a sip of coffee, "whether you know on what page your groundbreaking interview with the first lady ran in yesterday's papers."

Mrs. Jansen had given them to me, along with my mail, the night before, but I'd been too chicken to look. "I don't."

"A-one?" he asked. He gazed at me as he turned the pages on the *Times,* one slow pluck at a time.

"I doubt it." Why had I even come to face this humiliation? I thought. Why hadn't I let him lambast me over the phone?

"A-five? A-ten?"

I felt the back of my bottom teeth with my tongue. "Why don't you just tell me, Bill."

He finally stopped turning. "A-seventeen. No photograph. Sandwiched between a piece on parking in Midtown and" — he

skimmed the page — "an ad for office supplies."

"Well, we're the wire service," I said. My
stomach churned with coffee. "We provide
the reporting and these papers decide what
to use, where to put it. The president has
closed the banks — I'd say that makes for a
heavy news day."

He laughed. "They decide where to put it
based on what it contains. You gave them
cage liner."

I took a sharp breath. "Now, hang on. You
have no idea how hectic it was in that room.
We must have been interrupted a dozen
times. She couldn't speak freely."

"At the very least, I wanted drapes and
china and who's going to get to sleep in Lincoln's bed. But you didn't even get me that,
Hick."

Bill stuck out his chin and rubbed it with
his fingertips. He looked like he was ready
to blow. "Let's turn to another topic. I heard
quite a distressing tale from your fellows at
the Mayflower. It seems you were not in the
lobby with them but instead were seen taking the private elevator to the presidential
suite, where you remained throughout the
night. Do I have that right?"

I closed my eyes.

"There you no doubt had access to the

full text of the president's speech, to un-imaginable conversations about strategy, policy — not to mention the *fucking phone call* between FDR and Hoover about the banks."

He slammed his hand on the desk with each word. Bill was a hothead, to be sure, but I'd never heard him talk that way before.

"Yet — and I know this because I slept in my chair Friday night, Hick, like the rest of the news hawks *doing their jobs* — my phone did not ring. The only copy from you that has come over the transom in the last three days is this." He dropped his index finger on the stack of newspapers. "Do I have that right?"

What could I say? If I had been a man and Nora had been almost any other woman — particularly a lipsticked siren in a wiggle dress — I could have bugged out my eyes to Bill, held up my palms, and begged for mercy. *She got into my head, sir,* a man was permitted to argue. *What can I say — I'm weak!* And Bill, a fellow victim of feminine wiles, might clap me on the back. *Oh, buddy, I've been there. Just get your head in the game, all right?* But there would be no such allowance for a person like me. No fraternity, no sympathy.

I didn't want to lie, but I couldn't tell the

179

truth. "I know your hands are tied," was all I said.

A look of dismay came over him, and I saw that he really had been hoping I could explain it all away.

"Hick, your stock as a member of this organization is pretty high. Hardly anyone has been here as long as you, or written as extensively on so many different beats. You've trained half the guys coming up — you've certainly helped Bosco leap boldly into the realm of competence. I just don't understand." Sad Bill was worse than angry Bill. He looked heartbroken. "You spent two decades building your dream house, and two days ago, you drove a truck through it."

My eyes started to burn, and I felt my throat strain. But I would slit my wrists before I would cry in front of him.

"This is the end of the line, Hick."

"I'll clean out my desk," I muttered, and stalked out. I passed John at his desk, his forehead braced on the heel of his hand while he read through a stack of notebooks. I remembered his voice calling to me in the hotel lobby and how hard it had been to keep walking away from him. Though I tried to catch his eye, he kept his head down. He was freezing me out.

"Come on, boy," I whispered to Prinz, and

clipped on his leash.

On the walk home, a fierce wind pried its way down my collar and made me shiver. My old pluck rose and I tried to tell myself it would be all right. It was just a job and I could find another one. I had grown up poor and I knew how to live that life — I could be poor again. Screw Bill, if he couldn't understand the integrity I'd shown in protecting Nora. Screw John too — a fair-weather friend. I didn't need any of them.

But then I came to the corner newsstand where the morning editions fluttered in their racks, where each day I still checked to see my name in print and each time felt surprise that I was who the paper said I was. The sob that had been lodged in my sternum began to spread up to my mouth and all I could think of was drink, a bathtub full of enough bourbon to drown in.

Days later, Nora's letters had begun to pile up.

March 13

Darling,

I tried calling three times yesterday. Are you out of town on assignment? I fear I have lost track of your schedule. Send a telegram. You know how I love to follow your adventures.

Always,
Nora

March 14 (late!)

Hick,

Now I am worried that you are ill and no one is looking in on you but that dreadful woman across the hall. Please send up a smoke signal!

N

March 15

My silent darling,

Louis has heard a rumor that you have left the AP. What the devil is going on up there, and why won't you answer the telephone? Please send word, or so help me I will be on the next train.

Nora

This is the part of the story I'd rather skip past, but there is no way to explain what came next without providing a glimpse of my sorry state about ten days after I left the

AP's offices for the last time. It was half past noon, and I was still in bed with the covers pulled over my eyes to block out the sunlight. Prinz was draped across the foot of the bed like a worried mother who'd been nursing her baby all night. Suddenly, I heard heels clacking on the tile and an urgent knock on my door. Prinz lifted his head. I thought it might be the landlady, back again after her failed attempt to catch me the day before last. My rent was past due, but I did not want to pay it with what little cash I had on hand. Very soon I would be out of money.

But then I heard a familiar warble calling my name and lifted up on my elbows. My head felt like something being pulled by a tugboat. I'd managed to stay stinking drunk around the clock until I had made the mistake of falling asleep around nine the night before and put my body through fifteen hours of sobriety. I squinched my eyes shut and pushed myself up to the edge of the bed. Before I got up, I drained the lukewarm bourbon from the glass on the nightstand.

"Hick!" Nora shouted, true panic in her voice. Prinz let out a sharp bark and darted for the door. I had read Nora's letters and heard the phone ring and ring in the hall,

183

yet nothing seemed to break through my haze. But now Prinz was barking like a maniac and the noise was more than I could take. I padded down the hall and grasped his collar while I turned the bolt.

"Oh, thank heavens!" she cried when she heard it.

Her eyes were full of tears; she rushed into the entryway and took me into her arms. The sensation of being touched by her was overwhelming, and I saw that I had been keeping her at bay because I was afraid of being comforted. I wanted to be wretched and I knew she wouldn't let me.

"Oh, my darling," she whispered, and kissed my hair and forehead and pulled me against her again. Prinz sprang his paws up against her back and she gently pushed him down, once, twice, three times until he settled.

"I thought you were dead! How could you do that to me? I was minutes away from calling the police." Her voice was angry but she continued to hold me and pet my hair. It was nearly unbearable to be loved just then. I was so angry at myself, at her, at the warped world in which every thing that I wanted was, by default, wrong.

"You smell terrible," she said tenderly.

I laughed, and then, oh, how I began to

weep. And it was not the melodic weeping of a dignified Victorian woman in a novel, you can be sure. Instead, I sat down at Nora's feet and wailed, my mouth open, snot running from my nose.

She took her handbag off her shoulder and lowered it gently to the ground. She knelt down across from me, and from her pocket she took a handkerchief and handed it to me. I used it to try to muffle the terrible noise I was making, but the more I tried to contain it, the louder it became, as if some black thing were inside me, clawing, and had to come out. Nora just kept quiet and held my head on her lap, her arms wrapped around as if to brace it.

After a long time, when I had emptied myself of sorrow and noise, she said, "What happened?" and I let it all spill out. I confessed to every time I had compromised my work to protect her, how Bill had pressed me to write about her daughter's divorce, about Elliott, to get access to cabinet appointments and closed discussions and the text of the speech. In the end, I explained, I couldn't do both — be in love with her and report on her — and I should have admitted that to myself before I lost Bill's trust and my own integrity.

Nora looked stricken.

"This isn't *your* fault," I said, suddenly afraid that she would feel responsible. "You didn't ask me to do any of the things I did. But it's over now. Everything I've worked for is gone."

"Darling, I know how much your job means to you, but . . . you are *so* poorly. You're shivering!" She rubbed her hands along my arms. "Are you sure the job is all it is? There isn't something else?"

I kept quiet. I didn't know how I could make her see. My job was the only thing between the past and me. It was the moat that kept me safe.

Gently she nudged my head off her lap and I sat up and pressed my back against the cool wall of the entryway. Above me was a table overflowing with unopened mail — bills and the like. She went into the kitchen and changed Prinz's water, poured new kibble into his bowl; then she crouched on the floor with a rag to wipe up a puddle Prinz had made when he could wait no longer for me to take him out. I closed my eyes, ashamed at my negligence. Then I heard the light click on in the bathroom, the metal clink of the stopper, the rush of water.

I was so exhausted I could hardly move, but she eased me to my feet and led me to the bath. I sat on the edge of the tub and watched her take off her jacket and roll up her sleeves. Kneeling before me, she pulled pins out of my hair, one after another, and then unwound my frizzy bun as steam began to cloud the mirror. Her hands moved slowly through my hair and down to the small buttons on my nightgown. I raised my arms like a child, and Nora eased the gown up and over my head. She started to pinch the clasp on my necklace, but I clutched it with my hand.

"I have to keep this on," I said.

She gave me a curious look. "Why?"

"It's hard to explain."

"I have always wanted to ask you about it," she said, "but I've been afraid to. I don't know why. It seems to have a story."

I opened my hand and let the charm fall back down between my breasts. It was a flat disk of wood, sanded smooth long ago and rubbed to a sheen from years of my fingers worrying its surface. I had bought the plated gold chain with my first paycheck, but the charm had begun its life on a piece of string.

Nora turned off the water. "Won't you tell me, Hick? I want to know your stories."

"The water will go cold," I said.

She stuck her hand in and shook her head. "It's scalding now. It needs to cool."

187

Does every life take this shape, I wondered, where all things that happen flow through the keyhole of a single day?

I took a breath. Pulling the towel off the hook beside me, I draped it over my shoulders so that I wouldn't be quite so naked. "My father was a drunk. A mean one."

"So you've said."

"That was why we moved around so much, all over Wisconsin and Iowa and then to the Dakotas. The way he was . . . he could get a job but he could only keep it for a week or two before he flew off the handle. Once he beat a man so badly, he nearly killed him — we had to leave town in the middle of the night. My mother was terrified he would go to prison. She thought we'd all starve."

Nora shook her head. Her father had been a drunk too, but the world is kinder to a rich drunk than a poor one.

"The year when I was fourteen, we were living in Bowdle and he was churning butter for farms nearby. And . . ."

I felt my heart begin to accelerate.

"He asked me to go out to the barn to get the eggs. It was winter and we kept these three skinny hens that lived on weeds and the food I snuck out to them, and half the time they didn't produce anything at all.

188

That was the kind of man my father was —
he wanted the eggs, but he didn't want to
have to feed the hens to get them.

"So I wrapped up in a big blanket and
went out there. The barn was really a little
shack — we didn't have any horses or cows,
just those pathetic hens. And that morning
the wind was blowing over the scrap-tin roof
something awful, like a broken-down church
organ. Once I got to the barn, I didn't want
to have to go back out again. I decided to
stay and talk with the hens for a while. I
petted them. I tried to tuck more hay
around them to keep them warm. There was
only one egg and I stuck it in the pocket of
my apron."

I closed my eyes. "And then I heard him.
He was shouting for me and he banged into
the barn behind me. I knew what was coming and braced myself — he always used
the same old stave off one of his broken butter churns to beat us. But nothing happened. And when I finally turned around he
was just standing there staring at me. He
yelled that if I looked at him again he would
kick my head in. So I turned back to my
hens and that was when I heard his belt
buckle jangling, and he shoved me on my
face into the hay, all slick with fresh chicken
shit, and the hens squawked and went fly-

ing into the rafters, and . . ."

Nora's hand was over her mouth. "Oh, Hick."

I felt I might be sick, but I wanted to keep going. "He was very drunk. I could smell it. I don't even know that he knew what he was doing. When he rolled off me, I just lay there for a moment, stunned. I tasted blood — I had bitten my tongue. When I got up and pushed my skirt down, he was already passed out in the hay. I was going to try to get out without waking him, but, half thinking, I touched my apron pocket for the egg and of course it was broken.

"And then . . ." I swallowed, the ghosts rising up in me like steam from the bath, my heart hammering, "something happened to me. Before I knew it, that old stave was in my hands and I lifted it over my head and brought it down on his skull with all my might. Over and over."

Nora grasped my hands. She felt like the only thing keeping me on the face of the planet. "I just kept thrashing away until the stave broke in my hands. Can you believe it? That old thing had been used for God knows how many beatings over the years, and it just splintered and pieces of it went flying all over the barn.

"I didn't know whether he was dead or

not — he wasn't, it turns out, but I didn't know that at the time. I looked down and right next to my shoe was one of the pieces of wood. So I picked it up and took it with me. Then I walked the five miles into town with blood running down the inside of my legs, and I never saw that fucking place again. Once I landed where I was going, I pounded a hole through this with a hammer and nail, and put it on a piece of string. I haven't taken it off since."

Nora lifted my hand and kissed my fingers.

I took a shuddering breath, exhaled. "So now, do you see? Being a reporter isn't just a job to me. It *is* me; it is the thing I fought to be so that I didn't have to be that farm girl anymore. Without it . . ."

Nora dipped her hand in the water as she considered my words. I was glad she couldn't seem to muster any reply. It was a strange point of pride to have a problem so broken it couldn't be fixed, even by a woman who was known for solving impossible problems on a grand scale. My wounds, I realized, were precious to me; if she told me there was a way to heal them, I feared I might disappear.

Nora gently lifted the towel off my shoulders and hung it on the hook. Then, with her hand on my back, she helped ease me

191

down the slick porcelain into the heavenly still-hot water. She soaped a blue cloth with Ivory and washed my back, my arms and legs, in slow circles. Then she turned the tap back on while I tipped my head beneath it. Nora braced my forehead with her palm so that the water would not splash in my eyes.

When I sat up and squeezed the water out of my hair, she said, "What if . . . what if your story is still being written, Hick?"

I rolled my eyes. "Don't try psychology on me, Nora."

"It's not psychology. It's . . . it's the frame around the picture. What if what you are is changing? What if we all are? Look at me. I was a daughter until my parents died and I became an orphan. I was a mother and my baby died — I saw my baby go into the ground, and I thought I would die of grief. But I didn't die. I was a wife until my husband betrayed me, and the very definition of being a wife changed. And I tasted freedom." She touched my shoulder and ran her fingers down my arm. "And love."

I considered this, the possibility that there was hope for me yet. While she shampooed my hair, she kept her gentle eyes on me and under her gaze I felt an unrecognizable sensation run from between my shoulders

192

down into my fingers. Peace. The black thing I felt when I thought of Bowdle and that barn, a grackle thrashing in my chest, had gone out of me. At least for now.

When I was dry and dressed, Nora lay down beside me in bed and said, "Let's take a trip together, just the two of us. It will do us good to get away."

I looked at her. "*How,* Nora? The first lady cannot just 'go on vacation.' "

"If I say we'll do it, we will. I keep my promises, Hick."

When my face didn't lift, her voice turned stern. "The man who did that to you is dead. He cannot hurt you anymore. Your life is in *your* hands."

"But what can I do?" My voice choked. I was sick to death of crying. "What *is* there for me to do?"

Her voice was kind again. "A world of things. Let's talk about it. I have a hundred ideas —"

"Not now," I said, my eyes closed and my nose pressed against her collarbone. I thought I might be able to believe in divinity because of the solace of that collarbone; I wished I had known it was waiting for me years and years down the road from that worst day of my life.

"Tell me about our cottage instead," I

whispered. I could see it in the shade of two old trees. I could see the smoke coming out of the chimney and Nora walking up the path at the end of the day, coming home to me at last. "Tell me what we'll talk about when we sit on our porch swing."

■ ■ ■ ■

Part Two

■ ■ ■ ■

What happens to any of us as individuals, what we think or desire or hope to do, seems so trifling in the face of what I'm seeing these days.

— Lorena Hickok,
in a letter to Eleanor Roosevelt

CHAPTER ELEVEN

July 1933

When Nora first announced to the president and his staff that she would be taking a vacation north through New England and Quebec, driving in her own car with her journalist companion, the head of the Secret Service said, *No, absolutely not, preposterous.*

Nora called me at Mitchell Place, delighted. "They think they can tell me no," she said.

I sat down in the chair beside the telephone, and Prinz trotted out the open apartment door and sat on my bare feet. I hadn't really expected the trip to pan out, hadn't allowed myself to get my hopes up, so I was unperturbed. "And they can't?"

She laughed her lovely singsong laugh. "They say it has only been a year since the Lindbergh baby was kidnapped — that we could be abducted. Shoved into the trunk of someone's car."

A smile opened on my face, and the feeling was as inelegant as the wrenching of a wedged cupboard door. After a few months of drink and sorrow, of scraping by on savings and freelance assignments, I was starting to thaw. I kneaded the thick fur around Prinz's collar. "I'd like to see the criminal who could lift me into a trunk. Still," I said, "what can you do? If they say no, they say no."

"We'll see," Nora said.

A few days later, she called back. "Pack your suitcase, darling."

"No. I don't believe it." Mrs. Jansen's head popped into the hallway and the hem of her quilted dressing gown swept the doorframe. She disappeared with a huff when she realized that yet another call had come in for me instead of her.

"I promised you, didn't I? Never doubt my promises, Hick."

If she only knew how I lived solely for those promises these days. "But how did you get them to agree?"

Nora paused. "I told them we would bring a gun in the glove box."

"A *gun*? Do you even know how to shoot a gun?"

"I do," she said, "but this one is just for

show. I put the cartridges in the teapot in my sitting room."

She collected me in her gleaming Buick, and we drove Prinz out to a kennel on Long Island where he would have the run of the clover-pocked fields. Then we set out north, through the Adirondacks, with the top down. The scarves we wore tied over our hair whipped in the breeze and twisted their ends toward each other like fingers. We were giddy with the freedom of traveling alone and unnoticed, just two middle-aged biddies, anonymous in the way plain women are. But what we felt — the deep-down-in-the-bones gratitude at having found each other, the understanding that our long, lonely slogs had been leading us, step by step, to each other — was an aria in my mouth and I was not afraid to sing it.

Reaching Burlington and Lake Champlain felt like yanking open a grimy window shade. It was just so lush and green — enormous trees, crystal clear water, hawks in the trees and herons soaring over the lake. It was a breezy July day, and Nora drove the whole way because I still didn't know how, though she threatened to teach me. I rested the back of my head on the seat and squinted at the bright blue sky.

From this position, it looked like the very same sky that hung over the barren prairie, and one could almost be fooled, except for the scents the breeze carried. In Bowdle, it was eau de cow pies, the tang of iron in the dirt; in Vermont, everything smelled fresh and clean, of sap and rain. I thought of the trout as big as my arms that were likely swimming in the lake.

Nora glanced over at me, divining my train of thought. "Are you hungry?"

I smiled. I was starting to feel something strange. The muscles in my face felt loose and my shoulders had descended by about an inch. My skin felt warm. I wondered for a moment if I was about to have a heart attack — I reached instinctively for my cigarettes, as if they could save me — but then I realized what it might be. The phenomenon people called *relaxation.*

The gravel crunched beneath the tires as she pulled in to a roadside hamburger stand off Route 2. Its red-striped awning rippled in the breeze over two picnic tables. We ordered fish sandwiches and french fries and apple pie.

When the food came up, we took our trays to one of the picnic tables and dug into the deep-fried bliss. In the weeks leading up to the trip, I had gone around and around in my head about what the future held and whether I had made a huge mistake in leaving my job. But somehow, out in the fresh air and far from New York, I was able to make some kind of pact with myself. I'd get back to the fretting soon enough. For the moment, I wanted just to be in my skin, next to Nora, with a view of the mountains. In the morning, we would continue north to Quebec City, Le Château Frontenac, where, Nora had promised, we would dip strawberries from the hotel garden into our glasses of champagne. We would lie on the coverlet in the middle of the day. Nora would light a cigarette in her own mouth and then hold it to my lips for me to take a drag.

For now, there was a gull casually sidling toward us and our food. I laughed.

"Shoo!" Nora yelled, and it screamed at her and took off.

"Darling," I said, giggling, "you've a bit of mayonnaise on your lip." A few strands of hair danced around her face, golden in the sunshine.

She licked the mayonnaise off. "Oh, Hick," she said, taking my hand. "Why can't it always be like this?"

"Let's pretend it is," I said.

CHAPTER TWELVE

August 1933

To pretend that way was a refuge, but one that could not be sustained. After two weeks of bliss, we returned to Washington. Nora reclaimed her role as first lady of the land, and I traveled from Washington by train, then two hours by bus, on my way to Morgantown, West Virginia — the first stop of my new job.

Nora hadn't been exaggerating when she said she had a hundred ideas for what I should do now that I'd been, ahem, *retired* from reporting. The government was hiring, and my unpaid bills made the decision easy. I thought of the job as "itinerant paper pusher for Uncle Sam," but "investigator for the Federal Emergency Relief Administration" was my official title. It was a title trumped up by Nora, I knew, to make the task sound more journalistic and less like what it actually was — traveling the downtrodden swaths of this great land, shadowing local administrators at budget meetings and typing up dreary reports of their troubles. Politics, along with a healthy dose of old-fashioned bureaucratic incompetence, was keeping the people from getting the food, jobs, housing assistance, and other help the president had promised in his New Deal. Harry Hopkins, the head of the agency and my new boss, claimed he was depending on my reports to figure out how to get around the horseshit and actually help people.

It was a far cry from a front-page byline, and I missed New York and my evenings at Dom's. John, of course, still had not spoken to me since the day I'd left the newsroom. And I missed Nora. The worst part was that I'd had to sublet my Mitchell Place apartment — I'd be traveling constantly and it didn't make sense to keep it — and had to send Prinz out to the Long Island kennel indefinitely. But things had changed. I had to accept it. If I didn't die of boredom in the new gig, I thought I'd be all right.

The half-full bus to Morgantown smelled of sweat and tobacco juice that made slick spatters on the aisle floor. I wrenched open the small window next to my seat, hoping to get a whiff of the clean mountain air my travel book promised. The faint breeze did little to remedy the aroma of the bus, but I liked the improved view. The vast forests rolled up one side of the mountain and down the other, like waves on the sea, and here and there streams and chalky gray crags broke through the mass of green. The scene would have made a pretty postcard if it hadn't been framed by the grimy window.

Beside me, a man in a stained undershirt picked his nose with a dirty finger and examined what he pulled out of it. I puffed my cheeks in disgust and turned back toward the window. The man then unwrapped a sandwich that seemed to consist of raw onions, pickles, and horseradish so strong it made my eyes water. I inched slowly closer to the far edge of my seat.

"Say," said the man as he licked his fingers, "how about a drink before we go our separate ways?"

If ever I doubted that my preference for women proved I had both good sense and sound aesthetics, this man offered ample reassurance. "I'd love to," I said in the coy whisper of a debutante, "but I'm wanted for murder. Can't take the risk of being seen."

His eyes grew wide and he turned away just as we pulled, mercifully, into the Morgantown bus station. He stood, swung his bag over his shoulder, and began edging up the aisle, as far away from me as possible.

In the parking lot, a lanky man leaned against a car, squinting into the sun and holding up a sign that read HICKOK. I made my way over to him, my overnight bag banging against my knee, its contents sloshing. The humidity had turned mere breathing into a chore, and I was longing for a bath, a meal, and three fingers of bourbon, though not necessarily in that order. Nora had tried to extract a promise from me that I would not drink while I was on the road, but I'd said only, "I'll try," and made sure to pack the good stuff so I wouldn't be out combing the mountains for moonshine come evening.

"Clarence Pickett," he said, and put out his hand. "It's a pleasure to finally meet you, Miss Hickok."

I liked him instantly because of the unhurried way in which he spoke and his kind blue eyes. Clarence was the head of the Quaker relief services, volunteers from the Society of Friends who had spent decades serving the people of coal country in West Virginia. What seemed like the permanent poverty of this region had grown much worse when all the mines shut down a few years back. From my advance briefing, I had learned that Clarence and his cohort delivered food and first aid kits, blankets and towels and canning jars. But all of that was like a whisper in the gale.

"How did you get roped into being my chauffeur?" I asked. The county must be pretty bad off, I thought, if an administrator couldn't be bothered to pick me up himself.

"Well, the government people will have plenty to tell you, I'm sure," Clarence said as he folded the sign with my name on it and put it in his pocket. "But I wanted to get you out of town and into these camps so that you could see what we're dealing with."

That sounds ominous, I couldn't help but think. Clarence waited patiently while I sucked down a Pall Mall and then opened the passenger door for me. He crossed in front to the other side and took off his hat before settling behind the wheel. I smiled at the way he sat erect, with the top of his head gracing the car's ceiling. His face had a scrubbed look, and though I was entirely wilted, he seemed as cool as a swimming trout, as if those who were right with God could travel in their own pleasant weather systems.

Before long, we were outside Morgantown and sliding deeper into the hills on narrow roads that were dark in midday beneath the tunnel of trees. A pheasant wandered into the road, and Clarence braked gently to let it pass. On our right was a shack that was completely overgrown with honeysuckle, as if the mountain had reached out its arms to smother it to death.

"Where to, Mr. Pickett?"

"Osage, one of the towns that make up this region they call Scotts Run. I'm sure you've seen plenty of deprivation in your line of work back in New York City, Miss Hickok, but I feel I have to tell you to prepare yourself."

I didn't like the sound of Clarence's warning at all. I was only here to document the dull work of bureaucrats in airless rooms — not to see any *camps* for myself, not to have to steel myself against some devastating sight.

"Oh, and if anyone offers you a drink of water, don't take it," he said. "It all comes out of the same river as the diphtheria."

We pulled into a clearing, and Clarence parked the car in the bare dirt. A sloping lane ran along a stream, and shacks and tents dotted the side of the hill all the way down. After the smell — human waste mixed with something chemical I assumed had to do with the mines — the first thing I noticed was the black dust. I dragged my finger through it on the hood of the car.

"That's coal dust," Clarence said, gesturing to the headlights with his long finger. "The mines open occasionally for work and it all gets stirred up again. You'll find it in your teeth tonight, in the seams of your clothing. There's no avoiding it." We walked into the trees, many of them strangely bare, and over to the riverbank.

"And here we have the 'run' this place is named for," Clarence said. "More like a walk. A long, filthy one at that." The stream moved slowly and paused in eddies tinged an unholy array of colors — green with some soap-fueled overgrowth of moss, a foaming chemical red-orange, a slimy yellowish brown from God only knew what.

What in the hell have I gotten myself into? I thought.

I recoiled but then tried to conceal my reaction, but Clarence shook his head. "You don't have to try to be polite for their sakes," he said, sounding angry for the first time. "This here is a wretched place, and people living this way while others eat prime rib in Manhattan is a sin as egregious as murder. These folks aren't exactly proud of living here, so don't try to flatter them or pretend you haven't noticed the conditions.

Let them see your outrage. It's one of the few kindnesses we can give them."

We walked back to the lane and over to the first shack, a one-room hovel of nailed bare board and a cobbled-together tin roof. A curtain hung where the door should be, so, instead of knocking, Clarence called, "Hello?" A breeze stirred the fabric, and I saw what was behind it: a dirt floor, a table with a single chair. On the table was a bowl full of scraps most country people would feed their pigs: apple cores, potato peels. A pair of flies circled the food.

A woman with a weathered face and greasy clump of hair emerged from behind the shack, a heavy pail full of sopping laundry propped on her hip. Several small children orbited her skirt, each of them stark naked and streaked with mud.

We walked over to her. I drew in a breath at the sight of a girl about six years old, covered in sores all over her trunk. Some of them were scabbed, but the others were shiny with pus. She sat down in the dirt and whimpered.

"Good afternoon, Mrs. Johnson," Clarence said. "I have someone I'd like you to meet."

The woman set the pail down and wiped her hands on the front of her dress. Then she plucked up the smallest child, a little blond boy with a snub nose. He clung to the shoulder of her faded calico dress, which was threadbare at the hips and revealed her bare skin beneath. Even undergarments seemed to be a luxury these folks could not afford.

"This is Miss Hickok," Clarence said. "From Washington, DC." I opened my mouth to remind him that I was a New Yorker, actually, but then remembered I no longer lived there.

I held out my hand. As the woman stared at it, I got a whiff of her and the children, and it took everything in my person not to take a big step backward. I thought of the various pests that might be making a home in their hair and felt my skin begin to itch. There was something familiar about her — her posture, her wariness. It plucked at me, but I couldn't put my finger on what it was.

Clarence continued to broker our meeting in his unhurried way. "Miss Hickok has come to talk with you all about how things are going for you here, what you think the government should do to help. She is here to advocate for you all."

The woman's mouth twisted into a wry smile I could see she reserved for expressing disbelief in things she'd heard tell of but never seen — elevators, ice cream, talking pictures in movie houses with plush seats and electric fans. Never in her life, I could see, had someone from the government shown the slightest interest in her welfare. The boy on her hip buried his face in her hair.

"Ruth Johnson," she said, finally taking my hand with her free one. She looked back at Clarence. "What do you mean 'how things are going'?"

"I mean, is the relief helping you get what you need? Do you have enough food? Things like that."

I touched the pocket of my skirt where I kept my small notebook and pencil, but I decided against pulling them out at that moment. If Ruth clammed up, I wouldn't be able to get what I needed to write my report.

"Well," she said hesitantly, surveying her house and the shacks and tents beyond, as if I were the stupidest person alive not to know the answers to Clarence's questions, "I guess we're doing all right for now. We're supposed to get fifteen dollars a month from the county, but lately it has been just ten. And usually they run out of money that last week, so we have to make do. Last month, one of Mr. Pickett's people here got her

211

hands on a big sack of flour and passed it out. So we had that, but it weren't much."

The discrepancy in the payments piqued my reporter's interest and I nodded. "What do they say, the people from the county?" I asked. "How do they explain that they've run out of money?" I figured it could be corruption, dry coffers, or both.

"I never asked," Ruth said. Her bottom row of teeth looked like little brown pebbles, and I noticed a faint rash around her mouth and up the sides of her jaw. "All I know is, we got school starting in a month, and the older children need clothes. And shoes. They just reopened some of the mines, but it won't last long. And, anyway, my husband, Norbert, is blacklisted for talking to the union, the fool. He ain't worked in years."

Just then the little boy peed down the front of her dress.

I sucked in my breath before I could stop myself, my aversion all too apparent, but Ruth just glanced down at the wet spot and shrugged. She looked like the most exhausted woman in the world, as if it were her job to carry the entire mine-scarred hillside on her shoulders, with a baby on her hip besides.

"Is that all, then?" she asked. "I got to get that laundry wrung out."

I made myself take her hand again. "Thank you for telling me all this, Mrs. Johnson," I said, my voice too loud, too cheerful. I was facing a steep learning curve in this new endeavor, I realized. The job was nothing like what I'd imagined it would be. She stared at me, as if she were waiting for more. "I can promise you — Washington's going to hear about it."

Ruth looked at me like I was speaking Greek backward. "Oh, you mean that Roosevelt fellow? I heard about him. But I don't think Jesus Christ himself could make a lick of difference out here."

That makes two of us, I nearly said back.

For the rest of the day, as Clarence took me from one family to the next, the despair of the place engulfed me. I'd covered tragedies in my time as a reporter, but they were mostly accidents — fires, car wrecks — or one-off crimes of passion and drunkenness. This suffering seemed different. Perpetual. The mines had brought people here during the boom twenty years back and then left them stranded on the hillside when the coal market collapsed, Clarence explained. And no one but the Quaker relief people seemed to care.

"What's wrong with the children's skin?" I asked him, afraid to know the answer.

"Those sores come from bathing in the river. It's the pollution. And then there's the diphtheria, like I said, and the typhoid, the rickets, the dysentery." He counted them off on his fingers. "All of which could be resolved with proper sanitation, wells, and waste disposal. But we don't have the funds to do it."

I thought with longing, and then chagrin, of the room Nora and I had shared at Le Château Frontenac, decorated all in white and pale green like an ice cream sundae with mint candies. It seemed to be on another planet. Clarence introduced me to one sad story after another: young men who were as gnarled as old codgers, leaking tents, women wearing nothing but their slips. There was no livestock anywhere nearby, so no milk or eggs, to say nothing of meat. Most families kept a little garden, and Clarence had tried to help them can their yield, but they never had enough jars and often got too hungry to wait for the vegetables to mature anyway. He had seen them dig up bitter green potatoes, he told me, small as knuckles, and eat them raw.

It was too much, a Gothic melodrama, and I wouldn't have believed it if I hadn't seen it for myself. When we finally returned to the car, I nearly wailed with relief.

"Now you understand what I was trying to tell you," Clarence said as he switched on the ignition. "If only I could get other people down here to see it too. What we need to do is get these folks out of this polluted hollow. I've written letters about it to just about everyone I can think of, including the Roosevelts. And now they sent you here, which I've got to think means someone is listening."

I gave him a weak smile, afraid to make any promises. "All I can tell you is that this report will be one for the ages, Mr. Pickett," I said. But what a meager offering that was — a government report hardly anyone would read.

We retraced the dark mountain roads, and Clarence drove me to my hotel in Morgantown. He parked the car and stepped out, fitting his hat on his head.

"I'll be back in the morning to collect you," he said after he opened my door and helped me out of the car, "and we'll go see a settlement near Cassville."

There's more? I thought, not sure I could take it. He took my suitcase from the compartment beneath the rumble seat, and before he could offer to carry it inside, I grasped the handle.

"I just have the one," I said.

"Are you sure? You've got your portable to carry too."

"It's fine," I said, and thought of the promise of sweet relief secreted in my suitcase like the glimmer of quartz in an old stone. I was afraid the sound of its slosh would give me away.

"Have you got anything to read?" He seemed to be stalling, as if he were a little worried about leaving me on my own. "It's good if you can do something to take your mind off it."

We were both thinking the same thing: How do you sit down to a good meal after that? How do you brush your teeth and take a hot bath after you have seen a naked child with weeping sores and no doctor in sight?

"I'll be all right," I said. "I've got my report to type up, and I'll go get a sandwich. I brought a mystery novel too." *The Case of the Empty Bottle,* I thought.

He nodded once. "All right. I'll see you in the morning," he said, and crossed back to the driver's side door.

"Clarence?"

He looked back at me, his face open and gentle as the moon.

I felt a welling in my heart for him, for the steadfast way he went out to see those people day in, day out. And all the while, I had been lounging in my New York apartment listening to opera records, blissfully unaware. "You are doing good work out there. My hat is off to you, sir."

"Well, it has been a long haul," he said. "But now that you are here, Miss Hickok, maybe we'll see some progress."

My throat closed up a little at his words. I didn't like to imagine being responsible for delivering what those mining families needed. What if no one listened to me? What if I couldn't make anything happen? Why in the hell had I let Nora talk me into this job? "I'll do what I can," I said.

He gave me a grim smile. "I hope so. We're counting on you."

Clarence waved as he drove away. I trudged into the hotel and checked in as quickly as I could. With immense relief, I lugged my bag to my room, where I closed and locked the door. Immediately I fished a glass out of the bathroom. Too tired — hell, too eager — to go in search of ice, I unearthed bourbon and poured.

With my portable set up on the desk, I began recording all the details I could remember from the day. When he had hired me, Hopkins had warned me never to sugarcoat the details in my reports for his sake, and I didn't. I described the shacks and the people I had met — the naked, infirm children; the out-of-work men; the barefoot women. I passed along what Ruth had said about the fishy last-week-of-the-month business. The gardens, I explained, were set in the side of a hill so steep, the seeds must have been shot into it with a gun in order to make them stick.

I took a break to freshen my drink and stood at the window, looking out through the gap in the gauzy peach drapes at the gravel parking lot and the green mountains beyond. The dense trees made me think of the forests of New Brunswick, where, at the end of our vacation, Nora and I had spent a whole day driving as we made our way to Maine and points south. It was late in the day as we barreled through a tunnel of dark forest, no houses in sight, when we emerged suddenly into a bright clearing. What I saw made me gasp. All around the car, in every direction, stood thousands of blackened tree trunks. The ground too was covered in soot and nothing moved among the desiccated poles, no birds or butterflies or rabbits. I had never seen the remnants of a forest fire — back in Bowdle there were not enough trees to burn — and the destruction was staggering. Nora slowed the car and we watched as the black trunks passed one after another, hypnotic like the succession of frames in a moving picture.

"It will take a long time," Nora had said, giving me an uneasy look, "but the trees *will* grow back."

And I'd nodded, too haunted to speak. It was fitting, I'd thought darkly, that we would end our heavenly vacation in such a harrowing way. I wanted to believe her — I wanted to believe that eventually it would rain and the ground would give up the sprouts, and the soot would be concealed beneath the fresh layer of bark that would grow on the trees. Perhaps in a few years we could drive that same stretch of road again and not know the forest had been ravaged. But the trees would know. They would carry the memory in their bodies.

Standing at the window in the Morgantown hotel, I felt around the inside of my mouth with my tongue and, just as Clarence had predicted, felt the grit of coal dust. I took my drink back to the desk and sat down once more at the typewriter. The paper curled in the miserable humidity that made everything droop, and, as my hands went to the keys, I realized what was getting under my skin, just like that soot got under the trees: Ruth was the kind of woman I knew down in my bones. Ruth was my mother, my grandmother. And if I hadn't left Bowdle, hadn't found my way to the newsroom, I could have wound up just like her.

"Nora, just what in the hell — did I lose a bet I don't know about?" I tried to keep my voice light, but I was tired and a little drunk and it was hard to breathe in the enclosed space of the phone booth in the hotel lobby. It was about nine that evening and I had just wired my report — an opus in three pages fueled by sore feet and despair — to Harry.

Nora's voice was bright. "There, you see? I told you it wouldn't be as dull as you feared. Now, I have to run. We are dining with the attaché to Panama, and I just popped up here to check my messages before they serve dessert."

Her breeziness annoyed me. It had been such a trying day, and here she was off to crème brûlée and hot chocolate from a silver pot. "Nora, hang on for just a moment. I think you need to know that — well, something is very wrong down here in coal country. The way these folks are being forced to live . . . I knew it was going to be bad, but it's so much . . . worse."

I heard talking in the background and

then the crackle of Nora pressing her hand over the mouthpiece and giving someone an instruction. Another crackle, and she came back on. "And this is exactly why you're there, Hick. Put it all in your report. Wire it to Harry — then the wheels will start to turn."

I sighed, annoyed.

"I'm sorry, darling, I wish I could talk longer, but I really do have to go."

"Nora," I nearly shouted. "Wait. Just a minute. And listen. The report is in. But it's not enough . . ." In a rush, I told her everything I had witnessed on my tour with Clarence. And I could almost see how, as the horror tumbled out of my mouth, she paused in her rush to get back to the party, sat down with the phone cradled against her shoulder. I dared to hope she began to take notes.

"And no doctor has been out to see them?" she asked.

"No. Clarence says they won't come unless they are guaranteed payment. And of course these people don't have a penny. I just don't see how a three-page report is going to do them any good. This is a goddamn emergency down here," I said. "Like a natural disaster — except there's nothing natural about it."

Nora was quiet for another moment and then I heard more rustling, the squeak of a hinge. "Just a minute," she called to someone.

"I know you have to go," I said. "I know you are surrounded, every minute, by people who want something from you."

She did not reply and I heard still more noise, someone calling from the hallway. The suffering in Scotts Run was desperate, and I wanted Nora to conclude, as I had, that the situation was urgent, based on the facts at hand. But I had more selfish aims too: I wanted it to matter that those facts were coming from me in particular. What if the distance had eroded our connection? Only weeks ago we had been on a kind of honeymoon, but now she felt remote. What if I had become just one more voice in the throng, pleading for her attention?

I switched the earpiece to my left side and wiped my clammy cheek with the back of my hand. With the toe of my shoe, I wedged the door of the booth open to get some air. The lobby smelled of mildew and pipe smoke. Nora, I knew, would be fresh with lilac perfume, the lemon juice in which she soaked her nails to bleach them white.

"I'm sorry, darling — they are calling for

me and I have to go."

And then she hung up the phone.

CHAPTER THIRTEEN

August 22, 1933

When the alarm went off in the morning, I was tempted to slap it with my hand and roll over — I certainly had a headache for the ages. But then I thought of Ruth rising at dawn to scrape another day out of the dirt and it was enough to get me to the sink, where I marveled at the running water and my toothbrush and the unimaginable luxury of soap bubbles.

After all, I had a job to do. I tried not to think of Nora. When I did, I reminded myself that she was just one person. She could not be in a dozen places at once, and each demand on her time *was* a worthy one. The women garment workers and the NAACP and the children's literacy people and the delegation from some tiny nation plagued by a mysterious disease. All of them mattered too, and I had to try to understand and bide my time. President Roosevelt would not be president forever, and some-day Nora and I would have our cottage, our porch swing, all our private dreams. She had promised me.

With more than an hour to kill, I dressed and walked across the street to a diner in the hot morning sun. My shadow was long and lean behind me, a funhouse mirror twin trying to sneak up on me. Inside, at the chipped counter, a woman with silver hair and a faded uniform was just opening for the day. She raised her eyebrows in lieu of smiling and said, "What can I get you?"

"Black coffee and eggs, please," I said. I would have liked beef hash or bacon too, but somehow I felt it would mark me as a highfalutin out-of-towner to order meat with breakfast.

She nested a heavy porcelain cup on its saucer and poured my coffee, busied herself wiping down the counter that was already clean. I could hear the murmur of news coming from a radio somewhere in back, the hiss of the griddle, and I remembered the diner in Potsdam, where Nora invited me to ride the train with her for the first time.

"Did you grow up around here?" I asked.

She nodded. "Lived here my whole life."

"In town, or . . . ?"

She moved from one booth to the next, opening the blinds to the morning sun. "My daddy was the janitor at the city hall. We lived in a little house down the street."

"So he wasn't a coal miner?" I said with a smile, because of course she knew I was from out of town — there was no hiding that fact around here — and she was probably sick to death of the assumption that every West Virginian man walked around with black-smudged cheeks.

She didn't say anything for a moment as she moved back behind the counter. Finally, her tone stiff, she said, "No. But that's honest work."

"Oh, of course it is," I fumbled. She had misunderstood: I was trying to tell her I saw the complexity of the people here, that I didn't lump them all into one narrow category, but instead she thought I was making fun of them. "Of course it is."

A fan in the corner with a bent blade wobbled around its axis with a whine. It felt like eons passed, but finally my eggs came up and she set the plate in front of me on the counter. "You here with them Quakers?"

"Something like that," I said.

The waitress shook her head. "I don't see it doing any good. Those folks out there in the holler, they're too far gone. Children eating scraps? Never seen a man with a job? How you gonna do anything to fix that?" She said it not so much with empathy as with the particular disdain of one only a couple hard-earned rungs up the social ladder from the folks under discussion.

I nodded. "It's as bad as all that and worse," I said. "That's for sure."

"All the do-gooding in the world won't amount to anything."

"Is that really what you think?" I asked.

"It is. Of course it's sad to think of people living that way, especially the children, but nothing can be done about it."

I took a bite of my eggs, chewed. "Well, if you're right," I said, and the dark part of me had a hunch she might be, "then I am wasting my time down here."

Reporters typically were cynical as hell because they had seen it all and then some. Redemption was always temporary, so why bother working for it? But Scotts Run had me losing my edge. If we could improve life for these people, even by ten percent, by one percent, it would be something. I tried to think of what Nora would say if she were here. How did she answer the refrain of hopelessness that seemed to echo from every corner of the nation? I made my best attempt to let her voice speak through me to the waitress: "But what about this: What if the way things are for the people in the mining camps — the pollution, the unemployment, the lack of schooling and health care — aren't just bad luck? What if those problems are the result of choices the government made? And, if that's true, what would happen if the government made different choices?"

She stared at me with one eyebrow hooked toward her hairline, like I might be the most feeble-minded individual she had yet encountered.

"Are you talking about President Roosevelt now?" she said with a laugh. "You think he's going to come down here and do something for those hillbillies?"

I shrugged. "You never know," I said.

When she took my dishes into the back, I set the money for breakfast plus a sizable tip on the counter and left. I'd had enough pleasant small talk for one day. Back in the room, I lit a Pall Mall and looked at a map of the region to see where I'd be touring that day. Then I made my bed and put my notebook and pen in the pocket of my skirt. Since Clarence struck me as the sort of man who was always early, I looked out the window just before nine, expecting to see his car idling in the lot.

Instead, I saw a tall woman emerging from a blue convertible.

I watched in amazement as Nora pulled off her smart tan driving gloves and smoothed her hair from her forehead. She disappeared from view as she strode toward the lobby of the hotel, and delight bloomed in my chest.

A minute later, I heard her soft knock on my door and opened it to find her in her crisp white blouse, tanned from the drive. "Nora."

"Good morning, Hick," she said and stepped into the room. I went to embrace her and imagined calling Clarence to let him know we'd be a little late getting down to the lobby, but something in her demeanor made me keep my arms at my sides.

"How did you get here so quickly?" I tried to do the math. "It must be seven hours' drive."

Nora nodded. "I slept for a bit after the party and left about three."

I gaped at her. "In the morning? The president let you leave at three in the morning? What about the Secret Service?"

She gave me a little shrug. "It's better to ask for forgiveness than permission. I stopped on the road and called when I knew he would be at his morning swim. They'll get the message to him. And Mr. Pickett knows I am coming — I called him last night after I hung up with you."

I couldn't believe it. She had come to me — and faster than I would have dared to hope. "Oh, Nora." I took her hand and laced my fingers through hers. "Won't you sit down? I've missed you like hell."

We sat side by side on the edge of the bed. "Yes, darling. I've missed you too," she said, but the response sounded a little vague, a little diffuse, while my longing was a magnetic field pulling my mouth toward hers. I embraced her and she kissed me; then she smiled in a polite way that filled me with disappointment. She didn't move to take off her hat.

"He should be here any minute," she said, and looked at her watch. "Isn't that right?"

"Who?" I was trying to play it cool, but inside I was reeling. It was only nine o'clock, but I'd already experienced despair, stubborn determination, and a surprise that delighted the hell out of me. Now I saw that her reason for making the trip had nothing to do with her feelings for me and everything to do with her work.

"Clarence Pickett." She stood up and smoothed her jacket. "He'll take us around the camp near Cassville today — I have to see as much as I can before anyone finds out that I'm here."

"Right. Of course," I said. I tamped down my disappointment. Nora was focused, that was all, and I should be grateful. And she was right about the need to move quickly. As soon as people realized the first lady was tromping around out in the mining camps, the logistics of our day would get much more complicated. "I know he will be delighted to see you."

We went down to the lobby and out into the parking lot to wait. Nora took her blue satchel — the bag that seldom left her side — out of the car and secured the convertible top just as Clarence pulled in. Through the windshield of his car, I could see the grin playing at the edges of his mouth, but he retained his dignity as he stepped out to greet us.

"Mrs. Roosevelt," he said and put out his hand. "I have to say, even after we talked last night, I still wasn't sure you'd come."

"Well, Mr. Pickett, here I am. You have Miss Hickok to thank for bringing all this to my attention." She opened the passenger door before he could do it for her. "Now, let's not waste a minute. I want to see these camps for myself."

Clarence drove us out of Morgantown, on the winding mountain roads, through Osage once more and then on to Cassville, about three miles west on Route 7. He slowed a little as the dirt lane became the main road through town and cut between two empty buildings. One looked to have been a grocery store at some point, the other perhaps a doctor's clinic, but both were shuttered and there wasn't a stick left in the woodpile out front. I watched Nora taking it all in.

He parked at the top of a ridge and helped each of us out of the car. I sucked down a cigarette while he loaded a small pushcart with sacks of donated canned beans and stew, preserved vegetables, salt pork, and flour. Nora clutched her satchel. It looked to be stuffed to the gills and I wondered at the correspondence and reports and other evidence of important tasks that it might contain — and what she was doing bringing it with her into the camp.

The three of us walked down the tree-studded hill to a cluster of tent homes in a clearing. It had to be at least ninety degrees already — and just past 10:00 a.m. — and the humidity cast everything into a haze. In his measured baritone, Clarence delivered the same explanation he had given me about the pollution in the river and the effects of the sludge on the poor saps who lived here. I understood that he had been repeating this same address for years now, to anyone who would listen, over and over and over again. Poor Clarence, the oracle everyone ignored. I found it admirable that he didn't see any reason to soften the rough edges of the gritty details just because he was now in the presence of the first lady.

She walked beside him, nearly as tall as he was, her posture erect. I had come to know this as a kind of barometer: the straighter her shoulders, the more intense her focus. Besides having removed her jacket, she seemed undaunted by the heat, but a telltale oval of perspiration on her lower back was already soaking through her blouse.

"This place is just about the same as the one you saw yesterday, Miss Hickok," Clarence said. "But here we've got more immigrants. Greeks, Italians, Russians. Some Hungarians. The mine companies started bringing them in as scabs when the white workers organized years ago. Then, of course, the foreigners started to organize, so the mine companies brought Negroes up from Georgia to replace *them*. They mostly live a mile or so down the river. Same conditions, same troubles."

Nora nodded once, absorbing the details. Some heads poked out of the canvas as we approached, the children zeroing in on our cart of food, and Nora strode to the first tent, where a man with a dark beard and thick, black eyebrows emerged. Behind him stood a woman and three children. The smallest was about two years old, and she toddled out into the sun. All of them were clothed, which was an improvement over Osage, but none of them wore shoes.

"Well, hello," Nora said. She stooped down to face the girl, her navy skirt pooling in the black dirt around her ankles, and put out her palm. "What's your name?"

The girl peered at her with a suspicious squint and then glanced back at her father. His expression was no more welcoming. When she turned back to Nora, she noticed the small luminescent pearl studs in the first lady's ears and reached out to touch one.

"Ana," the man barked. The toddler withdrew her hand.

Nora stood up. "Good morning. I apologize for the intrusion, but could I take a few moments of your time? Ask you some questions? My name's Eleanor."

He hesitated, looking down at her black oxfords, but finally shook the hand she offered. Maybe her shoes had made him

234

uneasy; the fact that she had any at all marked her as an outsider. He probably thought she was a nurse, or a nun. This idea made me smile.

"Petros Riga," he said. "This my wife, Agnes."

They invited us inside the tent, though it was impossible for all of us to fit, so Nora went all the way in while Clarence and I hovered beneath the open flaps. Clarence handed Mr. Riga a bag of food, and Mrs. Riga rushed to put it away in the tin box where they stored their meager provisions before the children took account of everything that was inside. But their insistence wore her down and she opened a can of beans and scooped them into two bowls. The two older children devoured them with their hands before Ana even had a chance to smell them. Mr. and Mrs. Riga insisted that Nora sit down. She eased her satchel to the floor beside her chair, undid the clasp, and slipped her hand inside. When it emerged, her reedy fingers held three ripe apricots.

You would have thought she held a loaded gun, the way everyone froze. Nora handed one of the apricots to Ana, who scrutinized it and brought it to her nose. She opened her mouth then and licked its skin.

Nora laughed. "Let's cut it," she said. Mrs. Riga got her a knife and she sliced the fruit in half and pulled out the stone. Nora handed half to Ana and we all watched in silence as the little girl took a small bite. She chewed a moment and then her eyes widened and she emitted a tiny squeal. She turned to her mother and extended the arm that held the rest of her piece. Then she shrieked something that sounded like "yevsi!" — *taste,* Mr. Riga explained — and Mrs. Riga leaned down and took a bite. She smiled at her daughter, her eyes pooling.

Nora cut the other two apricots and passed them around, and Ana climbed into her lap and leaned back against her while Mr. and Mrs. Riga answered Nora's gentle but thorough questions about their troubles. I remembered how the body odor and my fear of lice or worse had kept me standing at a distance from Ruth and her children the day before. I saw that my shrinking from them must have been obvious, and I felt like such a heel now as I watched Nora hold Ana. The little girl could no longer resist the lure of Nora's pearl earring; Nora plucked it right off of her ear and handed it to Ana so she could examine it closer.

The Rigases' story was the same one we'd heard in the last town. Mr. Riga had been let go by the mines over a year ago. The children had no access to medical care or reliable schooling, not to mention clean water, or decent clothes for the coming winter months.

"I know it not seem," Mr. Riga said, gesturing to their meager belongings, "but I hard worker."

"Of course you are," Nora said.

"Some of mens in mine call me 'dirty Jew.'" He threw up his hands and laughed. "I not even Jew! But who care, Jew, not Jew, if every man work hard? All we want is to work."

Nora nodded and rose from the chair, setting Ana down on the bare dirt floor of the tent. She extracted the earring from the girl's tiny hand and put it back on her ear. Then she shook each family member's hand, including Ana's, and thanked them for sharing the information about their lives. I noticed that she was careful not to make any promises of a particular kind of help, but then the Rigases could hardly have expected that since they had no idea they were talking to the wife of the president.

We went to seven or eight other tents in the hollow and met families from places I might not have been able to identify on a map — Serbia, Lithuania — and people who didn't even seem to have a country, who had been roaming as long as they could remember, led only by the basic need for work. To each family, Nora gave a handful of apricots. The satchel was full not of reports and documents but fruit. Nora had known just what to do to put the people at ease so that they would talk to her.

I tried to crack a joke or two as we walked, but the place was so damned somber they didn't stick. Once I saw her nearly lose her composure when we passed by a little boy who stood in the opening of his family's tent, clutching a shivering white rabbit in his arms. His world-weary older sister stood behind him and when she saw us looking at them, she said, "He thinks we ain't gonna eat his bunny, but we *are.*" And the little boy, perhaps thinking we were the executioners coming at last, took off running with the rabbit under his chin. I glanced at Nora to see what gentle comment she would make to the girl, but instead Nora turned her face away, toward where I stood. I caught her eye and she gave me a pleading look, her mouth stretched briefly into the expression that precedes weeping. But, in a flash, the look was gone.

The rest of the tour was more of the same. We saw cases of the skin condition with the oozing sores again, and deformities that seemed to have occurred at birth. We saw plenty of bed bug bites and infections and broken teeth and blindness. Having lived in this place would be like a scar on these children's hearts forever, even if they did get out someday. There were some things you could never get over. I knew that for sure.

How is Ruth today? I found myself wondering, though I could have guessed the answer.

Even steadfast, patient Clarence was starting to look a little frayed as the hours wore on. "Mrs. Roosevelt," he said as we left behind a sobbing woman who had recognized the first lady, dropped to her knees, and begun a cadenced prayer of gratitude in Italian. "I wonder if it isn't time for us to call it a day."

Nora appeared not to hear him; she never seemed to notice that the people around her didn't have access to the same limitless energy she had. She took a small pad and pencil out of the pocket of her skirt and jotted down some notes, pausing to count the tents that were visible from where we stood, and wrote that down too.

The sun had slipped from view, but it stained the sky the color of Nora's apricots. All around us, fireflies sparked as we trudged up the hill. "I want to see more tomorrow," she said, and stopped again to take more notes. "I want to meet the families in the Negro enclave and hear about their children's schooling. We know they have to be worse off than all these others combined."

Clarence raised his eyebrows. If he had expected this politician's wife to sail in for a brief visit and then decamp for the country club, he was mistaken. "All right," he said, nearly laughing. "I'll come to collect you from the hotel first thing in the morning."

She nodded, and I thought about how it had been hours since she'd said a word to me. Where we stood on the hillside — Clarence and I side by side, a few feet apart, and Nora a bit farther down — we made a little constellation in the shape of an arrow. Nora was its sharpened tip, facing away.

CHAPTER FOURTEEN

August 23, 1933

It was dark by the time Clarence delivered us to the hotel in Morgantown, to what now felt like the height of civilization. We wished him a good night's sleep and made our way through the lobby to a small breakfast room, where two covered plates waited at a small table: spaghetti and meatballs Nora had arranged for the desk manager to bring from the diner before it closed.

"You think of everything, Nora," I said as we fell into our chairs, exhausted.

"Well, we have to eat," she said.

My back ached and my eyes felt heavy as sandbags, but I wasted no time in twirling my fork in the steaming pasta and relishing the sweet onion and beef. The manager brought me a telegram that had come in from Harry Hopkins. The first page was a message about my report — I KNEW YOU'D BE PERFECT FOR THE JOB — WELL

DONE. H.H. — and the second contained my upcoming itinerary. After Morgantown, I was on to Kentucky, and then, in a few weeks, upstate New York and New England. The thought of more travel, with crowded buses and dingy hotels, sounded awful. I already missed Prinz, the panting pillow of him on my feet. For now at least, I told myself, Nora and I were together.

For every three bites I took, Nora took just one and chewed it slowly, lost in thought. She gave me a distant smile. Her collar drooped and her hair was a wreck. "Hick, it was as awful as you said it would be. I have never seen anything like it."

"Isn't it?" I said. "It makes me so angry."

"Me too," she said, staring into the middle distance once more. I might have thought our shared outrage would draw us closer. But Nora had spent the day treating me with such impersonal professionalism. I couldn't shake the feeling that something was wrong.

"Well, we can be sad and we can be angry," she said, pushing the still-half-full plate away and dropping her napkin beside it. "But feeling things won't help those people a bit. It only matters what we *do*."

"And what is that?"

She opened her mouth to answer but then

stopped. She met my eyes, finally, and gave me a half smile. "Hick, this is the perfect place to launch the housing program I've been talking about for years. I've been thinking of it all day. I can see it now, how I might present the idea to Franklin. I won't say more yet, but I have a lot of work to do tonight."

"That's all right," I said, trying not to be hurt that she wouldn't confide in me yet. "I don't mind if you work. I'm so tired, I think I could sleep through the sound of *ten* typewriters, much less one."

"Oh . . . ," she said. Her hand was on the table, but it didn't come any closer to mine. "I went ahead and booked a second room."

My face fell before I could stop it.

Nora glanced over at the desk manager out in the lobby, who seemed absorbed in the task of sorting phone messages. She lowered her voice. "You know I'd rather stay with you. But I needed to make the trip look legitimate. And plus, I didn't know how long you would be staying, when you need to move on to your next assignment."

Of course, she could have asked me those questions, coordinated her plans with mine. But she hadn't. I wondered if I'd made some misstep along the way, on our vacation or here in West Virginia, that had

243

caused her to retract. What an awful feeling, to be punished but not to know what for.

I plastered a smile on my face. "It's okay, Nora. I understand."

After two big glasses of bourbon, I spent a sleepless night in my hotel room, rising twice for water to wash away the salty tang of the tomato sauce and then twice more to use the bathroom. Even with the small window wedged open, the room was stuffy, and I flopped from side to side on the bed, trying to get comfortable. My exhausted mind shuffled through a jumble of images. The sores on the children's skin morphed into the flesh of apricots, sticky sweet sirens for the flies. Nora's white, sweat-soaked blouse became the ash in the New Brunswick clearing where we'd seen the aftermath of the forest fire. My thoughts returned to the walk to Ruth Johnson's tent, but each dirt path I turned down in my mind led to my childhood home in Bowdle. When the alarm clock rang, I felt as though I had never closed my eyes. I called Nora's room and told her I had a terrible headache and that she and Clarence should go on without me. Then I pulled the covers over my head and finally slept.

Around two in the afternoon, she knocked

on my door. I wiped the sleep from my eyes and let her in.

"Good morning, Hick," she said, her smile warmer than it had been the day before. She set a mug of coffee and a turkey sandwich on the dresser and kissed me. "How are you feeling?"

"Better," I said, and it was true. Both the kiss and the sleep had done me good, and I was relieved to have skipped act three of the opera of human suffering that was playing out in these mountain towns. I had seen enough to last me the rest of my days.

"Well, eat that, have some coffee, and then get dressed." She opened the curtains and began tidying the bed with an efficiency that made me chuckle. I marveled at her. How was it that she was still here, still unnoticed by reporters? How was it that the president hadn't sent out the cavalry to bring her home? The answer, of course, was that FDR knew better by now than to argue with his wife. Once she had made up her mind to take on a project, neither death nor life nor angels nor principalities could separate that woman from her aim.

"Hurry up." She clapped her hands with deathly cheer. "There's something I want to show you."

Twenty minutes later, we were sailing in

her convertible southeast of Morgantown on a shoulderless paved road that dropped off on each side into deep gullies. The prospect of one of her tires slipping off the road and stranding us in the middle of nowhere kept my pulse racing. Here and there, we saw a shack or a roadside stand heaped with onions from someone's garden, but for the most part the winding road was empty as it cut through the deep green hills. I inhaled the scent of honeysuckle and the lush trees baking in the heat; behind us a cloud of dust curled up to the sky.

"Where are we going?"

Nora turned to me and smiled. "You'll see."

I could sense we were climbing in elevation. The air felt cleaner here, and there was more light than there had been down in the mining camps. An incongruously grand farmhouse came into view, surrounded by dilapidated outbuildings and a sprawling verdant meadow. Nora slowed the car and pulled off to the right. When she got out of the car, I followed and stood beside her with my hand shielding my eyes from the sun.

"This is a farm owned by a man named Richard Arthur," Nora said. The meadow was full of grasshoppers that sounded like a hundred hissing radiators. "It's about a thousand acres, all within Preston County. Before Mr. Arthur owned it, and before the man before him, a man from Virginia named John Fairfax did. He was a close friend of George Washington, I'm told."

I gaped at her. The big empty land was giving me the willies. "You didn't bring me all the way out here for a historical tour, did you? Because I wouldn't be surprised if that field is full of snakes."

"Better than bed bugs and lice," she said. "What I'm trying to tell you is that this land has pedigree."

"Wonderful," I said. "Let's put it in a telegram to the DAR. Now can we get back in the car?" The sun was blinding and I was still a little hungover, more from my unsettling dreams than the booze.

Nora didn't move. "Important things happen on land with pedigree. I believe in that."

"Meaning . . . ?"

She sighed at my dimwittedness. "Mr. Arthur is quite behind on his taxes."

My ears perked up then. "Is that right?"

"Yes, indeed. And for about fifty thousand dollars, he will sell the government this farm, including all its buildings, to save himself from going into foreclosure."

"And what would the government want with this old farm?" I asked. But I had an idea. I felt a little shiver whisk up my spine.

"I guess we'll have to call it Arthurdale, since the poor man is practically giving his land away. Each family will get a few acres — maybe five at the most to keep things manageable. A cow, a pig, some chickens, and seed. And we'll build them a house, which I'd like to find a way for them to make payments on, so that they will own it outright someday. We need a clinic and a school. There's an awful lot to figure out." She turned to me. "But, Hick, doesn't it sound wonderful?"

I thought of the terrible cases we'd seen on our tour and tried to imagine the under-nourished children running in this fresh field, drinking milk and eating chicken, vegetables, bread thick with butter. I saw neat little houses with a lane winding among them, flags hanging from porches. "Yes. It does. But how will you do it?"

"I already am," she said, and her eyes were filled with more temerity than I'd ever seen. "I was on the phone most of the night. Franklin took a little convincing, though I can't understand why. A place like Arthurdale fits perfectly with the subsistence farming initiative he has talked about for years. Around midnight, he got the secretary of the interior to release emergency funding, and Louis is drawing up the paperwork for the sale."

"Incredible," I said.

"What you really need to know, Hick, is that he was convinced to say yes because of *you,* because of your report. The homesteading idea is part Franklin's and part mine, but the fact that we are going to try it here, with these people from the closed mines, that part is because of the work you have done. It's very important to me that you see — it matters, this work. It's not the AP, but it matters."

I stood there watching the grasshoppers fling themselves out of the grass like water dropped on a hot griddle and tried to let her words penetrate my mind. She knew I missed my old life, the job that meant everything to me. She knew I was despairing that I might have made a mistake.

Nora took her hand out of the pocket of her skirt and reached for mine. I glanced over at her, my heart ever hopeful, but her gaze had turned back to the dilapidated Arthur house as she imagined what this land would become, at the way she could use her vision to change the fate of hundreds of people. In the face of an aim so grand, I could hardly ask her to attend to my trivial doubts by taking me into her arms, by kissing me hard and long in the safety of this place, with no one to see us but the grasshoppers. But how I wanted to slip into the car and feel her skin against mine. How I wanted her to whisper to me again about the cottage she had pledged to build for us — the lace curtains curling in the evening breeze, the table spread with chintz and a half-full decanter while we talked the night away, finally unhurried, finally just we two. I felt on that country road the words of my heart welling up and nearly spoke them aloud: *Oh, Nora, say that you still love me — that you always will.* But instead I said nothing, my hand in hers like an offering.

CHAPTER FIFTEEN

September 1, 1933

"Miss Hickok, what do you make of this duplicitous woman, giving all of us the slip?" Louis asked, grinning, as he rattled the ice and gin in his glass.

I gave him my *What can you do?* smile and shrugged, while Nora feigned outrage. "Just because a person escapes in the middle of the night without telling anyone where she is going, I hardly think you could call that duplicitous."

Louis laughed. "I believe that's the precise definition."

Nora held her ground with a smile. "And, anyway, look what I was able to accomplish."

It had been almost two weeks since our West Virginia jaunt. Nora, Louis, and I stood in the doorway of the private family dining room in the White House, about to head in for a working supper over which we planned to review preliminary documents for the creation of Nora's homestead town, Arthurdale.

"What I really can't believe," Louis said, "is that she managed to elude the press."

"Well, for a little while," Nora said.

The evening she and I returned to the Morgantown hotel after our trip out to the Arthur land, a photographer from the *Morgantown Post* was waiting for us and snapped a few pictures, and a reporter probed her about the reason for our visit. I'd felt annoyed with them for blowing our cover and a little worried they might be curious about why Nora and I were in her car alone together, why we were staying in the same hotel. But, as always, the notion of a romance between us was so preposterous, it couldn't have occurred to them. That we would always be able to hide in plain sight was both a comfort and a disappointment.

I'd watched as the reporter and photographer walked out of the hotel, and I was jealous that they were headed back to the camaraderie of a newsroom, however one-horse it might be. And that, of course, had made me think of John. We hadn't spoken since the day I left the AP. I wondered if he was still angry with me. I thought of him sitting at his desk with a pencil over his ear and his boyish cowlick splayed on the top of his head, thought of us at Dom's drinking our courage and decided maybe it was time to drop him a line. I hoped things were still going well with Marina, even though he didn't really deserve it.

The windows in the dining room were draped with voile curtains that billowed with the breeze coming off the South Lawn. We carried our drinks to the table and took our chairs.

Nora looked at Louis. "I didn't know he was in," she said. *He,* of course, could refer to only one man. She seemed more irritated than alarmed, but my pulse lurched to top speed. After Morgantown, she had returned to Washington and I'd completed another leg of my assignment in Kentucky, where I wrote other reports and slept in other depressing motels. With a subletter in my apartment, I didn't really have a place to stay between trips so, after some prodding, I'd accepted Nora's invitation to stay in the White House. The servants had made up a bed for me in the sitting room adjacent to her bedroom. Nora had arranged for the violets from my kitchen to be transported to the White House solarium, and at the post office I'd changed my address to 1600 Pennsylvania Avenue. I even had a box of

White House letterhead. I'd assumed she had cleared all this with the president, but now I wondered.

Louis glanced at his watch. "Nor did I. Our man of mystery."

We remained standing, and, a moment later, President Roosevelt was propelled into the room by Missy LeHand, who steered his wheelchair to the head of the table, where the ornate dining chair had been removed.

"Good evening, Franklin, Missy," Nora said, her voice sunny. I plumbed her tone for acrimony, but if she felt any she hid it very well. I wondered what we'd stepped in.

"Mrs. Roosevelt," Missy said. She took the chair beside the president, and we all sat down. I exhaled a tiny stream of breath through my lips.

The president clapped his hands. "Miss Hickok, I've read your excellent — and distressing — reports from the field. Now we really do have a healthy quorum to discuss this Appalachia business. I'm glad you could join us."

"Thank you for having me, sir," I said, though if I had to guess I'd say he knew just as little about Nora's plans and guests as she knew about his.

With clammy hands, I unfolded my dinner napkin. I kept my eyes on the crystal vase in the center of the table. Louis updated the president on a few matters of business — announcement of new domestic oil production quotas and the trouble in Germany — and Nora chimed in with her own take on the Nazis' bonfires of Jewish art and the newly signed pact between Italy and the Soviets.

While they wrestled the affairs of the world, I stole a glance at Missy; she wore her blond hair in an elegant twist and a chic blue dress with butterfly sleeves. The very tip of her elbow rested on the arm of the president's chair. She was photogenic, curved in that solicitous posture like a parenthesis around the man she loved, and I wondered whether she ever indulged in a fantasy that it was she who was married to the president instead of Nora. How strange for me to wish her fantasy might come true, so that Nora and I might realize our own.

"Now, let's turn back to West Virginia," Nora said. She seemed to feel there was nothing unusual about a husband, wife, and the two people with whom they were having affairs dining together. I, on the other hand, felt I was in the early stages of a stroke.

"The survey has been completed and the paperwork is with the lawyers," Louis said, combing his notes. "I expect the sale to close this week. And then we begin the planning."

"I've begun already," Nora said. "I've met with the architects, and drawn up an idea of the selection process."

"I think it's a marvelous plan," the president said.

"We have to think about how to make it as fair as possible, because there won't be enough houses for everyone, not at first." Nora pursed her lips in thought. "Clarence and I spoke about a few different ways we could approach a lottery, maybe reserve a certain number of houses for people from each camp."

Louis swallowed a sip of his drink. "Each of the ethnic camps?"

"Yes," Nora said, "it's crucial that the residents reflect the population of the region as a whole — crucial that the help extends to everyone."

"Have you asked the people what they think about that?" the president asked. He glanced at Louis, and I considered his point. It was ambitious to imagine that people who preferred to live with their own kind would happily integrate themselves in this new town. But Nora gave the president a chilly look. Woe unto any man who suggested she scale back her vision for this utopia.

We were saved by servants then. They came into the breakfast room, followed by the family's head cook, and brought our plates — chicken in a white sauce, steamed vegetables, and rolls. It struck me that Nora seemed to move effortlessly from a place so derelict as the mining camps to a room so fine as this. All dining tables were the same to her, each person worthy of the dignity of a place there. My heart swelled with admiration, and I waited for Nora to thank the cook first, so the rest of us could follow.

But it was Missy, who until that moment had been completely silent, who said, "Thank you, Mrs. Nesbitt. This looks lovely."

I felt my eyebrows climb and glanced at Nora to see what she thought about Missy slipping so easily into the role of mistress of the house, but she was busy asking after Louis's wife, Grace, who had had bronchitis.

The president echoed his mistress — "Yes, wonderful!" — and there was the merest edge in his voice that revealed his unease.

Mrs. Nesbitt bowed her head in formal deference. "Thank you, sir. We do our best," she said, and went back through the door to the kitchen.

Roosevelt's smile faded as she left. He

sniffed at his plate. "It smells a little . . . odd," he said. He sniffed again. "Well, it smells like nothing at all."

Nora dipped the tines of her fork in the sauce and tasted it. "I believe she has left out the butter."

"And the cream," Louis said, his lips pursed.

"So that would make this, let's see — flour, water, and . . . salt?" Missy said to the president. He shook his head in irritation, and it was clear the two of them had discussed the matter of Mrs. Nesbitt's failed dishes before.

The president set down his fork. "It's dreadful." He looked at his wife. "Eleanor, have you told her to ration?"

Nora, I noticed, wouldn't meet his eye. "Most people in this country are making do without rich foods. It sets an excellent example if we embrace the same prudence."

"Oh, it's not so bad," I blurted, sensing that there were sides to be taken, and I wanted to be on hers. "The vegetables are fine."

"Yes, they are," Nora said, and took a bite of green beans. "We should be grateful for simple, nutritious food."

"You and your crusades, Eleanor," the president said. Missy shifted in her chair

258

and took a sip of her drink. "Even with decent ingredients at her disposal, Mrs. Nesbitt is no cook, and you know it."

Nora sighed. "It's true that she does not have much experience, but, Franklin, she has done so much for us over the years. And you know her husband is not well — she needs the income."

The president closed his eyes and tipped his head back in exasperation. "Well, can't you give her some other kind of work and hire a decent chef? I don't know how much more of this I can take. International diplomacy may be at risk if she continues to serve this sludge at state dinners!"

Missy chortled at her lover's joke. "Really, Effdee, this meal is just not dignified," she said.

And then I saw I had been wrong to assume Missy's attempted coup a few moments before had gone over Nora's head. The first lady fixed her with a stare so cold I glanced at Missy's water goblet to see if frost had bloomed around the edges. Missy, going a little pale, moved her elbow an inch closer to her torso so that it no longer touched the president's chair. Beneath the table, I tipped my knee against Nora's and silently urged her to breathe. I myself felt both riled and confused — indignant on

Nora's behalf, but also unsure of my place in the table's pecking order. If Nora was the first wife and Missy was the second, what was I? At least Missy was afforded the dignity of causing tempers to flare, but I doubted FDR felt anything like jealousy when it came to me. Back at Christmas, Nora and I had been so worried that we'd be exposed, but I saw that something worse had happened: it didn't *matter* to him enough to wonder. He didn't care what was going on between us. Somehow, our love felt less powerful when I knew it held no threat.

Louis cleared his throat — God bless that man — and said, "If we might turn back to West Virginia for a moment . . ." And I thought of Ruth Johnson standing with her bare feet in the dirt and felt ashamed of my chicken dinner, as unpleasant as it was. "The money for subsistence homestead projects was appropriated through the Recovery Act, but Secretary Ickes will need to approve a budget for this endeavor."

Nora looked at Franklin. The business with Missy and the dinner was forgotten; she had snapped into strategy mode, her boundless work ever her refuge from the volatility of home life. "Ickes will want to scrimp."

The president gave her a scolding look. "My dear, he's balancing a whole host of projects. That is his job, to make the funds go as far as possible. To see the big picture."

"The big picture," Nora said, "is that subsistence homesteads cannot succeed across the country unless we launch them with a bold, successful pilot program. And Arthurdale is the pilot program."

"It sounds like it's a matter of degrees," Louis chimed in. "Anything we do is going to be an improvement for these folks, right, Miss Hickok?" He and the president both turned to me.

I cleared my throat, stalling. "Well, yes, that's true. Their circumstances are fairly deplorable at the moment —"

"So perhaps we do not need an architect," Louis said quickly. He pulled a brochure from the folder on the table beside him and handed it to Nora. "These are prefabricated houses and can be delivered in a few pieces by truck. We'll save thousands on labor if we don't have to construct the homes from scratch."

Nora opened the brochure and I peered at it across her forearm. "Prefabricated Cape Cod–Style Homes," it read. "Build It in No Time and Summer in Style." A line drawing depicted a tidy cottage on what looked like the Maine coast.

Nora slapped the brochure closed. "Louis, don't be absurd. These are summer cottages. They have no heat! What will these people do in the winter? And no plumbing? You can't be serious."

He signaled to the servant standing by the door for another drink. "We could install woodstoves. After all, that's the way most people in this part of the country heat their homes. As for plumbing — wells, outhouses . . ."

"Absolutely not," Nora said. "It is 1933, for goodness' sake. If we want to lift people out of poverty, they must have decent accommodations. Franklin, are you listening to this?"

Both Nora and Louis looked at the president, who had been watching with some amusement as they volleyed back and forth like tennis players. He flashed one of his signature smiles. I was starting to understand that he used them the way some men used a raised voice, to take control of a conversation, to bring it back in hand.

"I have faith in the two of you to hammer out a plan that will maximize the benefits to these miners and their families," FDR said. "And I know you can put this initiative in the best possible light so that we may replicate it elsewhere, within the confines of the legislation — and the funding." He pushed his untouched plate away. "Now, Missy has agreed to help me with some reports. Miss Hickok, it's wonderful to have you here. I hope you know that you are doing a great service to your country with these field investigations."

I had to admit that praise from the president himself was a pretty good consolation prize for the loss of my byline. But beside me Nora was tense, and I knew she was scheming about how to get her way on the matter of the Arthurdale houses, not congratulating herself on achievements already in the can.

"Good evening," Missy said to Louis and me and the space just to the left of Nora — she still couldn't quite look at her — as she stood and smoothed her skirt. She pushed the president's chair across the plush carpet and out through the door, and I heard her ask the servant to have a tray of sandwiches sent up to the president at his desk. Nora watched this exchange as she chewed the final bite of chicken on her plate, sopped up the last bit of sauce with a scrap of bread, and popped it into her mouth. She had eaten the entire wretched thing.

CHAPTER SIXTEEN

September 2–17, 1933

In the morning, I woke to find all of them gone. Nora's schedule and mine had diverged once again. The Roosevelt family was off to the rustic luxury of a Cape Cod vacation, while the itinerary Harry Hopkins sent by telegram said I would be investigating upstate New York and New England's shabbier byways — fishing towns in decline, counties that depended on quarries and dairy farms. Perhaps Harry would take pity on me, I thought, and reimburse me for two bus tickets so that I might buy the seat beside me and avoid any northbound nose pickers who tried to chat me up.

I had a vague memory of Nora's lips sweeping my cheek as she said goodbye in the wee hours, but, like most of our encounters over the last few weeks, the moment felt ephemeral and I partly doubted whether it had happened at all. I dressed in my little converted bedroom and tidied my things so that the maids wouldn't have to trouble over much. As soon as they heard me stirring, there was a knock at the door and one maid brought in a tray with a silver coffeepot and plate of rolls with butter and jam while another brought in a stack of freshly laundered clothes — mine, I realized, though I couldn't think of when they had taken them out. The White House staff moved with a silent choreography that was a marvel. It made me uncomfortable; I didn't like to think of anyone else but me having to rinse out my stockings at the end of the day.

The first maid came back once more, this time with a cryptic note for me in Nora's hand. *Go see Walt in the garage, darling,* it said. *You may not say no.*

I looked at the maid in confusion.

"I can show you the way if you'd like, Miss Hickok."

I followed her through the building's hallowed halls, past portraits of founding fathers and paintings of ships and bucolic farms and other scenes meant to stoke the embers of patriotism. We exited a door that led to a series of outbuildings, and, inside a large garage, she introduced me to a graying man in olive drab coveralls.

"Miss Hickok." He nodded as the maid

265

disappeared, back to her covert tasks. "Mrs. Roosevelt has everything arranged. Please come on through."

I followed him past several bays occupied by cars and trucks. The garage, noisy with whirring tools, was enveloped in the aroma of coffee and motor oil. We passed mechanics illuminated by caged bulbs as they worked beneath the hood and chassis of two White House vehicles under repair. At the back of the garage, pointed toward a wide door shoved up on its runners, was a gleaming blue Chevrolet.

I gaped at Walt.

"It's not new," he said, as if that made the gift any less extravagant. I walked slowly around the left side to the front, where the sun glinted off the bumper. It was a cabriolet model, with chrome headlights that stretched across the grille like a pair of eyeglasses, black fenders, and tires with unblemished white spokes. The top was down, folded back behind the seat.

"Why don't you sit in it?" Walt said. "Get a feel for it."

My chest tightened with disappointment. The car was such a grand gesture, but how could she have forgotten such an important detail? "Walt, it's a beauty — but I don't know how to drive!"

Walt wiped his hands on a greasy rag and tucked it back in his pocket. "I know. Mrs. Roosevelt hired a young man to take you on the first leg of your trip north. He'll teach you the basics, until you're ready to be on your own."

I peeked at the dash, which was littered with dials and switches, and noted a three-foot-long stick crowned with a black knob that jutted out of the floor. "It's a thousand-pound tin can of death," I said.

Walt smiled. "Oh, two thousand pounds, at least. Maybe three."

I let Walt get back to work and rushed up to my room to write to Nora to tell her that this plan was extremely harebrained. But before I could, I found another note from her waiting on the desk in my room:

Dear Hick,
Her name is Bluette. She will grow on you.
Love, Nora

On the twelfth of September, a stocky young man named Sam — Walt's grandson, I later learned — loaded my bags into the trunk lashed to Bluette's hindquarters and got behind the wheel. After a few tries he got the car — *my* car — started, and we

267

headed around the winding drive out to Pennsylvania Avenue and Foggy Bottom and up through the campus of Georgetown on the road that hugged the Potomac.

From Washington we drove north through Pennsylvania, toward Corning, New York. After a couple of hours, with the Washington traffic long behind us, Sam pulled off at a filling station. The attendant shined the headlights with a rag and washed the dust from the windshield; then he filled the tank and checked the radiator and the oil. When he was finished, Sam drove across the street to a nearly empty parking lot beside a church. He opened my door and offered me a hand.

But I stayed in my seat, my fingernails gripping the leather. "I don't think I'm ready," I said.

Sam smiled and his doughy cheeks lifted. "No time like the present, Miss Hickok."

I griped for a few more minutes but then gave in and crossed to the driver's side. In a calm voice, Sam explained about the clutch and the hand brake, the big stick for shifting gears, the pedals — everything I needed to do to make the big boat move. I stomped on the pedals a few times before I succeeded at shifting into gear and releasing the hand brake, and we began to crawl across the blacktop. I gripped the steering wheel so tightly I could feel my pulse throb in my fingers.

"Now turn to the left," Sam said.

Flustered, I cranked the wheel to the right instead and we jerked sideways.

"Or the right," he said, and chuckled. "We can try left next."

I turned to give him a withering look, thereby taking my eyes off the parking lot for a moment. When I turned back, a squirrel made a break for it across our path. "How do I stop again, goddamnit?" I yelled, swerving to miss the bushy tail that whipped out of sight.

"The pedal in the center," Sam said, his voice gentle even as I rocked us to a halt by stomping on the brake. He patted my shoulder. "I think you're doing just fine."

I jerked on the handbrake, switched off the ignition, and stalked out of the car, leaving the door open behind me. My cheeks were hot and I felt helpless and out of control. I stood with one hand on the back of my hip and lit a cigarette, thought as I smoked it about how the squirrel could have been a child on a bike.

I was furious at Nora. I should have been grateful for her generous gift, but why wasn't she here with me? Was she throwing money at my problems so that she could manage me from afar? So much had changed in a matter of months. There were no more taxis in my life; they'd gone the way of reporting, of evenings at the Met, of Nora passing notes to me in front of the fire in her sitting room. My life had become as unrecognizable to me as the dials on the dash of the car. But as John had told me that drunken night at Dom's, we all pay the price to get what we get. What we want doesn't always factor in, and there isn't a damn thing a gal can do about that.

When the cigarette was spent, I flicked it away and walked back to the car. Sam got out of the passenger side to take the wheel, but I waved him back and got behind it myself. If Nora thought she could ply me with gifts, I supposed she was right; moping around would get old fast. "I'll take it from here," I said. When I turned onto the empty road, I pressed down hard on the gas.

The next few days passed in a blur of tours — glass factories that made thermometers and red and green lightbulbs for railroad signs; dairies where farmers were shooting their cows rather than continue to pay to feed them when they couldn't get more than pennies for the milk. Lake Ontario blew autumnal breezes that made me glad for my sweater as I met with county officials eager to show off the public works programs they had established for men on relief. In Syracuse, men built a public pool, a museum, an athletic field; they dug up poplar trees whose roots ruptured the sewer pipes, and repaved the roads. Everywhere I went, I heard the same thing: men and women were itching to work, if only we could find enough for them to do.

On the first day in New York, I tried calling Nora at the Cape Cod house to thank her for the car, but no one answered. I imagined them out for a sail. On the second day, satisfied that I could handle Bluette on my own, Sam took a bus back to Washington, which left me to pull into the porte cochere at the Hotel Syracuse alone. A valet took the car, and I sailed with relief across the plush carpet of the lobby. I knew Bluette would deliver me from the many indignities of traveling by bus, but I felt an awful lot more relaxed when she was parked in one place and I was parked in another, preferably with a fresh drink in my hand.

"Good evening," said the manager when I approached the desk. He had dark eyebrows and a mustache as thick as a pelt. "Checking in?"

"Reservation for Hickok." I propped my cheek on the heel of my hand as I waited.

He consulted the book and made a mark in one of the columns. Then he plucked a key on a silver ring from its hook. "Four-seventeen. Oh, and you've got a letter too," he said, and pulled it from a cubby behind him. I glanced at the postmark. It was from Harry Hopkins's office in Washington.

I took the elevator upstairs to the room, left my bags and the letter, and went back down to the lobby and around the corner to a pharmacy I had seen on the way in. What I wanted was a drink. Repeal was on its way; though spirits still were technically illegal, the president already had lifted the ban on beer. But beer had never appealed to me. It was about as effective for what I was after as trying to clean the Taj Mahal with a toothbrush. Fortunately, no one in the state of New York worried much about enforcing the all-but-dead law, and "medicinal" liquor could be found at the drugstore.

I paid for my staples — two packs of Pall Malls, a ham sandwich, and a bottle of bourbon — and returned to the room to open the letter. The outer envelope, from Harry's secretary, contained another letter that had a Morgantown postmark. I opened that envelope and unfolded two pieces of paper. The first was from Clarence, explaining that he was trying to help the enclosed letter reach me and would write in another week to make sure it had come through. I flipped to the second page, a cheap piece of lined paper like the kind found in a child's school notebook:

August 31

Dear Miss Hickok,
Bet you thawt I did not know how to rite well werent you wrong. I went to school as a girl and tho I caint say as I use it much I do know my letters and how to read the scripcher which Norbert says is all we need. I like to ask him how well thats done for us so far but that is not a bright idea.

I asked Mr. Pickett to get this letter to you because he tole me you used to rite for the newspaper and may be you can help me. Rumors been flying round this camp since you visited. Some say the first lady came back a few days later tho I werent round to see it for myself. What I need to know from you is what all have they got planned? People are saying the govment is going to build houses where some families can live. Some of these women round here are dum as a sack of hair so as one caint take nothing they say to serius.

But I got to say Miss Hickok if it is true can you help us? We just have to get in to one of them houses. I hate to beg but to be honest with you I am pert near the end of my rope with more little uns than I can say grace over and another one on the way that my husband got on me. Even tho I tole him enuf is enuf. He means to provide but what can he do when there aint a job to be found? All of us been sick with one thing after a nother and these little babys are all the time hungry. We got winter coming all over agin now and I just dont know how much more we all can take. Please help us if you can.

Yours truly,
Ruth Johnson

I stared at the uneven scrawl so painstakingly written I could feel the ridges the words made on the back side of the paper. I wondered how many drafts Mrs. Johnson had made and discarded before copying out this last one, and whether she had really believed it would reach me. When we met that first day back in Scotts Run and her little boy had piddled down the front of her dress, she had seemed so defeated, so far out of reach of anything like hope. And yet here she was writing this letter, going above her husband, to try to get her family out of that mess. Which just went to show that you can't keep a good woman down.

I had half a mind to write her back immediately and give her my word that she would get one of those houses. I stopped myself, as I had been on the wrong end of a dubious promise and knew not to inflict that particular heartbreak. Secretary Ickes of Interior had yet to publicly announce the plans for Arthurdale, and, once he did, I was fairly sure the families who applied for consideration would have to endure enough red tape to wrap all the Christmas presents in America — not that there would be too many of them, based on the conditions I'd seen so far in my travels. Ruth Johnson needed help *now.*

I glanced at the clock on the nightstand. It was past midnight, too late to try calling Nora at the Cape Cod house again, though I was certain she was still up toiling away in the dim light of a hokey seashell-shaped lamp, over a draft of a speech or an appeal for funds for the women's trade union. Closing my eyes, I indulged in the thought

275

that perhaps, instead, she was composing a letter to me. I was still rankled by the gift of the car, but a red ribbon of tenderness curled through even that unpleasantness and I felt a surge of love for her once more. Love. Lord, what a pain in the ass it was.

I opened the drawer of the lacquered desk and pulled out a leaf of hotel stationery. With my pencil, I drew a line through the Hotel Syracuse address and, checking my itinerary from Harry's office, wrote instead the name and address of the hotel in Maine where I would be staying in a week's time.

My dear lady,

How's the family? Are you up to your neck in oysters? Upstate is not so bad — fairly quiet, actually, now that I have run everyone off the road. (What can I say but thank you for this outlandish present?) Tomorrow I am off to Vermont, New Hampshire, and Maine, and if I go missing you can tell the authorities to follow the trail of dead birds and squirrels until they find the ditch that contains Bluette and me.

Now, I am enclosing a letter from Mrs. Ruth Johnson, the woman from Osage, West Virginia, whom I met on my first day there. Please read it. Please read it three times. This poor soul — another baby on the way. What can we do for her? Where do things stand with the homes? You told me when I left the AP that I could turn the page, take on a new role in which I could actually intervene to help people instead of just telling their tales in the newspaper. Well, darling, you may wish you could eat your words because I'm making it my mission to get this woman a house, even if I have to build it for her myself. This may not be what you and Harry Hopkins intended, but I feel that I have been sent out into the great American expanse like a sponge, to absorb miseries various and sundry, from Appalachian to Yankee, from the babies to the codgers. Who will wring me out — and when? These folks are permanent fixtures in my heart now, and Ruth is chief among them. We cannot let her down.

Yours,
Hick

In the morning I woke with an aching molar that worried me a bit, and the desk manager kindly rustled up some aspirin for me while the valet brought Bluette around to the front. Soon, I was distracted by my desire

277

to stay on this side of the grave as I navigated the steep hills around Lake Champlain. At Rouses Point, I took the car ferry to Alburgh in Vermont and passed summer cottages closed up for the season, their shutters latched and their flagpoles bare. These were sleepy towns and, after brief meetings, I pressed on over the next few days to Burlington, then Montpelier, then through the Mount Washington Valley, into Maine.

Penobscot Bay's open water and sky was a shock after so many days in the green woods, and I slowed Bluette as I sailed along the coastal Route 73 to take it in. Rockland smelled of the lobsters no fishermen seemed able to catch these days, according to information in my brief on the region from Hopkins's office. Fishery experts claimed a lack of regulation had led to years of overfishing small lobsters too young to have reproduced, causing the population to plummet. That in turn led to fishermen spending a great deal on boat fuel and bait with nothing to show for it at the end of the week. I counted thirty empty storefronts along Main Street and wrote the figure in my notes.

At ten in the morning, I pulled into the McConchie Quarry in Saint George and hustled, already late, to the office to meet the foreman.

"Greger Hedman," he said without standing from his desk. He gave me a puzzled look as he attempted to size me up. "Your boss is outside?"

"My . . . ?" And then I understood; from sea to shining sea, America could be relied upon to underestimate its women. "I'm the one and only, I'm afraid," I said.

He leaned in toward me. "You are the field reporter? You drove yourself here?"

I smiled and tried to tamp down my irritation. My day was packed with appointments and I didn't feel like justifying my existence to a backwater oaf.

"Well, I've seen all of it now," he said, taking a sip of his coffee and making no move to commence with our meeting.

"Yes," I sighed, rather more prettily than he deserved, "it *is* shocking what women get up to these days —"

"Who had the bright idea to put a lady in this job?"

"President Roosevelt, actually. So. If you don't mind . . ."

We finally mended our cross purposes, and Greger showed me the quarry. He explained that when New York City halted all spending on street repairs, the granite paving-stone business of Saint George,

Maine, had fallen into the dumps from lack of demand. All of it was connected.

From there, I drove north along the coast. In Machias, I saw blueberry barrens plucked of the smallest harvest in twenty years. In Eastport, I met fish processors who had been optimistic about the first healthy sardine population in an age only to find that, when the schools of fish entered the Bay of Fundy, five whales followed them in and ate them all.

Now just what in the hell was anybody supposed to do about that?

After the potato fields of Caribou and Fort Kent, I finally turned Bluette south and arrived a day later in Augusta. Same hotel lobby carpet, same armchairs, same dusty lamps, different town. In a haze, I checked in and asked after my mail. There was nothing from Nora — my questions about Arthurdale went unanswered and my worries about Ruth flourished — but Harry's office had forwarded the itinerary for the next leg of my travels. After a few weeks off to recover, I would set out again to the towns listed in that envelope. Fall's chill would be upon us by then; I dared to speculate that I might be assigned someplace exotic, at least to the likes of me. Palm trees and umbrella drinks in Fort Lauderdale? Étouffée and

Sazeracs in the French Quarter?

As the elevator clanked and shuddered to my floor, I unsheathed my fate from the envelope. Hope springs eternal — usually right before I get sucker punched in the gut. In November, the paper said, I'd be going to South Dakota.

CHAPTER SEVENTEEN

November 1933

But not Bowdle is what I told myself in the weeks leading up to the trip. That no-horse town was not on my itinerary. Not the farm, not that barn I had fought my way out of all those years ago — the place to which I'd vowed never to return. Half the booze I'd drunk over the decades was meant to be a disinfectant, to rid my memory of Bowdle. I touched the lump my necklace made beneath my blouse. There wasn't a reason under the sun that I'd need to go *there.*

As I set out for my trip and starting driving west, I conjured Nora's reassuring voice: "Look at all that you have achieved, darling. Those long-ago days have no hold on you anymore!" That got me through until I crossed into Minnesota, where the temperature dropped and the wind howled its disapproval of my presence. Then I began to feel a little dread: Bluette seemed to shrink around me and I had to crack the windows in order to breathe. The cigarettes I smoked one after another sent embers whizzing onto the seat beside me and singed the leather upholstery. As I drew closer to that prairie and its washed-out hues, the years and the accomplishments I had stacked up around me like a wall began to fall away. Hick was back in the sticks. And the sticks was trying to get back into me.

I stopped for lunch at a diner in Benson with a red-striped awning and a wanted poster in the window that was half warning, half boast: Bonnie and Clyde had robbed the place over the summer. Somehow, seeing it helped me get my head on straight again. Folks here were down and out and upside down, and I had a job to do. While I waited for my meat loaf in the booth by the window, I flipped through a copy of the previous day's *Minneapolis Daily Tribune* and read the work of fine local reporters. Farmers in these parts were threatening to embargo the sale of their wheat if the government didn't do something to stop the plummeting prices, and the governor of North Dakota proposed calling up the National Guard to stop them.

On page three was a story penned by none other than John Bosco, Associated Press. It was one of those only-in-New-York tales that smaller papers printed for their readers' amusement: MURDEROUS MAID EXPOSED WHEN CANARY SINGS — to cops. I thought of John's goofy ears and his worn-out trench coat, the way he had stuffed the pockets full of hors d'oeuvres the night of the election. How fine it felt to see the words my friend had typed, even if they made me realize how very far I was from home. With careful fingers, I tore the article from the paper and made a few corrections — the copyeditor had neglected to replace *convince* with *persuade* where the latter was appropriate, and in the penultimate line John had used *then* as a conjunction, which was not strictly incorrect but still hard on the ear, so I penciled in a carat crowned with *and.* I would drop this little love note in the mail on my way out of town.

My next appointment took me to a farm outside Aberdeen to interview a wheat farmer and try to gauge his sympathies, if any, for the communist cause. People at the federal level were worried it would take hold in places like this with folks angry and desperate and likely to see the well-off as the villains. But I found no copies of *Das Kapital* lying around, and no man about the place — in fact, only a very pregnant woman and ten other children in a house without a stitch of bedding. I thought instantly, of course, of Ruth, of West Virginia, of the same sort of suffering in different terrain.

"The older ones are called Samuel, Catherine, Dorothy, Timothy," she said, pointing them out where they stood against the walls and in the rude little kitchen. "The rest . . ." She gazed helplessly around. "You see, it's hard to keep them all straight. But this little girl here" — she clutched the arm of the nearest one, about six years old, with two big crooked teeth — "she's real good. She doesn't give me a bit of trouble."

Anonymous smiled at me and I smiled back at her. "And your husband?" I asked. "Is he going to be home soon?" The man never gives you a moment's peace, I thought, judging by the size of this brood.

She waved her hand. "He's out picking thistle for soup."

Russian thistle. I remembered that from my girlhood. It dried up like barbed wire each fall and rolled up and down the road. When cows ate it, they got sores all around their mouths, but in hard times people boiled it with a few moldy potatoes, and it kept you from the brink. I could still feel the spiny fibers in my mouth, the way they would stick between your teeth. Just to feel something real instead of that awful memory, I pressed the tip of my tongue against the tooth that had been bothering me for a week or more and the firecracker of pain gave me a strange moment of relief.

Bowdle was only fifty miles from where I stood.

I went back into town to see what could be done about getting a doctor out to that woman when her time came and found one called Angstrom, who thought he might be able to get some of the supplies he needed from the storeroom the Red Cross kept in the back of the Lutheran church.

"They have a whole lot of good things over there," Dr. Angstrom said, a little stupidly, I thought, for a doctor.

I closed my eyes and took a deep breath. "Could you point me in the direction of that church, please?" My only comfort came from envisioning Nora's reaction when I shared the tales of these moribund towns with her. We would lament together over a bottle of wine how the people suffered not just from the crash itself but from the decades of isolation, the lack of education. We would talk about how Arthurdale would pave the way for change across rural America — what it would do when we got it up and running.

In the office at Holy Trinity, I met the church secretary, who was sitting on a folding chair behind a card table and talking on the phone. She wore a thick wool sweater over her dress and the tip of her nose was pink.

"My job," I explained when she hung up, "is simply to make sure that the local government here is doing everything it can to give people what they need."

"Well, you can't get blood from a turnip," she said.

"Don't I know it. And I realize that you are not a government official, obviously, but is it true that you have some kind of storeroom here? Donations from the Red Cross?"

Her gaze flicked to something behind my head and back at me. I turned to see a hook on the opposite wall; hanging on it was a key on a piece of red string.

"Would you let me see it? As you might know, there is a woman up the road planning to give birth on her bare dirt floor." Surely this secretary already knew of the family: it was a very small town. After a long moment, she nodded, then stood and crossed over to the key.

"I don't know about this 'Brains Trust,'" she said, miming quotation marks with her fingers as we padded across the carpet.

"Pardon?"

"I like the man — I voted for him — but he's getting pushed around by a bunch of eggheads."

"He" was FDR. I nearly smiled at the image of the president surrounded by a marauding band of professors in sweater vests, shoving him and shouting about the finer points of macroeconomics.

I shrugged in a way that I hoped seemed friendly. "What I know about fiscal policy, you could fit in a shoe," I said.

"What those men know about farming and cows . . ." She trailed off and shook her head. "Fools leading fools."

She turned the key in the padlock on the storeroom door and switched on the light. The shelves, from floor to ceiling, were jammed with wool blankets, thick quilts, cabled sweaters. Bolts of flannel were stacked on the floor next to sacks of new long underwear, still in its packaging.

Again, I only closed my eyes and took a deep breath. I felt a headache coming on, and my molar ached. "Don't you think," I said, and took a steadying breath, "that that woman, and everyone else in this town, could sure use some of these warm linens and clothes?"

She shook her head. "I'm sorry, but we are saving them for an emergency."

I stared at her and thought of the wind cutting through the expectant mother's shack, the sore-mouthed cows, the farmers destroying their crops in protest. "Well, just what in the hell do you think this *is*?"

Later, I took Route 12 west out of town, still fuming, and squinted at my map to find the road that would take me south. As Bluette sailed down the frosted lane, I thought about what I would put in my report. *People aren't going hungry for lack of food,* I'd explain. *We've got plenty of food, but a shortage of heart. And brains.* My cigarette gave me little comfort; when I brought it to my lips, my fingers were like ice against my skin and I tried to shake some warmth into them. I recalled the four seasons of the year in Dakota: flood, grasshoppers, dust, and frostbite.

The road scrolled by me for a long time and I let my mind roam free. On another cold day like this one, I had stood beside Nora in front of the tenor's window while we listened to him rehearse the aria that made my heart leap within me. Our hands hung just an inch apart, but, standing there on the sidewalk for all the world to see, we could not allow them to close the space between us. We might have looked a little like one of those drawings of an optical illusion, in which a second image can be seen in the negative space. That day in front of the tenor's window, would a viewer have seen a picture of two women standing together or a picture of an ache framed by the curve of their arms?

After a while, the sameness of the land in every direction played a trick on my eyes, and I began to question whether I had taken the turn to the south or had missed it. There were no signs on the road, no houses, no other cars. Just the pavement and the dishrag sky. Had I turned or not? Was I headed south, or west?

I felt the skin on my neck pucker with apprehension and I glanced at the map again, as if it meant something. When another road finally appeared, I turned left on it. Still I saw no road signs, no reassurance. And yet I began to recognize the road. My right hand went to my pendant.

On the right was the Houskas' farm, where a half-dozen skinny cows mashed their bodies together next to the barn to keep out of the wind. I smoked, listening to my breath. When the weathered fence ended, there was another open space, then another farm. I crossed a bridge over the ghost of a stream and arrived where I'd never wanted to go: Chateau Hickok, stamped on the dead land like a black eye on a face that was ugly to begin with.

The windows were dark. The door my mother had painted bright red in an act of rebellion against my father, perhaps her only one, was now pink-gray and hung askew in the frame. Bluette's engine chugged in the silence and I let it run. I knew if I turned it off in this cold, I might not get it started again. I mashed my cigarette into the ashtray and, as if pulled by the hand of a phantom, took the car out of gear and set the hand brake. I got out and started walking. But it wasn't the house I wanted to see. It was the barn.

The wind smacked my whole body, nearly knocking me off my feet. I was bareheaded — foolish city woman, with no wool hat! — and I felt the pins in my hair lift off my scalp. I picked up my pace and recalled the many times I'd walked this exact same way, crossing from the house to do my chores, a kitten tucked in my sweater so it wouldn't freeze. The cold scoured my cheeks.

I got inside and yanked the door closed behind me. The wind whistled through the gaps in the boards but the space was otherwise quiet. I stood very still and braced myself for the tidal wave of anguish I'd been dreading. Over the years, no matter where I went, it was here that my mind returned, like a dog sniffing around a grave. I had, after all, worn a piece of this place around my neck for decades, a talisman to protect me from ever coming back.

And yet here I was.

At some point, the barn had been emptied and swept clean. The floor was bare dirt and the buckets and crates were gone. The hooks on the walls were empty. But still there in the corner was the site of the hen-shit-covered hay where he'd pushed me down.

I thought about who I had been the last time I'd stood in this spot, lean fourteen-year-old little Hick with long brown hair and a fierce mien. A girl who'd just had the facts of life slammed into her by a miserable excuse for a father. But somehow instead of crumpling, she had picked up that stave and bashed her way out of this barn, of this prairie, of the life that fate had tried to pin on her.

A bubble rose in my chest and I waited for the tears to come. But when my eyes pulled back at the temples, what I heard was a belly laugh I usually needed three drinks in order to muster. The sound astonished me; it was so loud. I leaned over with my hands on my knees, cackling to beat the band.

This was just a goddamn barn.

There were no ghosts here, no undead buried body that might reach up out of the dirt to grab my ankle and hold me prisoner. I'd been telling myself a story for so long that had this place at the center — this old barn. But I saw now that it was just one place, and the day my father raped me just one day among many days. My life was a thousand times bigger than any one of them.

The clasp on the necklace gave easily, and I hung it on one of the empty hooks. Then I turned on my heel and went back out into the cold. The specter of Little Hick ran ahead of me, hurrying out to the road to hitchhike her way into town. But I walked at my own pace, despite the howling wind, because I had finally realized nothing was chasing me.

Back in the car, I switched on the little electric heater on the passenger side and watched the coils begin to glow red. The thin stream of heat thawed my numb face, and I thanked the god in which I didn't believe, and Hearst and his newspapers, and Louis Chevrolet, for delivering me, just as I was, into this moment. And Little Hick — I thanked her too.

"Office of the first lady. Mrs. Thompson speaking. How may I help you?"

Of course, it was the middle of the afternoon in Washington and Nora had to be busy with a thousand different things, but this was big — I couldn't wait to tell her. She had seen me through so much grief over that barn. I wanted to tell her how I'd left that necklace dangling on the hook, that I could finally put it all behind me.

"Hi, Tommy — it's Hick," I said, standing nearly breathless at the table in the shabby hotel lobby. "Is Mrs. Roosevelt in?"

"Hick! Lovely to hear from you. How is life on the road? Where are you calling from?"

"South Dakota," I said. "Listen, is she there? It's quite important."

"Let me check. Hold on for a moment."

I glanced around the dim lobby and felt the deflating effects of its nicked furniture, the mousetrap I spied in the corner that held a dusty cube of cheese. It seemed like a place that could drive a jolly man to suicide in under forty-five minutes. I pulled the chair out from the telephone table and sat down in front of a window that framed the barren Dakota landscape. In spring, I knew, this land could be beautiful — feathered with gray-green shoots of prairie grass that turned golden by June. That's what kept people here, the clean slate each new year promised, though it hardly ever made good. How a mere promise, so easily made, could keep us hanging on in hope, enduring against the odds, against the *facts.*

"Miss Hickok?"

"Louis?"

"How are you enjoying that beautiful car?"

My feeling of triumph was leaking away with every minute I sat with the phone pressed to my ear. "It's wonderful," I said. "I can't believe how long I got by without one. It was such a generous gift."

"Well," he said, "I know how much she was looking forward to giving it to you."

If that's true, I wanted to ask, then why didn't *I* know about it? Why did Louis know more about what Nora was looking forward to than I did? And when was the last time she and I had even spoken?

"Louis," I said, "I won't take more than a minute of her time — I swear — but could you please put Mrs. Roosevelt on?"

"I wish I could, but she is preparing for a meeting this afternoon and can't speak now, but I'll be sure to pass along —"

"Please," I said, my voice near to breaking. "Please just tell her it's about Bowdle. About the barn."

I heard the crackle of his hand covering the receiver. She was probably sitting next to him at the table, the phone wheeled over to them on some priceless antique cart.

"Miss Hickok, she says she'll call you back later —"

I scrambled for something to keep him, and my precarious connection to Nora, on the line. "Well, another thing, Louis — it's been ages since I've heard a status report on Arthurdale. Where are we on the selection process? The construction? Have you heard anything about Ruth Johnson's family?" I felt my cheeks getting hot. I knew I sounded desperate, but I didn't care. *Damnit* — why wouldn't he just put her on the line?

"Can't speak to individual cases, but everything's moving forward. Mrs. R can fill you in when she calls. We have your itinerary — she knows the hotel."

"But I'm not —"

In the background I heard voices, dishes, the shuffling of chairs and paper. "Okay, then," Louis said, "signing off now. Please travel safely, and we'll see you soon." The phone clicked off, and I lowered the receiver.

They had my itinerary, but my detour to

Bowdle had me off course and I was staying in a different hotel. *I'm not,* I had tried to say to him, *where I'm supposed to be.*

I tried John next, but the newsroom secretary — a new one, a voice I didn't recognize — said he wasn't at his desk. Did I want to leave a message? Sure. Just tell him it's Lorena Hickok calling from the middle of nowhere. Tell him I was elated a heartbeat ago, but now I'm lonely and full of regret, though I can't tell him why. Could you ask him to call me when he gets in?

"No, thank you," I said. "I'll try him tomorrow."

In my room, I poured a drink and tried to reclaim the victorious feeling from the afternoon. Even if I had to celebrate alone, finding freedom from Bowdle at last *was* something to celebrate. So I poured another drink, and then another.

As I lay in bed waiting for sleep to come, I listened to the mice moving in the tunnels they'd chewed through the hotel walls; what arduous work it must have been for them, forging their destinies one mouthful at a time.

■ ■ ■ ■

PART THREE

■ ■ ■ ■

Everything went into Eleanor and Hick's daily letters: the weather, their schedules, their sleep, their dreams. "And now I'm going to bed — to try to dream about you," Hick wrote from Texas. "I never do, but I always have hopes."

— Susan Quinn,
*Eleanor and Hick: The Love Affair
That Shaped a First Lady*

CHAPTER EIGHTEEN

December 1933

Ruth herself was the one to enlighten me
on the status of Arthurdale when a letter
from her caught up with me at my hotel in
Minneapolis in mid-December:

Dear Miss Hickok,

I guess you are prolly sick of me by
now but I am pert near the end of my
rope with the knot about to break off in
my hand. Mr. Pickett dont know what is
going on and the men in charge of these
homes do not or at least will not tell me
nothing. So here is your old friend Ruth
asking for help agin.

The good news is they got some of us
out of the tents. Me and mine and abowt
a hunred others are packed in to the old
Arthur manshin like hillbillys in a shaft
elevater. But it is dry here and we have
water and heat and my babys are sleep-

301

ing, thank the lord. The wives got a sked-gel going and we take turns cooking and washing up and all the folks eat in the big dining room.

The bad news is I am like to kill these fool women if I have to live with them much longer. And people are saying they don't got enuf houses for erybody becaus the ones that came off the trucks didnt fit the foundashuns. Some folks is going back to the tents. I don't know if that is a rumor but I caint risk it. So you see what I mean. I caint stay here but I caint go back. I come so far Miss Hickok. I got the baby coming at Christmas. Will you please help me?

Ruth

I looked at the postmark and saw that the letter was a month old. Four more weeks after the day she had written this, Ruth had spent wondering about her fate — or perhaps she knew it by now. There was no telling. In those same four weeks, I had received just two letters from Nora in which she spoke in vague terms about the frustrations of Arthurdale. Louis had prevailed in his parsimonious suggestion of the prefabricated cottages, despite Nora's warnings, and when the homes arrived at the building site on enormous trucks, the workers realized the specs provided by the company were incorrect. The foundations were the wrong size. Nora stepped in and directed that everything be sent back to the company. Then she found an architect to build proper framed homes, with plumbing and electricity, just as she'd originally planned. But the havoc had doubled the budget, and some within the administration were starting to speak out publicly against the project.

Nora and I had not talked by telephone; I'd given up on getting through. In my reply to Nora's first letter, I'd asked after Ruth in particular, but she had offered no details on her case. *Of course,* she wrote, *in a perfect world, every single one of those families would be living in a warm and tidy house by now, but as you well know we fall far short of perfection. The process is slow and we can make no guarantees for individuals — but the thing to think of is the big picture, the long-term outcome. We must get the houses right so that in twenty years, in fifty, they will still be standing. When these children are grown, when their children are grown, that's when we will see the fruits of our labor.*

Tell that to poor Ruth, I thought. Nora's high-minded reassurance that short-term sacrifice would be worth it in the end reminded me just a little too much of the current status of our entanglement — barely speaking but hanging on in the hopes that someday, when someone else was president, when all her other ambitions had been fulfilled, we'd have that little cottage in Hyde Park at last.

I was starting to wonder if it was horseshit.

After more than a month on the road, exhaustion was bearing down hard and I had to take more aspirin than was wise to keep the ache in my molar at bay. I was fed up with being a good little soldier — my hurt was hardening into anger. The big picture was one thing, but here's what I knew for sure: *somebody* was going to be first to get one of the finished houses, and I was going to make sure it was Ruth Johnson.

"Office of the Secretary of the Interior."

"Hello, this is Lorena Hickok. I'm calling to speak to the head administrator on the Arthurdale project in West Virginia."

"Yes, miss," the girl on the phone said, "and on whose behalf are you calling?"

I cleared my throat for courage. "The first lady," I said.

"Yes, ma'am. Right away," she said.

The line clicked and hummed. I sat at the

ornate desk in my hotel room; with its damask bedspread and plush ivory carpet, it was a vast improvement over some of the glorified boardinghouses in which I had laid my head over the past few weeks. I had elected to stay here the entire time I was in Minnesota and make day trips out to my various meetings rather than endure hopping from one bed to the next each night. And the Leamington Hotel was far from unfamiliar to me. A lifetime ago, my old flame Ellie and I had lived here together for seven years, until she caved to her family's pressure and moved to San Francisco to marry Bill. When I saw the hotel on the itinerary from Harry Hopkins's office, I did the only thing one can do when the past keeps coming back around, like a carousel from hell. I laughed.

"Office of Mr. Samuels," said the next assistant. I wondered if Washington was built atop a never-ending stack of women with tidy hair and smart dresses, answering phones and taking messages. Maybe the whole operation was just secretaries all the way down.

"Yes, is he in?" I asked. "I'm calling on behalf of the first lady with an urgent matter related to the Arthurdale project." Telling the lie a second time gave me a chance to refine it. I waited while she put me through.

"Zig Samuels."

"Good morning, Mr. Samuels. My name is Lorena Hickok, and I am a field investigator in Harry Hopkins's office —"

"Miss Hickok, of course. I've read your reports. You're a bit of a legend around here to us paper pushers, I must say. Out in the world with real people, making things happen. Your reports make fine reading — I hope you won't mind if I say that. Damn fine."

"Oh, well," I said, surprised and shameless when I saw his praise presented me with an opportunity. "Thank you. Listen, Mrs. Roosevelt has . . . asked me to take a special interest in the Arthurdale project and particularly to inquire about the status of the selection process for families."

"All right," Samuels said. "What can I help you with?"

"Well, first — who will be overseeing the process of moving the families out of the mansion and into the houses once they are complete? Are you staggering them by groups to make things run more smoothly?"

"It's a concern, certainly, but we've deferred to the Quaker relief people and the Arthurdale folks themselves to decide how they want to organize it all." He hesitated, and when he spoke next it was with trepidation, as if he were explaining something quite obvious and didn't want to insult me. "The idea, of course, is we get more buy-in if they make their own decisions."

I summoned up now what courage I had. I went to touch my necklace, but realized it wasn't there anymore. And then I forced out the words: "Well, Mrs. Roosevelt wants to be sure that the Johnson family — Norbert and Ruth and their children — are placed in the first completed home. So if you could let your people know . . ."

Samuels didn't say anything for a moment. Then he ventured, "Oh, boy, I hope I'm not talking out of school here — but doesn't this go somewhat against the policy we set at the outset? Not to interfere with the decisions they are making locally? Even Mrs. Roosevelt herself has said —"

I cleared my throat and put on the particular impatience of a woman who was in the know and didn't have time to explain things to the lessers. "I am quite sure Mrs. Roosevelt has her reasons, and she is insisting on the Johnsons. Would it be helpful for me to speak with someone above you on this project?"

"There isn't anyone —" he began to scoff

but then got hold of himself. He had been about to claim that no one stood above him on the project, but of course we were all serving at the pleasure of Franklin Delano Roosevelt, and anyone who had been in Washington more than a day understood that Nora wielded nearly as much power as her husband.

He cleared his throat. "Thank you for letting me know, Miss Hickok."

"I know Mrs. Roosevelt appreciates your attention to this matter."

"If I could just have it in writing, please," he said. "To assuage any confusion about the change in policy."

My stomach seemed to fold in on itself then. I was pretty far out on a limb to begin with; was I now really contemplating adding forgery to my list of crimes? And yet when I thought of Ruth, I told myself that one little document couldn't matter much. Nora must have been sending twenty memos per day making various requests. Who would notice one more?

"Of course," I said. "I'll speak with her and we'll send it over today."

I set down the phone and closed my eyes for a moment. Then, before I could think too much about it, I moved my portable to the center of the desk and rolled in a fresh leaf of the White House letterhead I had been too shy to use. *Dear Mr. Samuels,* I typed, *Regarding the Arthurdale selection process, I hope you will honor my request that special attention be paid in the case of Mr. and Mrs. Norbert Johnson . . . .* I tried to emulate Nora's crisp writing style and ended the memo as she often did, by typing only her initials with no closing.

Back in the lobby, I laid the memo on the polished wood of the front desk.

"Good evening, Miss Hickok," said the desk manager. He had a mustache so thin it looked drawn on by a woman's eye pencil.

"I need to send this, please."

"Very good, Miss Hickok," he said. As he slid the document to his side of the desk and took note of the header, he glanced up at me.

"I thank you for your discretion," I said. Now I had a second witness to my crime. "This is privileged communication."

"Of course."

"Please send the confirmation of receipt up to my room."

I tried to tell myself that I couldn't lose. Either Samuels would take the memo on its face and give Ruth a house, or Nora would find out and tear into me. But in order to do that she would finally have to pick up the telephone and call me.

That evening, I climbed onto the stool in the hotel lounge like a shipwreck victim onto a raft, and ordered a double bourbon. Repeal was only a week old, but establishments across the country had already changed their menus and stocked up with miraculous speed. Even if all of FDR's relief programs went to hell, I thought, he would still be remembered for making it legal to order a drink in a bar like a civilized human being again. Only the prim church ladies opposed him — and the gangster bootleggers he'd put out of work. Perhaps the New Deal would have to come up with a program to bail them out too. The thought of Johnny Torrio planting sugar maple saplings in some Jersey ditch made me smile. A tough guy on the dole.

The bar, crowded with businessmen, was situated in the middle of a large room and ringed by tables where guests sat eating dinner. The one at the back of the lounge, close to the swinging doors to the kitchen, had been Ellie's and mine. If I squinted, I could see her sitting there, holding her jade cigarette holder and sipping her brandy, looking down her long nose at me with laughing eyes. Ellie was a friendly ghost, and it did not pain me to remember our years together. I hoped her marriage had made her happy — though it was hard to imagine happiness was possible for a girl like her in a bed shared with a man named Bill.

I felt the air in the room change a little and looked to my right to see a woman take a stool a few down from mine. She was about thirty, with smooth, tan skin and dark hair cut to her shoulders. She wore it loose, tucked behind her ears, and a simple silk dress that was at once unfashionable and interesting. While every other woman in the room wore a variation of the dress of the moment, this frock looked like a piece of abstract art, an intense pink column that draped her petite silhouette, with fine details that were clearly the work of a deft seamstress. On her wrist was a thick bracelet of carved bone.

The bartender brought her a glass of water with lemon, though I hadn't heard her ask for it. As she sipped from the glass, she looked around the bar and seemed to take note of each man sitting there. One at a time, she waited to see if the man would make eye contact with her; if he did, she looked away and smoothed her hair or raised her wrist as if she were checking the time, though the bracelet was not a watch.

We were the only two unaccompanied women in the room. Just as I realized I had been watching her for longer than was polite, she turned to me and smiled.

I nodded. "Evening."

She wasn't smoking, but I was, and like usual I was grateful it gave me something to do.

"Freshen your drink?" the bartender asked. He was friendly enough — he knew my money spent just like everyone else's — but there was a tinge of pity in the way he looked at me. A woman alone. A woman alone who was smoking in public — commonplace in New York, unseemly in Minneapolis. A woman alone who was not pretty, who wore no ring, who had no lilt in her voice, who was plump and aging. He was trying to figure out what I was *for,* since he couldn't think how someone like me could be of any use to him.

Buddy, I felt like saying, *there are more kinds of women in heaven and earth than your dim-witted philosophy can dream of . . .*

"I'm Mae," the woman said suddenly.

I turned back to her in surprise. "Hick."

She squinted. "Not really."

"It's a nickname."

"Oh, thank goodness," she said, with a

312

charm that made me chuckle. "Are you waiting for someone?"

"No. I travel a lot for work. I don't think I know a soul in this town, though I used to."

Mae's eyebrows tipped in toward each other. "Oh. That's a shame. Well. Now you know one."

She lifted her glass of water toward me before she took a sip, her eyes on mine, and I felt a lightbulb flare in my brain as I realized what might be her intention. I sat up the slightest bit straighter, wishing I had stopped to reapply my lipstick before I'd come in. Again I thought of Ellie and wondered if perhaps she was sending me a gift.

It's bad luck to toast with water is what I should have said to her. But instead I asked, "What about you? Are you meeting someone?"

She laughed. "I'd say probably not — and I've gotten pretty good at reading this room. I come here almost every night, after all."

I must have given her a funny look because she held up her hand. "Not that! I'm not . . . a working girl or something."

"Oh, my, I wasn't —"

We both laughed then, and she put her elbow on the bar, rested her cheek on her hand. "I'm an artist," she said. "My studio is around the corner from here. But I'm broke, of course — that's part of the job. So most nights I come in here to see what I can see, and maybe if I meet a nice man he buys me dinner. How else am I going to keep myself in steak and potatoes?"

She was so trim, I couldn't imagine she ate more than the odd salad. But still, she had the age-old problem of women who preferred women: the only people who had money were men. "Sounds like an enterprising plan to me."

"It's hard out there these days for a gal on her own."

"Yes, it is." How I knew it! There probably wasn't another woman in this country who had seen the scope and the scale of ruin that I had seen over these few months. The knowledge of it was like a stone in my heart's pocket.

"But maybe not for every gal. Maybe not for *you*. What is it that you do?"

"Just a paper pusher," I said. I didn't want to talk about it. I didn't want to be sad right now. "What kind of artist — do you paint?"

She nodded. "Large-scale canvases — which was a fool move, in retrospect. They take too much space. If I had chosen miniatures, I could have kept on living in my father's apartment for free."

314

I looked at her unusual dress again. "You don't seem like the type to make something small." I had not intended that comment to be anything other than an honest assessment, but her eyes flicked to mine again, and I could see how she might read it. Reporters always knew how to put on like they belonged anywhere, but this kind of thing never happened to me — flirtation, smooth talking. I was already in over my head.

I took a long drag on my cigarette, and thought of Nora, the look that came into her eyes just before she started to laugh at something I'd said, how I'd prided myself on being able to amuse her, able to take her by surprise. Then I pushed the thought away.

I raised my hand to get the bartender's attention. "You sure you don't want a drink?"

Mae hesitated, maybe trying to size me up one more time, and then said, "No, thanks. I think I am going to head out."

Relief mixed with disappointment in my chest like a bloom of oil in water. "But you never got dinner. We could order something." I didn't want her to go. This was the first conversation I'd had outside work in weeks and I was just plain eager for any kind of company.

She shrugged. "I'm not that hungry." She pulled the strap of her tattered pocketbook onto her shoulder and hopped down from the stool. "Why don't you come with me? Studio's just around the corner. I'll show you my paintings."

The zipper on her dress was on the front instead of in the back, and it went from her sternum all the way down to the hem. I swallowed. "That sounds . . . really interesting — I'd love to see them — but unfortunately, duty calls."

"Time to push the papers, eh?"

"Time to push the papers."

She found a pen behind the bar and wrote her telephone number on a napkin. Then she wrote MAE and drew a sketch of a woman with a cigarette hanging from her lips, pushing against a mountain of paper with all her might.

"Let me know if you change your mind."

Chapter Nineteen

December 17, 1933

A few days later, I returned to the hotel late in the evening from a meeting in Red Wing to find three phone messages waiting for me at the front desk. One was from Tommy telling me I'd better call Nora quick. The other two were from Nora herself.

I took the elevator up to my room and set down my things. Then I picked up the extension. It was very late, and the telephone operator at the White House seemed to be under instructions to put me through to Nora immediately.

"Hello, stranger," I said when I heard her voice.

"Hick. I am so furious I can hardly speak. What in the *world* were you thinking?"

"About what?" I said, though of course I knew.

"You have no idea what a headache you have caused. Ickes will not let up on the

317

budget. He thinks our plans are too extravagant — bathtubs and refrigerators and electricity — he complains to Franklin every day. Someone from his office told the press I am spending like a drunken sailor. And now he thinks I am meddling in the selection process, something we all agreed was off-limits."

I said nothing.

"And all for this Ruth Johnson, Hick? Did you really think I would let her, or anyone else, be sent back to those tents?"

"I didn't know *what* to think, Nora. It has been months since you and I have really talked. And Ruth said in her letter that there weren't enough houses for all the families that were selected."

Nora sighed. "Rumors. There are always rumors. When things slow down, when they don't go to plan, people start to talk . . . But you should know better than that."

"So does that mean Ruth's family will be taken care of?" Nora had the luxury of objective distance, of thinking in terms of policy, cost projections, long-term outcomes. She could not understand the connection I felt to Ruth, how easily I could have been in her shoes: poor and uneducated, dripping with hungry children. I had only thwarted that destiny by the skin of my teeth.

"Hick, are you listening to me? Yes. The construction is behind schedule, and the houses probably won't be finished before the spring. But everyone who is living in the temporary quarters in the mansion can stay there as long as they need to. No one is going back."

"Well," I said, and felt a rush of relief. "As it should be. Poor Ruth — she has been through so much."

"Poor Ruth? Hick, do you know that we have hundreds and hundreds of families in West Virginia — thousands across the country — who need a place like Arthurdale? Do you know how hard the conservatives are fighting me on these plans, how eager they are to turn supporters against me? And now I find you going behind my back. Honestly, you should be fired, Hick. You forged a document."

"Then fire me," I said. I stretched out on the bed with the phone pressed to my ear and closed my eyes. "I'm tired."

She didn't say anything for a moment. "Hick."

"Do you miss me at all, Nora?"

"Of course I do. You have no idea what my life is like now. Every day is scheduled

319

down to the minute. I can barely find time to breathe. I wish you could spare some of your sympathy for *me*."

"I went to Bowdle," I said. I wanted so badly to stay angry enough that I would resist confiding in her, but the part of me that longed to connect with her was breaking through.

"Bowdle! *Why?*"

Something in her voice was so cold, so detached, I clammed up. She wasn't going to give me an inch. "Never mind."

"Did you finally get rid of that awful necklace?"

The sentence felt like a slap. She couldn't have found a better way to hurt me, to treat that part of my past as if it were merely a nuisance to her, an item on a checklist waiting to be crossed off. I thought of the day she had scraped me off the floor of my apartment, washed my hair so tenderly while she listened to my sad tale. Where was that woman? What in the world had happened to us?

"Now, are you coming back for Christmas?" Nora's voice had brightened and I was startled by how easily she could toss off her hurtful comment and then change direction. "I am making my schedule today. If it's all right with you, I have the twenty-second saved for us. The children won't be in yet, and Franklin will be busy with something, I'm sure."

I struggled to follow the thread. "You *want* me to come?"

"Of course I do. Don't be ridiculous. We can have London broil."

I laughed at the mention of the menu, as if settling on the dish could counteract everything that was going so spectacularly wrong. "I don't know, Nora. We don't have a very good track record on Christmas."

"What do you mean? Christmas Eve last year was one of the most wonderful nights of my life."

My hand flew to my brow and I covered my eyes, recalling the disgust on Marcus's face when he barged into my Mitchell Place apartment and found us entwined. After that lighting bolt of a moment was the long unbearable stretch of waiting for the storm that would mean humiliation, ruined careers, and reputations. The fact that the storm never came almost made no difference.

"Most wonderful? That was a terrible night."

"Oh, before that part." Her voice changed again and this time it was tender. "When we were together. When you gave me my

321

ring." I pictured her gazing down at it in her study, wondered if her long hair hung loose down the back of her nightdress. She had brought up the ring, but I noticed she had said nothing about the gift she had given me — the promise of a future together. "And even with that dark spot, everything came out all right in the end, didn't it?" she said.

"Things certainly have come out all right for you, Nora," I said bitterly.

She didn't take the bait. "Please say you'll come on the twenty-second."

"I'll think about it."

When we hung up, as I lay alone in the darkening room, I thought, *I don't want to be alone in a darkening room anymore.* So I got up and turned on the light and found Mae's napkin where I'd laid it on the dresser.

Her studio was in the tower room of a dilapidated church. The room had two enormous windows, one that looked out over the street and one that looked down on the sanctuary. Mae turned on the lamp to reveal a table with brushes in glass jars, crimped tubes of paint, and, on an easel in the center of the room, a ten-foot-tall canvas.

I whistled in genuine amazement. An enormous impressionistic tree spanned the canvas, bare roots curling to the bottom edge, and leaves splayed at the top. It was a free-form idea of a tree, more light and shadow than realistic detail. But scattered throughout its boughs were sharply drawn figures: Two men lunging at each other, one with a cocked fist. A woman wearing a coat made of layers of money. A Negro man being lynched not far from where a couple was entangled, the woman's red gingham dress pushed up above her hips.

"I call it *Tree of Life*," Mae said.

"It's . . ." I trailed off. I didn't want to say beautiful — that seemed condescending. The stylistic contrast between the soft brushstrokes that made up the tree and the precise detail of the figures' faces was striking, and the raw depiction of the violence and sex made me feel uneasy. "It's remarkable."

Mae wore her hair tied back with a pink ribbon and reached to tighten it. "Thanks. I'm not very good at explaining the paintings. I suspect I wouldn't make it too far as a paper pusher."

She climbed the ladder that stood beside the enormous canvas. At the top, she lifted the lid on a box perched on the open rafters and took out a bottle of clear liquor. "Guess I don't have to hide this anymore, now that we have repeal. Though I don't think the Holy Rollers are going to change their view overnight."

I offered my hand to help her down, and she took it. She'd recently had a manicure, and her fingernails were painted red, like cherry-flavored candies. I thought about how a woman artist on the make could not afford to walk around with bare nails marred with paint, could never really be free the way a male painter probably could. Men could fall headlong into the tunnel of their work, but women would constantly be called back to the surface: show a little leg to get some dinner, get your hair done so no one starts to wonder whether you're off your rocker, go home to check on a father who is getting on in years. The world had no tolerance for a woman who wanted to make a life out of her interests alone, to be an intact thing instead of a loose collection of fragments.

"Brave girl, keeping liquor in a church. But does this one still have a congregation? It looks like an ancient ruin."

"Oh, yes. They still come every Sunday, but it's a dwindling lot and the minister mopes around complaining about it the rest of the week." She gestured to two tattered armchairs beneath the window. I took one while she went to fix our drinks. "He takes it very personally, says the preacher at Good Shepherd a few blocks away has *charisma,* says he is stealing the parishioners away."

I laughed. "Well, I guess it's hard to be passed over," I said.

She rolled her eyes and took two glasses from a cupboard. "Mixed or straight?"

"Mixed," I said, the aroma of the gin already filling my nostrils. Mae added a splash of juice and handed me the glass.

"Everybody gets passed over at some point," Mae said. "Do you know how many times I have been rejected from competitions, classes, grants? The trick is not to get stuck. That minister is stuck something awful. He feels so *wronged,* keeps waiting for somebody to come around and fix things."

She sat down in the opposite chair and we touched the rims of our glasses; I took a long drink. Mae sat straight and still like a rabbit; she balanced her glass on her knee. She wore slim black trousers and a man's oxford shirt with the sleeves rolled up above her elbows. I liked the ease of this outfit but had been hoping for a second appearance of the endless zipper on the pink dress from the other night. I tried not to fidget, but I couldn't stop myself. One of the lapels on my jacket did not lie quite flat, and I smoothed it with my free hand, wishing I had a cigarette.

I looked up at *Tree of Life* again. "It's really something — thank you for showing me. Are you usually shy about letting people see your work?"

Mae leaned forward and set her drink on the cold slate tile at her feet. She placed her hand on my knee and left it there. "I'm not shy about much. How about you?"

I laughed and, with my cheeks growing warm, I threw back the rest of my drink. I felt surprise, but this was what I had come for, wasn't it? I took in her broad cheekbones and dark eyes, the curved smile. She wasn't pretty, exactly, but she had the confidence of a doyenne. With one little tug I knew I could pull the ribbon from her hair.

"You seem like someone who could meet anyone she likes," I said in a quiet voice. Her hand still rested on my knee. "Why in the world would you invite *me* here?"

She thought about it for a moment, her head cocked to the side. "I guess because you were friendly but you seemed sad," she said. "And because I could tell you were thinking about what it would be like to be with me."

She stood and pulled me to my feet, and with her body pressed against mine she began to kiss me. My mind flashed with alarm — this was going too far — and I thought of Nora and her ring, Nora standing beside me in the cold as we listened to the aria from *Aida*. Nora's kiss, always more chaste than this one, more chaste at first, until I could coax the wolf of her hunger out into the light.

Mae threaded her fingers beneath the lapels of my jacket and eased it down my shoulders while I stood very still, watching her arms move. *I'm spoken for,* I should have said. *I've made a promise to somebody.* I thought about where my purse hung on a hook by the door. How I should walk across the room and take it, go back out into the cold.

But Mae's fingers trailed the bare skin of my arms. She dragged her warm lips along the line of my jaw. A woman can only take so much, I thought, half laughing, half full of grief, and I pulled the tail of her pink ribbon, until it fell, loose, to the floor.

CHAPTER TWENTY

December 18–21, 1933

I returned to my room around one and fell into a restless sleep in which I dreamed of rain falling on the unfinished homes of Arthurdale until a flood coursed through the rooms and the water rose up the freshly painted walls. Furniture bobbed down the hallway. Then came Ruth with a big white belly that floated like a buoy and made her captive to the current. On her face was a serene smile, and she floated on her back headfirst down the hallway so that she could not see what was coming up ahead.

My eyes blinked open. I sat up and gulped the stale air of my hotel room, relieved that I could make the dream disappear. Then, as I registered my aching head and the throbbing in my jaw around my sore tooth, I remembered what I had done.

With a moan of remorse, I threw off the covers and shuffled toward the bathroom but stopped when I saw the top half of a telegram someone had slipped under the door. I opened it:

DARLING, WHEN THEY WRITE ABOUT YOU (AND THEY WILL), IT WILL BE TO SAY HOW YOU HELPED THE RUTHS OF THE WORLD. I THANK GOD FOR YOUR STUBBORN HEART AND I AM SORRY. LET'S BEGIN AGAIN AT CHRISTMAS. — N

Oh no, oh no, oh no rang like a bell between my ears. I switched on the light to see the clock — it was four in the morning — and then threw on my clothes and grabbed my purse and room key. Rushing to the elevator, I shoved pins into my hair. At the front desk, I had to ring the bell to rouse the night manager from his office, and he staggered out, his collar unbuttoned and a red crease bisecting his cheek. Along his chin was a line of yellow mustard, and I wondered if he'd fallen asleep on his sandwich.

"Is everything all right, ma'am?"

"I need to send a message," I said, breathless. Let him think someone is dying. Someone is!

He pulled a form from a cubby beneath

the desk and a pencil from the pocket of his uniform shirt and passed them across the desk.

Mia Regina, I scribbled, *I was a fool to flounder. If you'll have me, I'll be there with jingle bells on. — H.*

I gave him the form, with my recipient's infamous name and address at the top. He peered at it and then at me. Certainly he had been trained never to comment on messages, but perhaps his sleepiness had rolled back the curtain of his discretion. He was giving me the same look the bartender had fixed me with the night I met Mae: puzzlement and pity. How deranged must I be to be sending a love note to the first lady of the United States, to be sending a love note to anyone at all? Love was the reserve of the beautiful, or at least the common — love was a reward bestowed upon women and men who shaped their desires in the mold the world provided. Clearly I had strayed from the path and, to him, that made it impossible a real person could be waiting on the other end of this telegram. Love was not *for* someone like me. This narrow world, this disdain was the ocean I'd been swimming in my entire life, and I was goddamned sick of it.

"Is there a problem?" I barked.

"No, ma'am. Not at all. I'll send this right away."

While I stood waiting at the desk to make sure he did, I swung from righteousness back to remorse. Mae had been a moment of weakness, but I shouldn't tell Nora about it, should I? I wanted badly to be forgiven, but it seemed selfish to ask for that. And what if she wouldn't give me forgiveness? Better to tell myself it hadn't happened, to leave it behind in Minnesota and start driving east. Maybe it was not too late for us.

The man came back to the desk. "Would you like to pay now, or when you check out?"

I pulled my wallet from my purse and opened the flap that held my cash. When I stuck my hand in, I winced.

Mae hadn't taken it all. She had left enough for meals on the road, cigarettes, bourbon, fuel. But the rest of my money — all I had to my name until I could get back to Washington — was long gone. I thought back on the tender things she'd said about my smile and the curve of my sturdy hips, things I'd found hard to believe, and I saw now that I had been right to doubt them. While I had lain on her bare mattress, she had slipped over to my purse where it dangled from the hook by the door and

331

made me pay for my delusions.

Good, I thought, standing before the night manager as he waited to be paid, my eyes prickling with tears and shame scraping my lungs until I could hardly breathe. *This hurt is what I deserve.*

Two monotonous days on the road later, I pulled into a mechanic's garage in Indianapolis and asked him to give Bluette a once-over. I had put hundreds of miles on her over the last few months and it was my kind of luck to be sidelined by car trouble just as I was finally making my way back to Nora.

I walked across the tree-lined street to a lunch counter to wait. My knees were stiff and the muscles around my eyes were sore from squinting at the road. Indianapolis was merely chilly compared with the biting cold of the upper Midwest, and I was glad to leave that place behind. The further east I traveled, the more I started to feel like myself.

"Soup du jour is corn chowder," said the waitress as she poured my coffee.

"I'll take a cup," I said.

The waitress wiped an invisible drip of coffee from the counter. "Anything else?"

"No, that's it." I needed to preserve my meager funds, especially with Christmas coming. No matter how I scrimped, I'd never be able to compete with the extravagance of Nora's gift giving — a car, the house we'd live in together someday. Still, I couldn't show up empty-handed on Christmas.

Down the counter was a disorganized pile of newspapers, and I pulled them closer. The feel of the newsprint gave me the old tingle. Was there anything more marvelous than ink-soaked paper, still smelling of the oiled machine parts and the mill's bleach, the heft of labor present in its perfect creases? I scanned the headlines. Ambassador Bullitt had dined in Moscow, where Stalin greeted him with a kiss on the mouth. Hitler had placed all the newspapers and radio broadcasts in Germany under government control: a worrisome development, to say the least. A headline on A2 caught my eye: BUDGET OVERRUNS DOG FIRST LADY'S PET PROJECT.

I groaned so loudly that I saw the cook glance up at me from behind the window to the kitchen. Another of the kind of headlines John Bosco and I had lived for back at the AP. It was our habit to promise extra booze to the copyeditor who could come up with the best — or *worst,* depending on your point of view — pun and get it past the managing editor. These headlines alone made it worth saving the free press from the humorlessness of totalitarianism.

I realized as I read that this was the article Nora had been talking about on the phone:

First Lady Eleanor Roosevelt is confronting strong opposition to some details of her subsistence homestead project in rural West Virginia, called Arthurdale, that will resettle hundreds of impoverished citizens. Construction errors have cost the government time and money, and while there is widespread support for government-sponsored housing assistance, conservative lawmakers deride what they call extravagant amenities in the newly constructed homes, including central steam heat, indoor plumbing, and even refrigerators.

"Will coal miners use a bathtub for any other purpose but to store their coal?" one Connecticut congressman has asked. Mrs. Roosevelt, he said, is using humanitarianism as a cover for her real agenda — Communism.

Discord over Arthurdale has permeated even the highest office administering the programs of President Roosevelt's New Deal, the Department of the Interior. One official, who asked for anonymity because he fears retribution, expressed his concerns over the project's cost overruns. "The first lady and her friends are spending money like drunken sailors." Those close to Secretary Harold Ickes say he is "reassessing" the budget.

For now, at least, the Arthurdale project continues to have the president's full support. But this year's White House Christmas dinner is sure to be a tense one.

Poor Nora, I thought. No good deed goes unpunished. The reporter had failed to include any detail about what the people of Scotts Run would be up against *without* the first lady's intervention: another winter spent shivering in their tents. More illness and death, more despair that the promise of America had turned out to be a lot of horseshit. How much longer did these lawmakers think people would endure this way of life before they rose up to demand a decent existence? Nora was working to prevent a revolution.

I pulled my map from my purse and unfolded it on the counter. I had two days of driving left, and on the second day my route would take me across the southwest corner of Pennsylvania, not fifty miles north of Arthurdale. I wanted to see it for myself.

It was a cold morning, and my tires made two black stripes through the frost as I pulled onto Route 7. The dense forest east of the Monongahela darkened the road even though the branches were bare, and, with each sharp turn and blind hill, I braced myself to dodge the deer that were just waiting to leap into my path. In Reedsville, I turned south on the country lane that led to the Arthur estate. This time there were no crickets leaping out of the grass, no danger of the car overheating. But I could still see Nora and me, where we had stood beside this empty field in the blazing August sun. She'd had the broad vision to imagine an entire town. All I could think about was Ruth.

The old Arthur mansion sat atop the fallow straw-yellow hill like a Victorian outpost on the moon. It had once been grand, built with the profits of the mines back before the war, when coal was easy to get and in high demand, but the decades had taken their toll on the grandeur. The soaring turrets sagged and the dormered windows were rimmed with chipped paint.

At the bottom of the hill, spreading away from the road, I could see homes in various states of construction and men moving among the stacks of lumber. Each one wore leather work gloves and a wool cap, which I knew Nora had likely chosen herself. Everything would have had to be purchased for them — each hammer, every last nail. The government had hired well diggers, technicians who could design roads, an architect too. "Extravagant," the newspaper had called these costs, but what did they expect when Nora was attempting nothing short of building an entire town from scratch, practically overnight?

I parked Bluette behind a few other cars, one of which I recognized as Clarence Pickett's, and climbed the half-rotted steps to the mansion's enormous double doors. Just as I lifted my hand to ring the bell, a woman's face appeared in the glass and she opened the door.

"Hello," she said. She wore a man's wool cardigan over a cotton dress, and a line of children stood behind her.

"Hello." I extended my hand. "My name is Lorena Hickok. I work for the —"

"— for the government?" She smiled and I saw that I was likely the fifty-first such official to pass through here this week. "Come on in."

The children stood behind her waiting to

resume their parade. Some of them held paper, string, and fabric; one little girl had a bowl of popped corn and a spool of thread. I glanced ahead of them into the parlor where a grand blue spruce about eight feet tall stood in the corner.

"Mrs. Roosevelt had it sent," the woman supplied. "It's too much, really." I could imagine that the growing scrutiny of the endeavor to build this town made the residents feel they had to justify or denounce each expense.

"It's gorgeous," I said.

"It's the first one most of these children have ever had. Are you looking for Mr. Pickett?"

When I nodded, she pointed me back down the way I had come, toward the kitchen. I waved goodbye to the children — all of them were wearing new shoes, I noticed — and walked back through the entryway, where cut paper snowflakes hung on red thread from the tarnished brass chandelier. They undulated in the drafty space and filtered triangles of yellow light. I couldn't help myself: I untied one of the red bows and slipped the snowflake into my pocket for Nora. Here was something I could give her for Christmas.

Passing through the dining room, I saw a

handful of older students sitting around a long table copying a list of words written on a blackboard on wheels: *surface, cauliflower, applause.* A cacophony of chatter and clanking pans filled the kitchen as the preparations for lunch unfolded. Two women faced off beside the sink with their arms crossed, Clarence standing between them. One looked to be about seventeen, her brown hair pulled back in a thick braid down her back. The other could have been her mother, except they looked nothing alike. The older woman was as pale as a worm, with red-gray hair and nearly transparent eyebrows.

"Now, gentlewomen, I know we can come to an agreement." Clarence spoke with the same steady patience that I remembered from my first visit. I smiled at this use of such a mannerly term and could see both gals in question trying hard not to roll their eyes.

"Mr. Pickett, I'd rather be back in my tent than do one more week's laundry in this loony bin. It ain't right."

"Now, you don't mean that, Mrs. McNamara. Your tent had no running water and hardly any food. We all have to divide up the work here. That's part of communal living. Each one does his or her share."

"Well, all's I'm saying is some's doing their part and *more,* and some's sitting around reading the first lady's magazines. For example," she said, narrowing her eyes at her foe.

"Oh, you're just jealous cause you can't read, you old cow."

Clarence closed his eyes, and when he opened them again, they were as placid as a summer pond. "This is a hard time for all of us, but remember that this arrangement is temporary. Soon, you'll all be in your own houses, with your own land. A little space is going to do us all some good. Besides," he said, "when you hold it up against what the Lord sacrificed for us, laundry and cooking and tolerating each other isn't so awfully hard a thing to bear, is it?"

It was the first time I'd ever heard Clarence invoke religion, and I knew it had to mean he had reached the end of his tether.

"Well, the way I learnt religion," Mrs. McNamara said, "is each wife is supposed to minister unto her *own* husband's underwear and nobody else's. Half of these men don't even know how to wipe their behinds properly."

"Hi, Clarence," I said.

He looked up at me like I'd saved him from a couple of nails through his own palms. "Miss Hickok! What a wonderful surprise!"

The women turned and gaped at me.

"Miss Hickok, allow me to introduce Mrs. McNamara and Mrs. Kilch, two members of our new Arthurdale family. Ladies, please meet Lorena Hickok. She is a field agent —"

"Let me guess — another *official* here to watch us like we're animals in a zoo," Mrs. McNamara griped as she turned to the pot in the sink and leaned over to scrub the bottom of it.

"Are you gonna take our picture?" Mrs. Kilch asked.

I shook my head. "Actually, I'm here to visit Ruth Johnson. Is she upstairs?"

The women exchanged a glance and then looked at Clarence. He put his hand under my elbow. "Yes, she is. I'll show you the way."

We walked toward the foyer, where a grand staircase curved to the second floor. At the bottom of the stairs, a sign with the letters LH hung on the wall.

"What's that?" I asked.

"Ladies' Housing," Clarence said. "Just a reminder to the gentlemen to use the staircase that leads to the rooms on the other side of the second floor. It's not ideal for married couples, but for now we're trying to keep the peace and separate quarters seems to help."

Our footsteps echoed in the oak stairwell. A wide, pale stripe ran down the center of the staircase where a lavish oriental rug had once made climbing the steps a quieter endeavor. It was gone now; gone too were the oversize pictures that had hung on the stairwell walls, leaving behind only nail holes and isosceles triangles of grime. I tried to imagine what the pictures had depicted — symbols of wealth or the ghosts of wealth past, surely. Probably show horses, hunting dogs, a brood of children in sailor suits and Sunday dresses clustered around Grandfather Arthur in his carved armchair. The pictures had all been sold, no doubt, and now hung anonymously in some hotel.

Once we were out of earshot of the women, I said, "Well, besides those two killjoys, everybody around here seems to be doing pretty well."

He didn't say anything for a moment, contemplative Clarence. He stooped to pick up a doll that had been abandoned on the landing halfway up the stairs. She had a hand-sewn cloth face and hair made of brown yarn, and he slipped her into his jacket pocket with her pale feet sticking out over the flap. "It's true that everyone is warmer now and better fed," he said, leaning against the wall and crossing his arms. "And that certainly is an improvement."

"I saw the men working on the houses outside. They're reworking the pieces to fit properly this time?" I glanced out the picture window, clouded with steam from the radiator, that faced the yard behind the mansion.

"Mm-hmm," he murmured with a single nod.

"It sounds like you had an awful lot of trouble with the last ones. If only they'd listened to Mrs. Roosevelt in the first place." And along with the people of Arthurdale, *Nora* was the one paying for that mistake now, not the men who had failed to heed her good advice. "I saw the tree," I said. "The children's decorations."

"Mm-hmm," Clarence said again.

"You don't like it?"

"Well, Miss Hickok, it has me worried."

"The tree?"

"All of it."

"Clarence," I sighed. "Could you please say plainly what you mean? I'm on my way to Washington this evening. If there's something you need me to pass on, some information, I can get it through to the right people. I can get it through to Mrs. Roosevelt."

He pressed his lips together in thought. I glanced nervously at the closed bedroom doors on the second floor that I could see from the landing. Ruth was inside one of them.

Finally, Clarence answered. "I believe that Mrs. Roosevelt's intentions are entirely good. And that she means to see this thing through to the bitter end. But the United States government is not made up of Eleanor Roosevelt alone. Would that it were! The problem is that these people's hopes have been raised. I've always told them that things could be different for them, that I would do everything in my power to improve their lives. They know they can count on me, because I've turned up faithfully . . ."

"Of course you have," I said and touched his arm.

But Clarence bristled. "Let me finish. I've turned up, year after year, with my trunk full of clean linens and warm socks and canned food. And they know why I do this — because Christ has called me to it. That kind of thing makes sense to them — they can trust it. It's not personal, if you see what I mean. It's not about me in particular, and it's not about them in particular. It's about living life in a certain way. Do you understand?"

I winced. I wanted to. "Not really, but I'm trying."

He shifted his weight and relaxed his shoulders, bringing his hands together. "In all the years I've been coming to Scotts Run, I have never said to anyone that someday he would have a house that didn't flap in the wind, because I myself had no money to build that house. Of course, privately, I hoped and prayed that the homes would come. But I've been careful about promises because of what I said before about these folks trusting me. I have to honor that trust. I can't be careless with it."

"Ah," I said, beginning to understand. "And suddenly they've been promised the moon."

"Which would be fine," he said, "provided that the one making the promises was the moon's rightful owner."

"I see your point," I said. Clarence had read the wire story in the newspaper this morning too, I thought, and felt the same rumble of dread that I had. But I had the benefit of knowing that Secretary Ickes was no match for Nora. "Don't forget, Clarence — this project has the president's support.

And I wouldn't underestimate Mrs. Roosevelt. Once she sets her mind to something, you can bet she will make it happen." I thought of the threadbare elbows of Nora's dresses, the reams and reams of paper that flew beneath her pen when she went on a tear about something. To love her was to love the whole world more, and better — to want to be a part of the effort to save it. How I missed being near her.

"Yes, but, you see, she can't simply will these things — the school and the roads and the clinic — into being. She's got to convince these other folks in Congress to approve the funding. They've made Arthurdale into a symbol, though what it symbolizes depends on where you're standing."

"If you think it could work, that makes you a socialist," I said with a wry smile.

Clarence nodded. "And if you're the type who doesn't like the government in general, doesn't like paying your taxes, then Arthurdale *can't* be allowed to succeed. Because where would that leave one's beloved capitalism? It's not about the people from the mining camps anymore. They're a case study now. And if Mrs. Roosevelt can't change lawmakers' minds, what am I going to tell these folks? 'Sorry, go back to your tents'?"

I thought of the poor-quality houses Louis had tried to push through, the delays and uncertainties around the project's completion. "If this isn't done right, it *will* fail," I said, echoing Nora's words from our meeting in the White House with Louis and the president.

"Mm-hmm," Clarence said once more. "Which may be exactly what a lot of people want."

At the second floor, we made our way down the long, narrow hallway. The house had at least ten bedrooms, and each doorway was adorned with carved oak trim and cast iron hinges that looked to weigh about ten pounds each. The floors were bare up here too and they creaked; from inside the bedrooms, snippets of conversation, drawers opening and closing, pipes and radiators clanking echoed around us. Clarence stopped at the last door on the right. "Here you are. She'll be surprised to see you, I think."

He turned to go. "Clarence," I said, and he looked back at me. "It's not going to fail. She won't let it."

He gave me a dim smile and started down the hall. Over his shoulder he said, "Well, either way, I'll be here."

I smiled back. "I have no doubt of that."

"Come in," Ruth said when I knocked on her door. She was sitting on the bed, half lying down, really, like a fallen mountain climber pinned by the boulder that was her enormous belly. I had only seen her the one time back in the summer, but I remembered her face, the weathered skin that made her look far older than her years. Her limp hair was caught up in combs above her ears; she had deep creases around her eyes.

"Good morning, Mrs. Johnson," I said, keeping to the doorway. "I'm Lorena Hickok. Do you remember me?"

She clapped her hand to her chest in surprise, as she tried to wriggle upright. She reached to smooth down a skirt she could barely see. "Oh Lord. Of course I do. I had no idea you were coming."

"Well, here I am," I said, with a little trepidation. "I hope it's okay that I came. I wanted to see how you and your family are doing." I stepped over to the bedside and offered my hand to help her sit up. "You look like you are about to burst, my dear."

She moved closer to the headboard and rested her back against it. "I wish I could say it's going to be any day now, but I think I have at least a week or so. And I swear I don't usually lie down in the middle of the day like this. It's just . . . they have the children occupied downstairs at the moment, and I was feeling so tired."

"Rest," I said.

She patted the bed. "Please, sit."

I tried not to stare at Ruth's belly, but her current form seemed to defy physics. She had a petite frame — as fragile as a sparrow's, her shoulders like featherless wings — but somehow her torso had swelled to accommodate an entire baby. She looked *occupied.* I knew she had done this before with her other children, but nevertheless, I wondered if she was afraid. What did it feel like to be wrenched open and then sewn back together and handed a mewling stranger?

"You getting enough to eat and all that?" I asked.

She nodded. She certainly seemed less agitated than she had the last time I'd seen her, and the rash on her chin had healed. "I have you to thank for getting us in here."

"Oh, I don't know about that," I said. I brushed my hand across the red and blue stars on her quilt, which had been pieced, no doubt, by some industrious mountain woman sitting beside a dim fire.

Ruth shook her head and leveled her eyes

at me. "You are an instrument of the Lord, Miss Hickok. He worked through you."

I restrained the laugh this comment would have called up if I'd been in different company — as instruments go, I was probably something like a pocket knife rusted shut — but who was I to tell her what to think? "I'm just glad it worked out, Mrs. Johnson."

"I never would have believed I would have a *real* house," she said. Her brown teeth showed when she smiled. "They're saying we're going to have bathtubs and hot running water!"

"Well," I said, feeling uneasy, "your men have to build the houses first. And we've got to get the government to appropriate enough money to make sure they can give you everything you've been promised."

She waved her hand. "They will." She had lost the cynicism that she'd worn, like a beetle's hard shell, back on the sweltering summer day when we'd first met. This both heartened and worried me.

"And you've gotten to see the doctor? The baby's doing all right?"

Her jaw tightened at her temple. "He ain't said nothing, but there's been two babies born not right this year. From the chemicals, you know? So we just got to wait and see. 'Play the odds' is how he put it — a gambling man, I guess."

"Oh," I said, but stopped, despair strangling my voice. So the damage might already be done. The poison was in everything; it leached into the potatoes they grew, the wildflowers that spilled unbidden across the hillside and dried to husks in the heat, scattering their seeds. And now that poison was slicing up the branches of their family tree like an ax blade.

"It must be hard not to worry," I said carefully. "But think of the healthy babies you've had. This one will be just fine too."

She peered at me as if I might actually be able to see the future, and she was wondering whether to trust what I'd said. In the end, she didn't nod or shake her head, just shrugged a little. Ruth was practiced in helplessness, in surrender to forces outside her control. Those were the only kind of forces she'd ever known. What would happen with the baby was not up to her, and she would accept whatever came. It was hard to watch. One of the things I loved about opera was that, in those grand stories, people get what they deserve. Villains get punished. The wronged and misunderstood might die at the end, but they died redeemed. In real life, nothing was so certain.

"So your job, Miss Hickok — it's just to drive from place to place, checking on people?"

I smiled. "That's one way to put it. The nicest way I've heard, actually. I used to have a different job that I loved. But I like this one too."

"They don't make you work on Christmas, do they? That don't seem right."

"No, they don't. I'm on my way home to Washington, actually, after a long time away." *Home,* I thought. Where Nora waited. Where we could finally hold each other and make everything else disappear. If it wasn't too late.

Ruth gave me a knowing look, as if she too were acquainted with the soggy sandwiches and bleak diners that made up life on the road, though she'd likely never left Preston County, West Virginia. "Where abouts you coming from?"

"The Dakotas. I spent part of my childhood there."

"No kidding. And that's where your people are?"

I shook my head. "No. I guess I don't really have any more people. My parents died a long time ago. One of my sisters ran off and we never heard from her again. The other lives in New York."

"Huh," she said and gave me a sympathetic smile. Suddenly we had switched places; now I was the impoverished one. "Well, I got people coming out my ears. And I can tell you you ain't missing much."

Goddamn, she's a good egg, I thought. I felt like I'd pay just about any price to make sure things came out all right for her. "I should let you rest," I said and stood. "Now, you make sure to take good care of yourself. Take good care of that baby. All right?"

"Yes, ma'am," she said with her eyes closed, ready to slip off into sleep. "I'm going to dream about what I want to eat for Christmas dinner."

"And what's that?"

"I don't care, as long as it has butter on it. I'm going to put butter on my butter. I'm going to eat every single thing but the bones." She cracked one eye open. "Do you know, these little'uns are such fools. They never seen milk before, and when we poured it for them after we moved here, they said, 'Momma, there's something wrong with my water.'"

"Oh, good heavens!" I said, just the way she wanted me to. But in my heart, I wondered which was worse — never having milk, or having it for a month and then never again.

"They ain't got the sense God gave a stump. But they liked the milk pretty well."

"Sweet dreams, Ruth," I said from the doorway. "You take care."

In the hall, I put my palm on the wall and had to stand there for a moment before I could walk toward the stairwell. Out the big picture window, I could see the men working on the skeletons of their houses and hear the rhythmic *pop, pop, pop* of their hammers. If that article was to be believed, after the homes they planned to build a school and convert one of the outbuildings into a factory where they could bring in jobs. Next they wanted a clinic, and a hall where they could hold meetings and dances. They could already see all kinds of things that didn't exist yet.

I said my goodbyes and pulled out onto the winding lane back to Route 7, one hand on the wheel, one hand lighting my cigarette and holding it to my lips for the first long drag. I felt the crinkle of the paper snowflake in my pocket. We all wanted hope, but hope was a dangerous thing. It operated like the roots of an old tree that grew in all directions, bursting up through smooth concrete, muscling through a house's brick foundation. Once you set hope loose, there was no telling. It made you sure that things could change, that you *wanted* them to change because anything was better than what you had now. But you might be wrong about that, and you were sure to find out, one way or another.

CHAPTER TWENTY-ONE

December 22, 1933

I crossed the Potomac at three in the morning and shuddered down the deserted streets to Pennsylvania Avenue. Bluette was a little worse for wear, having seen over the course of my journey drought, dust storms, coal smog, pine pitch, floods, and hail, not to mention a good deal of inebriated driving and a lifetime's worth of cigarette burns on her upholstery. Her finish was pitted and chipped, and she was every inch of her absolutely filthy. It might have been easier just to melt her down and make a new car, but the capable White House mechanics would whisk her away and restore her, I knew, like a fallen woman taken in by a millionaire and passed off as a true lady. No one would know what she had seen; Bluette and I would keep our secrets just fine.

When I cut her engine under the portico at the entrance to the East Wing, the machine seemed to cough its last breath. I must have looked awfully out of place in my old tweed coat and scuffed shoes, and I wouldn't have blamed the Secret Service agents for barreling out the door and tackling me as they would an intruder. But it seemed they were expecting me. A steward met me with a polite smile, relieved me of my luggage, and led me through the east colonnade to the stairs.

At the open door to the Monroe Room, which Nora used as a parlor, I waited in the hallway while the steward stepped into the room to announce me.

"Mrs. Roosevelt —"

"Hick!" Nora cut him off and I heard a lapful of books and papers slide to the floor. "You made it!"

The steward backed out of the way, and I stepped into the room to face Nora. To see her in the flesh, after these months of separation, of wondering and racking my beat-up heart over what love might be left for me, was a balm I could not have imagined. She wore a dark green dress and jacket with a white collar, and clusters of pearls at her ears. My eyes locked on hers.

"Thank you, Anthony," Nora said to the steward without looking away. I heard his footsteps retreat and she pulled the door closed partway.

"We aren't really alone," she warned me as our fingers entwined, "but it's quiet here today. Franklin and the children are away until the twenty-fourth." She pulled my hand toward her waist and kissed both my cheeks. "Come and sit. You must be exhausted."

I was. And elated. And ashamed. We sat down on the flowered sofa beneath an enormous painting in a gilded frame, and I couldn't help but think of Mae standing on the ladder beside her provocative work. Next I saw our glasses of gin and orange juice clink and slosh; I saw her fingers unhooking my garters. I squeezed my eyes shut for a moment and tried to shake the thoughts of the depth of my betrayal away.

"I can't believe you waited up for me," I said.

"Darling, I have been counting the hours. We have so much to catch up on. Arthurdale, Minnesota. And I want to hear about Bowdle — really, I do. I can only imagine what it must have been like for you to go back there."

I wanted to confess so badly to what I had done, but I knew it would be a selfish act meant only to relieve myself of guilt. Nora had been through betrayal before, with her husband — the thick stack of letters tied with red cord, the handwriting that filled the page and crawled up the margins with passion unrestrained, unseemly. I wouldn't make her go through it again. We had waited so long to be together. I couldn't bear to puncture this bubble of happiness.

Nora gave me the airy smile of an unburdened conscience. "Is there anything you want, dear? Are you hungry? I can call for a tray."

"I just want you," I said, and leaned forward to kiss her. She indulged me for a moment but then hunched her shoulders and pulled her head away. "Now, now," she whispered. "We must be good."

I sighed. "Of course. You're right. Well, it's the middle of the night. We have to get some sleep, don't we? Or we will be wrecks tomorrow."

"Yes, and I have a busy day." She stood and stretched, and I followed her out into the hall as she lowered her voice. "But we can have breakfast together. And we'll have our Christmas together at three. I've cleared the evening. I have you set up in the drawing room just like before. We'll be near each other all the time."

I felt a yawn creeping up my ears as we settled in our adjoining rooms and Nora pulled off her earrings and kissed me good night. Then she closed the door that kept our arrangement proper to anyone who might take notice. This yawn was as much a sign of relief as exhaustion. My whole body felt calmer. Even my aching molar seemed improved. The proof I needed — that I had not imagined Nora — was taking hold. I could rest easy knowing I had not deluded myself into believing that we shared the kind of love that kept the poets in business. It was real. Whatever happened next, whatever people might say about us someday, whether they ever said anything about *me* at all, I knew that our love was real.

I opened my eyes the next morning to searing sunlight and the realization that I had overslept. Through the open door to Nora's room, I could see that her bed was made; she had probably been up for hours, planned a state dinner, and spurred three new pieces of legislation in the time that I'd been drooling into my pillow. Her lilac perfume lingered in the air.

In the bathroom, I dressed and splashed water onto my face. With the soft towel pressed to my cheek, I stared at my reflection in the gilded mirror. I looked old and tired, I thought, like someone's spinster aunt. One would never guess I had bird-dogged crooked cops and searched for a kidnapped baby, typing at the speed of light to get the truth out into the world, that I had swallowed operas whole until their melodies streamed out of the ends of my frizzy hair, that I had loved and been loved like Aphrodite. You'd never know any of that to look at me. There's the story we know, and the story the world wants to tell about us, stubbornly, based solely on a glance. How looks could deceive.

I hung the peach-colored towel and snapped off the light. In the hall, an usher found me wandering and led me to the family dining room, where a single place setting waited for me. Another servant entered and poured orange juice from a carafe into a slender cut crystal glass.

"Will Mrs. Roosevelt be able to join me?" I asked.

"I believe the first lady is occupied with meetings all morning," she said, "but I can take her a message if you like."

I shook my head. "That's all right. I don't want to bother her." Hadn't Nora said we'd eat breakfast together? I couldn't be sure. Maybe I had slept through the time she had reserved for us — I certainly couldn't blame her for that.

I consumed the platonic ideal of an omelet and then returned to my room to find a basket full of the mail that had arrived in my absence. There were bills, solicitations, letters forwarded by the AP. Those were mainly pleas from the crackpots who wrote to every reporter with a byline, begging us to investigate alien abductions and shadowy government conspiracies. The Long Island kennel where Prinz was staying had forwarded a bill from the veterinarian. And I had about fifty envelopes labeled PROSPERITY CLUB CHAIN LETTER, each one instructing me to send a dime to the name at the top of the list of recipients. I smiled. John Bosco was finally getting me back for my feed corn prank. I felt a pang of longing for my newsroom days — and the utter peculiarity of the brass letter opener in my hand, my current location at a table in the White House.

My most pressing task, now that I had returned to civilization, was the need to organize the jumble of receipts in the bottom of my handbag and submit them to my office for reimbursement. I was down to my last few dollars. In search of a pen to begin my calculations, I stepped over to Nora's escritoire by the window.

I plucked an ink pen from the drawer and

noted the stack of memos and file folders that leaned dangerously toward the edge of the desk. Nora had never been a neat freak; she was too busy for that. When I closed the drawer, the top-heavy pile shifted, and I nudged it with my palm so that it leaned back toward the wall. Though I had no intention of snooping, a clipped newspaper article on the very top caught my eye. BUDGET OVERRUNS DOG . . .

It was the same article I had seen in the diner the day before yesterday. It was clipped to a folder labeled ARTHURDALE — TEMPORARY ACCOMMODATIONS. There was a memo sticking out beneath the article and, though I knew I shouldn't touch it, I couldn't resist lifting the square of newsprint to see what it said.

Mrs. R:
I think you will agree that we are in a delicate phase with Adale and cannot risk losing POTUS support. Ickes has his ear right now. Won't you budge on LH accommodation?

— Louis

So Louis was on Nora's case about Arthurdale too. The project was bleeding money on construction of the homes, and

363

now it seemed even the temporary housing was ruffling feathers. Were the men really complaining about having to bunk separately from their wives? Having met some of those women, I'd imagined their husbands would be thanking their lucky stars for a nightly respite from the henpecking.

Then I considered Louis's words further and grew more concerned. No one in the White House was more in the know than Louis, and if he had decided to warn Nora — in writing no less — that she must not lose her husband's support for Arthurdale, that meant the shift was already underway. Secretary Ickes's doubts had begun to infect his boss. Just as Clarence had said, so many people wanted Arthurdale to fail, and without President Roosevelt's backing, that's exactly what would happen.

I set the memo back on the pile and shrugged into my coat, eager to get some air. Harry Hopkins's office was just a few blocks away, so I decided to walk there to file my expense report and kill time until the early dinner Nora and I had planned for our private Christmas celebration. As I went out the east entrance, Louis Howe came in, wearing one of the unfortunate brown suits he favored, a cigarette at his lips. A brief look passed over his face when he saw me

— surprise, concern — and then it was gone.

"Miss Hickok," he said, and shook my hand with both his as his smoke dangled. "How nice to see you back in Washington."

It was a sunny day and I squinted, trying to see him in the glare. "Thank you, Mr. Howe. It's nice to be back. Life on the road takes its toll."

"I don't doubt it," he said. "And when do you ship out again?"

"You know, I'm not sure. After the holidays, I imagine, but I need to talk to Mr. Hopkins. Here's hoping he sends me somewhere warm."

"Well, wherever he sends you, I know you'll serve your country well. Merry Christmas, Miss Hickok. I hope Santa brings you a big bottle of bourbon."

And then he set off toward the West Wing, with that tense walk that made him look almost crippled. I tried to brush off the odd feeling the exchange had left me with. Louis was a behind-the-scenes man, a broker of deals and counterdeals, and he lived for his work. The interruption of the holidays probably drove him crazy, I assured myself. Too many cocktail parties and tree lightings getting in the way of his machinations.

CHAPTER TWENTY-TWO

December 22–23, 1933

Three o'clock came, then four, then five. For the second time that day, I sat alone at the table in the family dining room in the White House. A cuckoo clock acquired on some diplomatic mission of a past decade proclaimed the passing quarter hours. With each squawk, a servant appeared to refill my wineglass until I took the bottle out of his hand and set it in front of me to save him the trips.

To pass the time, I took a long walk through the hallways, expecting to return to find Nora waiting for me. When she wasn't there, I retraced my steps and, outside a closed door, I found a serving cart that held an empty coffeepot and a pile of discarded newspapers. In the dining room once more, I read them front to back. Finally, at six, Nora sent in an aide with a message — *Trying to get free, I swear. Will explain all later.*

— and I set the scrap of paper down and kept on drinking.

If only I'd had the sense then to call it a night. But I'd taken unusual care with my appearance, choosing a black crepe dress with velvet cuffs that I was actually quite fond of, and pearls — I'd even made up my face — and I didn't want it all to go to waste.

With an abundance of time on my hands, my mind wandered back to Louis's memo and my worries about the fate of Arthurdale, and of Ruth. I wondered what would happen if the baby was sick, if it died, and I prayed the nonbeliever's prayer that Ruth and the child would come through all right. They weren't so far from Morgantown. If the homesteading project fell apart, I thought, maybe I could set the family up in an apartment there, help Ruth's husband find a job, and send them some money each month. I made more than I needed. I thought of what Clarence had said, that he'd stick by those folks no matter what happened. I wanted to be good in that way; I wanted to *do* good.

It was hard to believe that, just a year ago, I knew nothing of West Virginia or Kentucky or western Maine. Back then, I'd lived in blissful ignorance, a news hawk who stuck around a story just long enough to file eight paragraphs and move on to the next day's news. Had I been better off back then? Did it matter, since the choice was never mine to make?

When Nora finally came in at seven, I was fairly pickled and primed for a fight.

"Hick, I am so sorry," she said.

When I saw her face, my anger shriveled and my desperation to have her attention took over. I tried to swallow my hurt. "It's all right," I said. "I understand."

Looking drained, she sank down into the chair across from me and glanced at the empty wine bottle. "I hope you ate without me."

"I didn't, actually. I waited. I figure you must be starving."

The eyes and ears that surrounded us took this signal and delivered two plates that looked to have been reheated a few times over. London broil, just as Nora had promised on the phone a week ago. It was a marvel, the way she could orchestrate things exactly as she wanted them, down to every detail. Was that the power of the first lady, or just the power of Eleanor Roosevelt? I couldn't be sure. And yet she had been unable to get herself to our planned date. Couldn't she have moved mountains to be here if she had really wanted to?

"You aren't angry, are you?" Nora asked. "I have a gift for you."

"And I have one for you," I said, "though it isn't much."

I glanced at the servant who stood by the kitchen door. "After we finish eating," I said carefully, "let's go to my room so that we can talk."

She smiled but didn't nod.

"So," Nora said, "there's so much to talk about. Where do we begin?"

I shrugged. I was bothered by the way I had so willingly waited for her, and waited and waited and waited — when had I lost my self-respect?

"Now, please, Hick, let's forget it. I know I was late. I did apologize." Nora never did have much patience for my petulance.

"And I forgave you," I said, my voice terse.

She swallowed. "Here's one surprise I have for you. I've made an appointment for us with a real estate broker. She's the best in Washington."

"What for?" I said.

Nora dabbed her mouth with her napkin. "Well, I imagine you won't want to stay here too much longer. Aren't you eager for a place of your own?"

The cuckoo bashed through its little door

again and startled us both. I set down my fork and stared at her.

Nora put out her hand. "I mean, of course you are welcome to stay here as long as you like — you know I love to have you near — but eventually . . . ."

The realization unfolded slowly in my brain, and even as it did, I couldn't be sure I had it right. I recalled my strange encounter with Louis in the east entrance, his surprise at seeing me. I thought back further to his memo about Arthurdale, his appeal that Nora "budge on the LH accommodation." And now Nora wanted to help me find my own apartment.

LH.

Not ladies' housing, but Lorena Hickok. Nora should consider asking Lorena Hickok to find another place to live because Louis or maybe the president was uncomfortable with her presence in the White House, and in order to hold the line on Arthurdale, Nora needed to keep his favor.

"Oh, what a fool I've been," I said. I set my napkin on the table and stood.

"What are you talking about?"

But I said nothing, just walked out of the dining room and down the hall to my makeshift bedroom, opened the closet, pulled my suitcase from the floor and splayed it on my bed.

Nora flew into the room on my heels. "What are you doing?" she asked, putting her hand on my wrist to stop me. "What happened just now?"

"I understand," I said. My voice was strangely calm, as if the information had yet to reach my nerve center. It wasn't even that the president wanted to get rid of me, though of course that brought its own brand of shame. It was that Nora would have done it. "You don't have to conceal it from me. This is not working."

"I don't —"

"Do I make him uncomfortable? I do that to men sometimes. Because of how I look, and how I talk. Because they know what I might like to do with their wives."

"*Hick,*" she warned.

"I saw the memo from Louis," I said.

She glanced over at her desk and then back at me, her eyes flaring. "You read through my papers?"

"I didn't mean to. I just saw it. I recognized the article on Arthurdale, and I've been worried about the feud with Ickes, but I couldn't get time to talk about it with you — anyway, I saw it."

Nora cleared her throat. "First you forge a document, and now you're reading my mail?" She could be cruel that way, my darling strategist, could change gears on a dime. She saw an opportunity for the moral upper hand, and she took it.

"Yes," I said, "and you lied to me." I took a breath, felt the room sway and my goddamned tooth begin to throb once more. "I gave up everything for you," I whispered so that I might not have to hear the words. "My job. My home. New York City. Prinz. My friends. *Everything.*"

"Oh, Hick . . ." Nora's arm went to her stomach, as if guarding against the blow.

"The cottage you promised just one year ago that we'd have together someday. The life together. The porch swing —" My voice broke into a sob then. "It was never real, was it? You never really meant it."

It was so easy to dream up a vision of how things could be, so hard to build a bridge between the present moment and that place. It was the same with Arthurdale — she had made promises, raised hopes. It was cruel.

Her forehead creased with pain. "Oh, Hick, I *did* mean it. If this were a different world, my dear heart . . ." She tried to pull me into her arms, but I wouldn't let her. "A different life! If only I could live it over again, with you."

"Well," I said, and slammed the suitcase

372

closed, snapped the clasps, "you can't."

"I have so many regrets."

I laughed. "Look around you, Nora. Look where you are standing. I don't think you have a thing to regret."

She fixed me with a hard look. "I have tried to help you understand. When Franklin became president, I knew I had only two options: either be swallowed whole or set aside my fears and the idea of the life I wanted to have so that I could do something that mattered. Don't you see? This is bigger than us, Hick. Bigger than me. I have a duty to use these years to do all I can to help the people of this country. That doesn't have to change things between us, but you do have to try to understand. My life is no longer my own."

I looked around the room at the expensive drapery chosen by some former first lady, each piece of furniture mired in history, none of it hers or mine, none of it personal. The place had never felt more like a museum, more like a dollhouse with its rooms on display.

Nora had decided to embrace this life, but it was time for me to make some decisions of my own. "Of course it changes things between us, Nora. Your life is not your own," I repeated. "Your love either."

I lifted the suitcase off the bed. There was my portable typewriter, my mail and papers scattered on the table I'd been using as a desk. I would have to send for them. "I can't keep hanging on, hoping for a day that will never come."

This time she didn't try to argue. "Where will you go?"

"To New York. I'll get a room at the Sutton, take some time. I have to go back. I have to try . . . to get back to who I was."

"But you can't drive now. It's dark, and you've had so much to drink —"

"I'm fine," I said. I pulled my coat from the hanger in the closet, shrugged into the sleeves, and thrust my hand into the pocket. I pulled out the crushed paper snowflake and put it in her hand. She stared at it.

"Merry Christmas from the children of Arthurdale. I'm glad to go if I know it will help them. Just promise to keep looking out for Ruth."

Nora did not follow me into the hallway, and so she did not see the way I stumbled on the carpet and careened into the wall. Downstairs, an usher was waiting by the entrance, and when he saw my tense face concentrating so hard on putting one foot in front of the other, he opened his mouth to speak, alarmed.

"Please bring my car," I said. I knew my mascara was smeared down my cheeks.

"Are you all right?"

"Just get it," I barked.

It had begun to rain. It was strangely warm for December and the falling water steamed as it washed over Bluette's hood. They had polished her up, but when I slipped behind the wheel I saw that the burns in the upholstery remained. I was glad to see that something I'd made, even if it was the mess that came from carelessness, remained unchanged.

I released the hand brake and shifted into gear to take the long winding drive onto the street. As I eased onto Fifteenth, a dozen cars zoomed around me and the glare of the lights forced me to pinch my eyes closed and then open them as I tried to regain my bearings. I knew I should not be driving. When the streets turned residential, I pulled off on one, switched off the ignition, and lay down across the seat. I half expected a Secret Service agent to knock on my window, sent by Nora to check on me. But no one came, and I fell asleep.

The bright morning brought an ax blade of a headache between my eyes and down the side of my aching jaw. I started driving north in the holiday traffic. December twenty-third, the day before the day before the holiday. The cars crawled like potato bugs on a bumper crop, and I could almost hear them consoling themselves: *O come, O come, Emanuel. Let's get it over with.*

Somewhere around Edison, New Jersey, a sudden excruciating pain sent white sparks across my field of vision. I would have screamed, but I couldn't take a breath. It took me a moment to realize where the pain was coming from — my molar — and another moment to realize that I was still driving a car in dense traffic.

Malaise over love's vicissitudes was replaced by the urgent need to get to a dentist, or, failing that, find someone on a street corner willing to hit me in the jaw with a hammer for any price he could name. If I had stayed one more day in Washington, I'd have been in the chair of the president's dentist, getting the best care in the country. Instead, I was in the right lane of Route 1, crawling through Avenel, Linden, and Elizabeth with tears streaming down my cheeks.

Passing through Newark, I saw a sign with the letters DDS and threw the wheel to the curb, set the brake, shifted, released the clutch, hoping against hope I was doing it all in the right order. I heaved myself out of the car and leaned on my elbows on the hot chrome grille for support. A bell tinkled when I opened the office door, and a woman in a crisp hygienist's uniform said, "Good morning," and then, when she took a look at me, "Oh, my heavens!"

She pushed a call button for the dentist and rushed around the counter. Cradling my elbow in her arms, she led me to the first exam room and helped me into the chair. The dentist came in. While the hygienist prepared the novocaine injection, the dentist looked inside my mouth and furrowed his brow. My ears were ringing with pain and all I could do was whisper *please.* He nodded, and, before the nurse could even bring the anesthetic over, switched on his drill and pressed the bit into my tooth to release the pressure that had built up around the nerve.

The relief was so astounding; it felt like euphoria. All I could do was weep.

Only later would it occur to me that most things in this life that feel good only feel that way because they are the end of something awful: good food that ends hunger, good love that ends loneliness. But at that moment, analysis was beyond my capabilities.

As the novocaine took hold and the dentist

worked to repair my tooth, my mind drifted in numb bliss. I saw now why I'd had to leave Nora. My poor tooth had made it plain: mine was a case of neglect on every level. I had neglected my teeth and my health and my heart, all for the sake of winning Nora's love. I had forgotten that I'd once been the star of my own opera, *Le Journaliste Libre,* and I had let myself become a subplot at best. My heart was broken, but I felt a strange relief that I did not have to wait anymore for Nora to tell me what my life would be. I could take the reins back. I could decide for myself.

CHAPTER TWENTY-THREE

Christmas Eve 1933

Around ten in the morning, I called John's desk at the AP from my room at the Sutton Hotel.

"Bosco," he said.

"Yes, hello. I am calling to let you know that you have been enrolled in the Fish of the Month Club."

I heard the crackle of John's lips pulling back from his teeth into a broad smile. "Is that right?"

"Yes indeed, sir. For the next year, on the first of each month, a freshly caught whole fish will appear on your doorstep in a brown paper bag. January is catfish month."

He snickered. "Is that right?"

I nodded. "Mm-hmm, yes, sir. Now with catfish, that comes from New Orleans. So we do tell folks north of Virginia to expect a slight odor. There is a man who brings them up from Louisiana on a bus, and it does take a little time . . ."

"Where are you calling from, Hick?"

"Fifty-Sixth and Second."

John's chair creaked and I pictured him sitting up. "No kidding?"

"Nope. I think I'll be in the city for a little while at least."

"You haven't gone and quit your job, have you?"

"Oh, no. Nothing like that. Just . . . taking a little holiday. There's nothing like the Big Apple at Christmas."

John hesitated for a moment and I could tell that he knew I'd had my heart broken, that this was no victory lap.

"What are you working on?" I asked him, eager to steer him from pity.

"Bullitt's trip to Moscow. He's wrapping up there. And once I file that, a piece about a truck full of presents someone delivered to the children's ward at New York Prez. Bill gave me tomorrow off for good behavior. So if you think you might be thirsty later . . ."

"Let me check my schedule." I pretended to be flipping through the pages of my calendar. My mouth was sore and I wanted nothing more than a drink, but I had vowed to stick to the dentist's orders not to mix the pain medicine with booze. I'd have to choke down plain seltzer. Today was my new leaf. I was determined.

"I think I can move some things around," I said.

"Great. I'll see you and my catfish at five."

I hung up and lay back to rest my eyes for a moment. Hours later, I woke to a soft knock on the door of my room. A bellman handed me a telegram. I thanked him, closed the door, and braced myself, knowing good news hardly ever came this way.

I sat on the edge of the bed and looked at the message in my lap. Nora and John were the only people who knew where I was. It could be an emergency at the AP, at the White House. Something could be wrong at Arthurdale. *Ruth.*

I tore off the envelope.

RUTH JOHNSON SAFELY DELIVERED HEALTHY BABY GIRL, GLORY JUNE, THIS A.M. FIRST THING SHE SAID WHEN BABE WAS IN ARMS WAS "PLEASE TELL MISS HICKOK SHE'S ALL RIGHT."
MERRY CHRISTMAS,
CLARENCE

I stared at the words in wonder.

How marvelous it felt to be wrong about

bad news! How marvelous to be wrong about the fate of the baby! I felt like my heart might stampede right out of my chest with joy. In my mind, I could see Ruth in her bed in the Arthur mansion, surrounded by her children and the other families, all of them smiling down at the baby. I wished I could be among them. *Welcome to this big old hopeless case of a world, Glory June. We've done a shit job taking care of it so far. Maybe you will come up with some better answers.*

For a minute I considered picking up the phone to call Nora; she must have been the one to tell Clarence where to send the message, and it would have been nice to share my joy with someone who understood what it meant to me that Ruth was all right. But I couldn't bring myself to do it. And, plus, I had plans.

When I yanked open the heavy door and walked into the dim light of Dom's, the smell of cigar smoke made me grin.

"Hiya, Hick," John called. When I turned toward his voice, I glimpsed tawny fur and a slobbering snout.

"Prinz!"

I knelt down on the sticky floor and he nearly knocked me over with joy. First he brought his paws up to my shoulders and licked my nose. Then he leaped back down and galloped in a circle around me, howling.

I rubbed my fingers in the thick collar of fur around his neck, felt tears running down my nose as I patted his white belly. He flipped over and kicked his back legs in the air. "Hi, pal. Hi, hi, hi. Boy, is it good to see you."

I wiped my nose on my sleeve and looked up at John. "How did you . . . ?"

He shrugged. "I thought you might like the chance to see him while you're in town. I borrowed a buddy's truck to go get him."

I pressed my face into Prinz's fur. "Well, goddamnit, John. That was a pretty swell thing to do. I'll be goddamned."

"One more goddamn and you get a free drink!" Dom called from where he stood behind the bar that was draped with cheap gold tinsel.

Prinz, back to leaping around in a circle, tipped his head back and bayed what, I swear on my life, sounded exactly like German shepherd for *goddamn*.

"Good old Prinz," I said as we all laughed.

I paused to give John a once-over. He hadn't taken his coat off yet and I noticed that it was new, a fine gray-and-burgundy herringbone tweed. It sure beat the frayed number he had worn last year. Maybe he'd gotten a raise. Or maybe he was on a winning streak. I hoped not.

I hated to think about his age because it made me feel old, but the truth was that John Bosco was a young man in his prime, in the greatest city in the world, engaged in what I thought was the noblest vocation a person could embrace: telling the truths of people's lives in the newspaper. I was a little jealous, but mostly just proud. And glad to know him.

"Merry Christmas," Dom said as we bellied up.

"Santa Claus brought you repeal," I said. "Are you going to fix up this dump now that you can come out of the shadows?"

"Hell no," Dom said. "What'll you have?" He already had the stopper out of the bottle of bourbon and was ready to pour.

"Actually," I said, bracing myself for their guffaws, "nothing for me tonight. Just a glass of seltzer if you have any around."

Dom set the bottle back on the bar and smiled at me, waiting for the punchline. When none came, he nodded slowly and filled a glass with fizzing water. "Sure thing, Hick."

John gave me a sidelong glance but he knew better than to ask, and we ferried our glasses to our table and sat down. Prinz was still snorting for joy as he settled on the floor near my chair. It was too cold in the room to take our coats off, but the growing crowd would soon fix that.

"The newsroom isn't the same without you, Hick," John said. He leaned back in his chair. "Everybody misses you."

I smirked. "Save your flattery, rookie." The pang I felt when I thought about the AP wasn't quite as sharp as it had been even a month earlier. Maybe it was because I'd gone out to Arthurdale and seen those houses going up. Maybe it was knowing that Ruth had a roof over her head now, and a healthy baby. I would always be a reporter down in my bones, but my new gig wasn't so bad.

"How's Marina?"

He sat up and pinched the air with his fingers. "I am *this* close to convincing her to take me back."

I groaned. "I've lost count of how many times we've had this conversation. Don't you know when to give up, man?"

He shook his head. "There's no escape from this infernal thing."

I laughed. "From love, you mean?"

He raised his eyebrows in the affirmative and took a gulp of his drink. "You have to keep throwing your hat in the ring, over and over, until you croak. But this time it's going to be different."

"How?" I asked, with my lips twisted to the side.

"I'm going to ask her to marry me."

My mouth dropped open like a January catfish's. "Now why in the hell would she do that?"

"I'm serious, Hick. I've given up gambling."

"Again?"

"No, I mean it. I haven't placed a bet in three months. I really think I've licked it."

I gave him a weak smile, hoping he was right.

"Look at you — you quit drinking!"

"I had a root canal! I'm thirty-six hours sober and I'm ready to drink a bottle of mouthwash."

He sighed with a kind of sympathy only another failed quitter could offer. "Well, this is it for me — really — and now I just have to prove to her that she can trust me. And what better way to do that than to make it official, in front of God and everybody?"

"I don't know, John. Maybe you should take it slow. Prove it to her over time . . ."

He shook his head. "It's got to be tonight. And I need your help."

That is how, an hour later, I found myself standing on the stoop of a row house on the corner of Mulberry and Broome, ringing the bell marked BERELLI. John was hiding just out of sight, holding Prinz's leash, and he needed me to ring the bell, he said, because so far every time Marina had seen him, she'd slammed the door in his face.

"I thought you said you were 'this close'?" I'd shouted when he explained his plan.

"I am, Hick — I swear I am."

I'd only been able to roll my eyes.

The curtain whisked to the side and Marina looked relieved, and then confused, when she saw me. She opened the door, her dark hair loose on her shoulders.

"Hi, Marina," I said. "Merry Christmas."

"Miss Hickok. What a nice surprise." Her smile was interrupted by a sudden spreading panic. "Is . . . is everything all right? Is John all right?"

"Oh, yes, he is. It's nothing like that. Actually . . ." I glanced over my shoulder, "John is here." John stepped out from behind the car where he'd been hiding, and Marina's expression hardened with exasperation. "Honestly, he is dying to talk to you, if you

387

would just give him the chance."

"Please leave. Both of you. You're lucky my father didn't answer the door."

I could tell that she had promised herself she would say this the next time John came around, no matter what. She had promised herself she wouldn't let him wear her down. But her mouth, striped bright red with lipstick, twitched a little in its frown. Now that she had seen his hangdog face, those pitiful ears of his, big as saucers, she was wavering.

"Marina, I don't like him much more than you do — believe me. In fact, you would be doing me an enormous favor by letting him get what he has to say off his chest. If I have to hear one more time about how his heart is breaking, how he is going to die without you, blah, blah, blah, I might have to kill him."

Her eyes flicked to mine and a tiny smile was forming. She crossed her arms and sighed. She wore only a pale pink dress, with tiny buttons like small shells at the cuffs, and I shivered looking at her.

"All right, John," she said. "Let's get this over with."

He stepped to the bottom of the stoop and after he handed off Prinz's leash he shook my hand. "Thanks, Hick. You're true-blue."

"Good luck. You're going to need it." That was my cue to leave, but when I heard John begin talking as I started up the sidewalk, I couldn't resist turning around to listen. The stoop on the building next door was mostly hidden by a low brick wall and I slipped over to it and got Prinz to sit quietly by rubbing the ridge of bone between his ears. Anyway, those two fools were so focused on each other, they didn't even notice me.

"Hurry up, John," she said. "I'm freezing and we've got to finish supper before mass."

He took off his coat and held it up to her, and Marina shrugged. John took a few steps up to hand it to her, and though she draped it over her shoulders, she pointed to the sidewalk. "Go back down," she said.

He held up his palm to show he wouldn't argue. From the bottom step he said, "I'm done with gambling. Done."

"Hm. Where have I heard that before?"

"I know. You have no reason to believe me, but I'm going to prove it to you." He reached into his pocket and pulled out a small book.

"What's that?"

"Look at it."

She took a few steps down, took the book and flipped through its pages.

"It's my bank register," John said. "All my

account information's in there, all my deposits and withdrawals."

"So?"

"So, I'm giving it to you. You're in charge of it all."

I was suddenly aware that I had no business listening in on a conversation so intimate, but when I got up to leave I saw that the iron gate around the row house had swung closed behind me and I didn't want to risk making noise opening it. I sat back down.

"I don't want your money," Marina said.

"It's our money. For our apartment." He reached into his coat and pulled out a key.

Peeking over the brick, I saw Marina's eyebrows jump just a hair. She glanced over her shoulder at the front window of her parents' house, worried that they might be standing there watching but intrigued too, I could see, by the idea of living somewhere else. Anywhere else. She surveyed the building, from the iron rail to the broken terracotta roof line, and then looked back at John with her hand on her hip.

"So what — first you want me to be your accountant and now you want me to keep house? No, thanks." She pursed her lips to keep from smiling. She knew what he was getting at now, but she wasn't going to make it easy for him, not by a long shot.

John got down on his knees. Not on one knee as protocol demanded, but on both, and he lowered his forehead down onto the black bows on the tops of Marina's shoes. *Oh boy,* I thought. I winced with embarrassment. But still I couldn't look away. The man was prostrated by love, praying to it.

"What the hell are you doing?" Marina cried.

"Marina," John said, and reached for her hands. When she let him take them, I heard myself exhale; I knew it was going to be all right. "If you will be my wife, I promise you that I will spend the rest of my life trying to be worthy of you. Every single day."

"God, you are an idiot," she said.

He laughed and rocked forward so that his face pressed against her torso. She slipped her fingers into his hair and tipped his face up to look at him. I was over the moon for my friend, though not convinced he wasn't going to bungle it all again. But it hurt to watch the way they touched each other now — John's fingers curled into the backs of her knees and Marina running her hand down his hair and into his collar — right out in the open on the stoop where anyone might pass by. They didn't have a clue how lucky they were. They would never

391

have to hide.

"You got a ring or something?" Marina said.

"Oh, Christ, I forgot." John stood up and pulled one more thing out of his pocket, slipped it on her finger. "I hope it's all right. I knew if it was too nice, you'd wonder where the money came from."

Her full-throated laugh rang out through the street. "You're not out of the woods yet, *tesoro.* Now we have to go inside and tell my father."

She took his hand and they walked up the stairs, Marina leading the way. When they reached the door, she turned the knob and John extended his long arm, palm turned flat, to push the door open and hold it wide so that she could walk through first, so that her petal-pink dress wouldn't brush against the doorframe and get dirty. The door closed behind them and a light went on in the living room. And then I was alone on the street with Prinz.

It was the time of day when people whose fates were entangled with the fates of others sat down to dinner, poured wine or wiped up spilled milk, held hands across the table or threw a dish on the kitchen floor in anger. I tried to feel glad at being unencumbered, free as a bird. I could do whatever I pleased with my evening now — Christmas Eve, no less — while all around me people fell in and out of love, like delivery trucks crashing into each other, backing up and crashing into each other again. Their wreckage was all around me.

Was there any place where the road was smooth and flat? Was there any place not pocked with the graves of dead love, the broken gears and stripped screws of lives lived off plumb? If such a place existed, I sure wanted to see it. But then I wondered how long I could walk that bare lane in the hot sun, whistling with my hands in my pockets, before I turned and ran like hell back to the beautiful junk heap. Because of course Nora and I were entangled too; I had her love and she had mine, though what that would mean in the months and years ahead I could not say.

I decided to take the long way back to my hotel. By now, I knew that any way *I* decided to go would be the long way. I could tell Prinz didn't mind by the cheerful way he jangled his collar, and we made our way toward Macy's to see the Christmas windows. In one was an enormous blue spruce like the tree I had seen in the Arthur mansion, sent to West Virginia by the first lady herself, Eleanor Roosevelt, Nora, the love of my life. But instead of strung popcorn and paper snowflakes, this tree was adorned with electric lights, delicate glass ornaments like the ones I had bought for my own tree just a year ago. Beneath the tree, on a red velvet skirt embroidered with reindeer, was a heap of gifts covered in silver and gold paper, each one crowned with a bow.

In Herald Square, a ragtag choir began singing for tips, off-key but jolly as hell — anything for a coin or two in these dark days — and it made me grin at my reflection in the window. I thought about John and Marina, and Glory June and Arthurdale, and Nora and me, and the truth socked me in the side of the head: The future is a wrapped present. Who knows what the hell is in there? *You pay the price to get what you get,* John had told me. But damn if I didn't want it anyway, whatever it would be.

And so, on Christmas Eve, with a dreadful rendition of "O Little Town of Bethlehem" competing with the car horns on Thirty-Fourth Street, and a fine snow falling on my beloved avenues, sparkling in my old pal's fur, I set off north, a cigarette keeping me warm, into the undiscovered country of days yet to come.

EPILOGUE

Thanksgiving Day 1934

The cellars of Arthurdale are lined with canned tomatoes, green beans, peppers, and peas. Whole raspberries glow like cut rubies when you hold your lantern close to the glass jars that contain them. There are jars of strawberry jam and whole cored apples in cinnamon syrup and, in baskets that line the wall along the foundations of the four-room houses, pumpkins and potatoes and squashes with necks that curve like elves' shoes. From the hogs, steaks, chops, roasts, feet, and ears, smoked and preserved and stored in the cellar too.

Inside, upstairs, radiators hiss with warm air from the boilers. Well-oiled hinges, shaped in the Arthurdale forge, make not a sound as the doors open and close. The kitchens smell of fresh bread and soap.

The occupants of Arthurdale were once invisible, even to themselves. They were the men who, like shades, went down into the earth to bring up coal, and the women who waited for them up on the ground, specters in shabby aprons, seemed transparent too. Now, on the sitting room walls of all fifty houses at Arthurdale, hang mirrors in which the homesteaders can see themselves. There are no ghosts here; there is no magic either. Only men and women who begin before dawn and work into the night, wresting dignity out of the land. And it could all go away at any time — the government support, the collective spirit, the agricultural good fortune — all that they have worked for could come undone. But I guess you could say the same about anything.

"You and Mrs. Roosevelt ought to be very proud," Louis Howe said to me once about Arthurdale. "You really started something there." But all I could take credit for was that first report, the way I had tried to tell the truth about the people living in those tents, that I had tried to see them and make them seen. Everybody deserves that much. Everybody.

AUTHOR'S NOTE

Historians have spent forty years now wrestling with what to make of the relationship between Eleanor Roosevelt and Lorena Hickok. Was it "intense, intimate . . . passionate and physical" as Rodger Streitmatter posits in his collection of their letters, or merely a "belated schoolgirl crush," as Doris Faber claims in her biography of Hick? Of course, this question can never be answered entirely; only the two people in a relationship know its true nature. Outside of academic circles, the story of Hick and Eleanor hasn't had much staying power. In popular imagination, Eleanor Roosevelt has become a caricature — an asexual schoolmarm whose stirring quotations are plastered on coffee mugs — and Lorena Hickok continues to be largely and heartbreakingly forgotten.

Happily, a novelist can ask different questions than a historian. Why is Lorena

Hickok, who clearly had an enormous influence on Eleanor Roosevelt's life and career, elided time and again, when gallons of ink have been spilled probing the lives of FDR's mistresses? Why did Ken Burns sidestep Eleanor and Hick's relationship in his otherwise modern examination of the Roosevelts? Surely there is a lot of pearl-clutching at work here, but that alone cannot explain why we are capable of seeing a man like FDR as complex and multifaceted and yet cannot afford the same courtesy to his wife. Why has this failure of imagination persisted?

If you guessed misogyny, I see you have been paying attention! The election of 2016 underscores that, despite the many advances this country has made, women's lives, bodies, imaginations, intellects, dreams, anger, and joy continue to be diminished and denied by the stranglehold of sexism.

While I have certainly taken many liberties with the facts, some of the most implausible parts of this story come straight from the record. Between the election in November and the inauguration in March, Hick and Eleanor roamed New York City freely together — they went to the opera and museums, dined out in restaurants and alone together in Hick's apartment. There really was a sapphire ring and the promise of a home of their own someday; they really did go on vacation together, and Hick really did live in the White House.

The widely known details of Eleanor's family life are intact here, though of course any novel about Eleanor Roosevelt fewer than five thousand pages in length will omit countless important people and fail to render the complexity of her relationships, interests, projects, and the simple matter of her Herculean daily schedule. In order to tell the story of Hick and Eleanor, I had to draw a tight circle of focus around them, and this approach, by nature, leaves a lot of people and events out.

Hick really did survive a childhood of abuse by her father and set off on her own at age fourteen to work her way up as a journeyman reporter, from the *Battle Creek Journal* to the *Minneapolis Daily Tribune* to the Associated Press. Hick's field reports from her time as a federal investigator offer a remarkable portrait of Depression-era America and also capture her wry, vivid voice. In those pages, she reveals her flaws too — racial prejudice and lazy thinking due to her lack of historical perspective, which sometimes made her less than objective. But she also showed deep empathy for people of all backgrounds who were living in poverty. Her report on the conditions in Scotts Run, West Virginia — and her frantic calls to Eleanor about the place — helped launch the creation of Arthurdale, a project that rescued many families from sickness and starvation and ultimately made an impact that echoed through those families' future generations, just as Eleanor predicted it would.

Prinz the German shepherd really was a fixture in Hick's life. Ruth, however, is a fictional creation based on a real woman Hick met on her visit to West Virginia. I also created the character of John based on some of Hick's tales of her beloved colleagues, to give her an ally in an industry dominated not just by men but by a definition of women that simply did not include an individual like Hick. Hick was as "out" as a person could be in 1932; she didn't talk openly about her preference for women, but, as she said, she "made no bones" about who she was. Her colleagues respected her, but the truth is her work life was probably lonelier than the one I've depicted.

The longer I worked on this novel, the more I came to feel a sense of responsibility to engender the imagination that has so far failed us: to wonder about the secret heart of Eleanor Roosevelt, the woman whose ethics and compassion we claim to admire so deeply. And to finally give Hick a chance to speak for herself.

ACKNOWLEDGMENTS

As part of my research for this novel, I drove from Chicago to West Virginia in one day. I arrived in the tiny town of Reedsville very late, only to career, aimlessly, up and down hills so enormous they posed an existential threat to this flatlander. I could not find the place I'd booked online. It existed, in theory, but the darker it got, the more I started to doubt that the house that had looked so welcoming in the pictures could be real. I'd been driving for nine hours. With no cell service, I had to keep pulling over to turn on the dome light and consult the printed map, but that didn't do me any good since I had no clue where I was.

The process of writing, revising, submitting, absorbing many rejections, rethinking, rewriting, and revising many times more was exactly what it felt like to be stranded on that hill. These are the people who kept reminding me there really might be a room

403

out there waiting, with a light in the window: Kate Harding, Molly Backes, Claire Zulkey, Wendy McClure, Susan Gregg Gilmore, Lori Nelson Spielman, Kelly Harms, Eleanor Brown, Ellen F. Brown, Erin Blakemore, Julie Mosow, Mary Bisbee-Beek, Renee Rosen, Tasha Alexander, Anne Hawkins, Ruth Mills, Bonnie Perry, Emily Williams Guffey, Mary O'Connor, Steve O'Connor, Matt O'Connor, Julie O'Connor, Ann McNees, Bob McNees III, Andy McNees, Megan McNees-Smith, Kelley Smith, and all my other long-suffering friends and family who have listened to me talk about Hick for years. And thank you to Beverly Donovan, Katie Viernum, and Jenna Koph for the magical and loving haven that is Loyola University Preschool.

Gratitude to Jeanne Goodman, executive director of the Arthurdale Heritage site, for driving me around to see some of the original homes in Eleanor's "Little Village." To Rick North, for help with Bluette. And to Virginia Lewick, archivist at the Franklin D. Roosevelt Library and Museum, and all the dedicated archivists, historians, and guides who bring Springwood and Val-Kill to life. Hick's framed portrait sits in a place of honor on the mantel at Val-Kill, just where Eleanor always kept it.

I am grateful to the work of Blanche Wiesen Cook, Susan Quinn, Rodger Streitmatter, Doris Faber, Hazel Rowley, Michael Golay, Richard Lowitt, and Maurine Beasley. And I am particularly indebted to Lorena Alice Hickok herself, for her extraordinary reporting that amounts to a vital oral history of the Depression. It goes without saying that I take full responsibility for all flights of fancy and outright mistakes in this novel.

I am grateful for every rejection I received (really!) because they made the book better. Thank you to Kate McKean for seeing what this novel could be, and to Iris Blasi for giving it a home; to Claiborne Hancock, Katie McGuire, and all the other members of the outstanding Pegasus team.

Willa, to love you is to love the whole world more, and better. Thank you for keeping me from giving up. And to Bob, for everything.

I used to think long acknowledgments pages were embarrassing. But the more time I spend at this, the more I see I am one lucky soul to have so many people to thank that it has probably bored anyone still reading this to tears.

ABOUT THE AUTHOR

Kelly O'Connor McNees is the author of two novels, *The Lost Summer of Louisa May Alcott* and *In Need of a Good Wife.* Born and raised in Michigan, Kelly found that books made good friends. Mary Lennox, Winnie Foster, Kit Tyler, Will Stanton, and a dozen other characters were as real to her as any of the kids on her block, and she decided that the best way to keep them around and provide them with some company was to become a writer herself. Kelly received her first rejection letter in tenth grade, from the fiction editor at "Seventeen," and has been writing her way back ever since. In the meantime, she has worked as a teacher and editor, and lives with her husband and daughter in Chicago.

The employees of Thorndike Press hope you have enjoyed this Large Print book. All our Thorndike, Wheeler, and Kennebec Large Print titles are designed for easy reading, and all our books are made to last. Other Thorndike Press Large Print books are available at your library, through selected bookstores, or directly from us.

For information about titles, please call:
   (800) 223-1244

or visit our website at:
   gale.com/thorndike

To share your comments, please write:
   Publisher
   Thorndike Press
   10 Water St., Suite 310
   Waterville, ME 04901

Sept.1/20
TC~3
Last Sept.19